Other Books by Lauren Filarsky

The Star Horses Series

Emma and Starfire
The First Seahorse
Starlight Dancer Saves Christmas

Breaking Expections

Blood Shadows Book 1

KHAFYRI

L.M. Filarsky

Bink Books
Bedazzled Ink Publishing Company • Fairfield, California

978-1-949290-82-0 paperback

Cover Art
by
Trish Ellis

Cover Design
by

Bink Books
a division of
Bedazzled Ink Publishing, LLC
Fairfield, California
http://www.bedazzledink.com

For Brian, my favorite (and only) brother.
Thank you for your inspiration.

Acknowledgments

Writing is a solitary activity, but publishing a book takes a strong support network of family, friends, and fellow writers. They help in a variety of ways, including giving constructive criticism of works in progress, critiquing completed manuscripts, and fine-tune editing the finished novel. Thank you to everyone who has been a part of my writing career.

Vacaville Town Square Writers, thank you for your continued valuable feedback to my writing. Special thanks to those who took the time to read and "roast" my first draft: Betty Lucke, Laurie Rawlinson Evans, Kelly Hess, Sierra Janisse, Don and Syl Bestwick, Genevieve Monks, Scotti Butler, Joan Coulson, and Beth Cantrell.

I am especially grateful to Sub and Felicia Bloem, Brian Filarsky, Cheryl Filarsky, Alyssa Lundberg, Laura Lundberg, Betty Lucke, and Laurie Rawlinson Evans for taking the time to beta read my manuscript and give me their honest comments and reactions.

Thank you to my editor, C.A. Casey, for all the polishing and perfecting of *Khafyri*.

Last but certainly not least, thank you to my family. To my dad, for a lifetime of support while I pursue my various dreams. To my mom, for the priceless gifts of books and horses. To my brother, for encouraging (and participating in) travel adventures, both domestic and international.

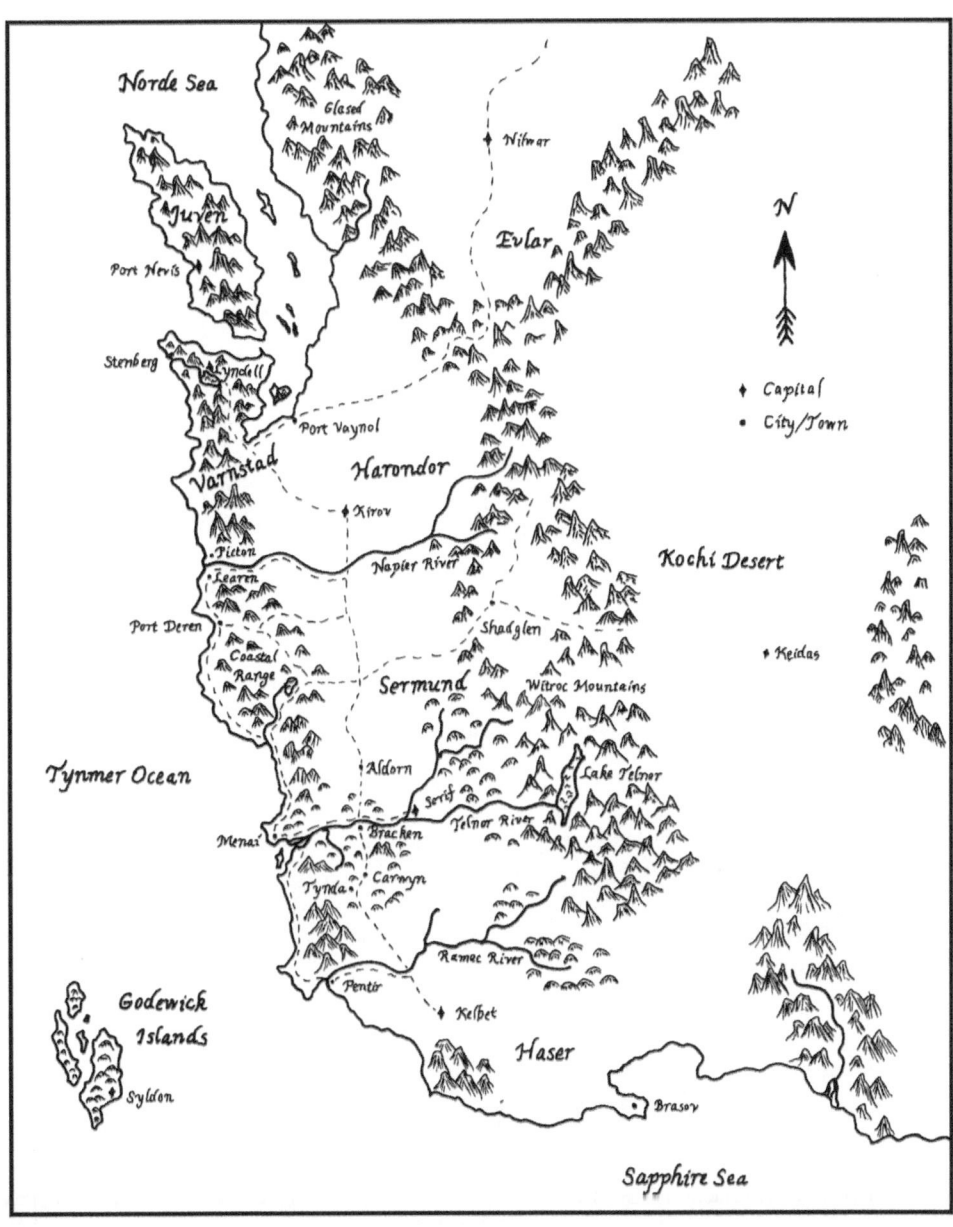

Prologue

I MUST NOT fail. The thought filled her mind, spurred her fear into action. *Not now. Not after we've come so far. Survived so long. I must be strong. For them.*

The clatter of horseshoes on cobblestones grew louder behind her as she raced through the town, sprinting around corners and slipping through alleyways, trying to shake her pursuit. But knowing, deep down, that there was no escape. At least not for her.

Another turn brought her to the market square. It was empty of all vendors—the local humans had obeyed the khafyris' orders to remain inside while they searched the town. But though the square was free of merchants, it wasn't vacant. A line of mounted warriors spread in a half-circle before her. Two dozen human knights in shining steel armor and, even worse, eight khafyri, some of them bearing strieborna shields.

She skidded to a stop, intending to run back the way she'd come, but it was too late. Her pursuers had finally caught up with her, and they were fanning out behind her, tightening the noose of the trap.

"Surrender," a soft, refined voice said. "There's no escape."

She whirled to face the speaker and found herself looking at the hard emerald eyes of Tav Arawn.

Not him. Why did he *have to come?*

"Never," she spat, forcing anger and defiance into the word, masking the dread that filled her.

Movement at the far edge of the square caught her eye. A pair of khafyri on foot dragged a bloodied and bruised captive into view.

"We caught him, sire," one of them said.

A malicious smile spread across Arawn's face. "Finally. I've been waiting for this moment for so long. At last I can—"

"No!" she shouted, channeling her rage and fear into heat and fire and death, unleashing an inferno that exploded outward in an all-consuming firestorm. Horses and men alike shrieked as they died, but over the screams and roar of the fire, she heard Arawn shout, a wordless sound of fury and loss. *It has to be enough,* was her last, desperate thought. And then she heard no more, saw no more. Was no more.

Chapter One
Aderes

THE STALLION BUGLED a challenge, tossing his head and arching his pale, muscular neck.

"Easy, Sahnden," Aderes said, stroking the young stallion to calm him and looking to see what had caught his attention. A small party of armored knights had crested the hills at the northern end of Carwyn valley and was trotting down the road toward them. The group's banner-man carried their standard, a black eagle clutching a sword and swooping across a crimson field. Aderes had only a brief moment to wonder why a member of Sermund's ruling house was in Carwyn before Sahnden claimed her attention, bellowing another challenge at the approaching horses. He reared, front hooves flashing through the air in a show of strength, and tugged at his lead rope, which was securely fastened around a sturdy oak tree.

"Sahnden," Aderes scolded, and the young stallion turned his blue gaze toward her. He snorted in irritation, pawing the grass impatiently. "That's better."

Aderes resumed saddling him. She needed him to behave himself, today of all days. Her father, Horse Master Torvald, was coming to see how his training was progressing, and Aderes didn't want to disappoint him.

Torvald was one of the finest horse breeders in the country, and Sahnden was the pride of his herd. Her father was no longer able to ride, ever since a colt he was training had misjudged a turn, skidding sideways and crashing to the ground with the horse master pinned beneath him. The accident had disfigured his leg, and since then Aderes had taken over the majority of her father's work. She hoped her progress with Sahnden would make him proud.

Aderes paused in her work when the approaching riders reached the stone wall that bordered Sahnden's pasture. Both she and the stallion watched them pass by, Sahnden grumbling throatily at the other horses, who mostly ignored him. Aderes, too, looked at the horses, barely noticing their riders as she studied their gaits and conformation. None were particularly eye-catching, save for the black gelding ridden by the leader of the group. He was a tall, graceful creature, and his sable coat paired beautifully with his rider's crimson cloak draped over his haunches.

When she glanced up to see what sort of man rode the dark horse, she noted that he was a superb rider, well-matched to the elegant strides of his steed. Together they made dignity look effortless, though the look was slightly spoiled by the rider's constantly shifting gaze, taking in every detail of his surroundings, even flicking briefly over Aderes and Sahnden before continuing to study the pastures full of horses, the fields of grain and vegetables, and Carwyn Castle, rising in the near distance from its island stronghold in the valley's narrow river.

I thought the eagle banner only flew for the khafyri, Aderes thought. *But there's nothing remarkable about that man; he appears merely human, not all-powerful like the legends would have us believe. Surely he can't be a khafyri.*

In a matter of moments, the group had passed, leaving Sahnden chomping at the bit in a clear desire to follow. Aderes watched them for a moment longer, seeing them ride by a stooped figure leaning on a walking stick next to the road. Her father.

Aderes turned back to Sahnden, tightening his cinch and flipping the reins over his head.

"Ready, boy?" she asked. Sahnden snorted and tossed his head. "Let's show Father what we can do."

Chapter Two
Jarond

A KHAFYRI WAS coming. Jarond saw the blood-red standard streaming from a banner-man's staff as a small party of armored knights thundered down the Northern Road toward Carwyn Castle. From his position atop the western gate tower, Jarond couldn't make out the black device on the banner, but his mind conjured up the swooping eagle of the khafyri line, its outstretched talons clutching a jagged black blade. He lifted his horn and let out the sequence of blasts that signaled the arrival of a member of Sermund's ruling house.

As Jarond let the horn swing freely from the strap crossing his chest, he studied the approaching riders through the gap in the crenellations. All were armored, save their leader, who wore dark-gray garb and a crimson cloak that matched the fluttering banner. Jarond leaned on his spear in an attempt to relieve some of the weight of the chainmail hauberk hanging from his own shoulders. The wool jerkin he wore under his mail, so necessary for warmth in the cold hours at the start of his watch, was making him sweat under the warming spring sun. He idly reached a hand up to scratch his head, his light brown hair plastered against his scalp beneath his arming cap and helm, and glanced up; the sun's position seemed unchanged as it stubbornly refused to reach its zenith and the end of his guard duty.

Below him, the clanking of chains announced the raising of the portcullis and lowering of the drawbridge, and Lord Kuval of Carwyn rode through the open gate with a pair of knights. Kuval's own sigil, a golden stallion rearing proudly on a green field, floated from the banners affixed to both knights' lances. Jarond watched as they intercepted the incoming party, both groups halting as formalities were observed and Lord Kuval bowed deeply in his saddle. They regrouped and started riding back toward the castle, the gray-and-crimson garbed figure leading the way, Lord Kuval on his right flank and the standard-bearer on his left, with the knights bringing up the rear.

When the party reached the drawbridge and trotted across, Jarond was able to get a closer look at the newcomers. The knights, their suits of plate mail shining in the noontime sun and clanking with every stride of their muscular steeds, had their visors lifted for ventilation, revealing an assortment of skin tones, from sun-burned ivory to the ink black of a Haseri. Despite the variation in coloring, all the faces were the same: the stoic, proud faces of experienced warriors in their mid-twenties. It was their leader who caught Jarond's eye and held his attention.

So, that's a khafyri, he thought, studying the man—or was it monster? Hundreds of years' worth of legends surrounded the khafyri, each myth claiming to be able to define what Sermund's powerful rulers truly were. But the tales themselves were at odds, some upholding the khafyri as mankind's saviors, others vilifying them as demonic overlords. The only consistency in the portrayal of khafyri was that they weren't human. They were something else. Something that the king and lords of Sermund paid tribute to.

Jarond's sharp blue gaze focused on the khafyri, trying to discern for himself what the differences were in the visitor. The khafyri looked human, and yet at the same time everything about him indicated he was something more. He flowed smoothly with the movements of his steed, perfectly balanced, looking even more natural atop a horse than Jarond's twin sister Aderes, who had been riding before she could walk. A longsword hung at his left hip in an elegant, jeweled scabbard, more gemstones studding its hilt; Jarond briefly wondered if the weapon was there for ornamentation or use. The jewels undermined its practicality, but its owner carried himself with a balance and grace that to Jarond's trained eye looked like the marks of a formidable swordsman.

The feature that stood out to Jarond was the khafyri's eyes. They were in constant motion, scanning the castle's walls and defenses. Jarond noticed slight pauses as the khafyri's stare picked out each sentry atop the corner towers and on either side of the gatehouse. He had the piercing eyes of a predator, and it was clear to Jarond that not even the smallest detail escaped them. An involuntary shudder shivered through Jarond as those eyes glanced at him, taking in his chainmail hauberk, steel half-helm, crossbow, and spear in one glance before moving on to study the walls. He recognized the look as a quick evaluation, and a quick dismissal, of yet another simple guardsman from a simple fief.

A moment before, Jarond had been silently cursing the sun; now he was grateful for its warmth in the aftermath of the cold, calculating gaze. It was with a sense of relief that Jarond watched the group disappear beneath the thick arch of the main gate. He heard the clatter of the steel-shod hooves of their mounts when they reached the cobblestone courtyard, but the width of the wall and the inner ramparts shielded his back from the unnatural gaze of the khafyri.

Jarond returned to his watch duties. Before him, Carwyn Valley lay cupped between gently rolling green hills, the twin peaks of Mount Piru reaching toward the sky over the northeastern end. The Northern Road skirted the mountain's western base, but from his vantage point Jarond could only see the road as far as the northern end of the valley floor, where it began winding through the foothills. Sprawling farms covered the far end of the valley, but closer to the castle, the land had been devoted to bright green pasturelands, watered by the middling-sized river that bisected the valley and formed the moat around the castle walls. The pastures were filled with horses, the pride of Carwyn fief, their coats—burnished copper, pale cream, or spun gold—glinting in the sun.

The golden steeds of Carwyn were renowned for their strength, stamina, and beauty. If Jarond looked carefully, he could just make out the yellow glint of his sister's hair amongst the horses. Their father, Torvald, and every man before him as far back as Ashwin, who had originally bred the famed Carwyn Gold, was the master of horse, a renowned position in a small fief not known to any other great honor. To their father's great disappointment, Jarond had preferred a life of sword and steel to that of breeding horseflesh, but his sister had been eager to uphold the noble family tradition. She was now the one with primary responsibility for training the young mounts, and although Horse Master Torvald made the final choice on bloodlines, Aderes had great influence on his decisions.

The heavy step of boots on stone announced the arrival of Jarond's replacement sentry as the new guard climbed up the narrow, spiraling stairs of the gatehouse tower.

"It's about time," Jarond said when Kamin appeared. "I can't wait to shed this damn mail."

"Keep waiting." A mischievous crinkle around blue eyes matched the impish grin of Jarond's fellow guardsman and closest friend. "Lord Kuval wants all the sentries coming off duty to form an honor guard for the khafyri. They're going out to inspect the herds."

Jarond cursed soundly; normally he'd welcome a chance to ride out to his sister's domain, but not after he'd just finished a shift. And certainly not in the presence of the newly arrived khafyri. At that moment, he wasn't considering that the duty would put him in close proximity to the khafyri; he worried about their unusual guest getting within a league of his sister. Some of the legends claimed that khafyri kidnapped maidens and took them back to their strongholds, never to be seen again, and after seeing the predatory glint in the khafyri's eyes, Jarond was more willing to believe the fantastical than he had at the beginning of his guard duties.

Kamin, always unperturbed, laughed at his outburst. "Are you going to be putting salt across your sister's doorway tonight?"

"What?"

"You know—the story my gran used to tell. That khafyri can be stopped by salt. Because it's a clear white crystal. The darkness in them can't abide the purity of it."

"An old wives' tale," Jarond scoffed. *But might be worth trying out.*

Kamin smirked. "Maybe so. But you'd better hurry up and get down to the courtyard; the grooms were saddling mounts when I passed the stables."

With a scowl that was answered by another grin, Jarond dutifully tromped down the stairs, stopping briefly by the armory to drop off his crossbow and exchange his spear for a sword. When he emerged into the yard, ten saddled horses waited for him and his fellow guardsmen. They were plain brown, an unfortunate byproduct of the breeding program to produce the famed Carwyn Gold, but that was expected. Lowly guards were not worthy of the renowned mounts.

Jarond cast his eye over them before choosing his steed—he may have not followed his family trade, but his sister and father made sure he knew exceptional horseflesh from average, and the gelding he chose was the brother of Sahnden, the magnificent stallion who was the epitome of Horse Master Torvald's breeding efforts. Jarond took the gelding's reins from the groom, whose hands were full with leads for half the horses, and swung into the saddle. The horse chomped restlessly at the bit, but Jarond quieted him with a gentle touch of the reins. Once they were all mounted, the guard moved into formation, waiting for the lords to emerge. When they finally did, it was only three—Lord Kuval, the khafyri, and one of Lord Kuval's knights, who now bore the standard of the khafyri in place of his lord's banner. All three were mounted on fresh steeds, whose golden coats shone metallically in the sun.

The khafyri swept his gaze over the assembled guard, and Jarond was relieved to see that he wasn't the only one unable to refrain from shuddering under the raptor gaze. This close, he saw that the khafyri's eyes were an emerald green, as cold and hard as stone. Apparently satisfied with his brief assessment, the khafyri rode past them toward the raised portcullis. With a clatter of hooves and jingle of mail, the guard wheeled to follow behind the lords as they passed through the stone arch of the castle gate.

Jarond rode in the first line, as suited his status as the best swordsman in the fief. Even the court-trained knights at Carwyn rarely bested him. As he followed the nobles, he studied the back of the khafyri, instead of keeping an eye on his surroundings. He didn't feel guilty about his neglect of duties; the grassy valley had no hidden refuge for bandits, and he knew the squad of guards was merely for ceremony's sake. From behind, there wasn't much to see: the crimson cloak spread over the gold horse's hindquarters, lifting and flapping as they sped up into a trot once they crossed the drawbridge. Black hair hung to shoulder length, smooth as a raven's feather, and the brief glimpses Jarond caught of the khafyri's face as he examined their surroundings showed lightly tanned skin and handsome, refined features. Jarond was grateful to be behind the khafyri, safe from the piercing gaze, but his stomach churned uneasily as every step took them closer to his sister. Aderes was strong-willed, but her fair face had attracted unwanted attention before, and this noble guest was not a drunken villager who Jarond could throw through a door.

Chapter Three
Aderes

THE STALLION SURGED under Aderes, hooves skimming across the grass as he galloped in a wide circle, his cream-colored coat shining pearlescent in the sun. Aderes flowed with the rhythmic stretch and pull of his muscles, the powerful animal an extension of her own body rather than a separate creature. Together they raced forward, warmed by the heat of the sun and cooled by the wind whipping across their faces and through their hair. For a moment, the stone walls of the pasture were nonexistent, as if they could gallop to the ends of the world unhindered.

But even Sahnden couldn't run forever, and when Aderes felt his strength wane she sat up straight, gently touching the reins, and the cream stallion eased back into a walk, sides heaving like the bellows of a forge as he snorted, still eager to race the wind.

Aderes patted his sweat-streaked neck, then rode him to the corner of the pasture and the gnarled oak tree that Horse Master Torvald had claimed as his throne. Her father sat in the cupped seat formed by the twisted roots, watching her from the comfort of the shade. His crooked leg made walking to the pastures an onerous task, but nothing could keep him from watching the progress of his prized young stallion.

Aderes couldn't keep the smile off her face as she pulled the horse to a stop in front of her father. "He feels like he could go forever."

Torvald nodded. "He's improved his form too. You've done well with teaching him the correct lead. Sahnden's looking balanced now, not like a gangly colt. He has his sire's strength and his dam's grace, with the strong lungs of both of them. When next year's foals are born, I'm sure we'll see some improvements from his influence on the bloodline."

Sahnden pawed impatiently, fidgeting from boredom. His head swung to the right, ears pricked forward as he spotted the group of riders coming down the road from the castle. He bugled a challenge at them, then tossed his head in annoyance when Aderes didn't allow him to charge down the pasture toward the approaching horses. Aderes looked at the mounted group in surprise; the guards wore the green livery of Carwyn, although they bore the newcomers' red-and-black banner instead of the majestic golden stallion on his green field.

As they drew closer, Aderes recognized Lord Kuval riding at the front, next to a man dressed in gray, a crimson cloak spread across his horse's haunches. It took a moment for Aderes to recognize him as the one who'd arrived on the beautiful black gelding, but seeing his perfectly balanced seat triggered her memory.

Just behind the stranger, Aderes spotted Jarond. Her twin looked tired and grumpy, no doubt wishing that his guard shift had ended at its appointed time. She flashed him a quick grin, then schooled her face into proper blankness as the group drew to a halt.

Her father had heaved himself to his feet when he saw the riders approaching. He walked toward the fence as quickly as his crippled leg would allow, leaning heavily on his walking staff. Aderes dismounted and followed, keeping Sahnden on a short lead. The young stallion snorted restlessly, his pale blue eyes sizing up the new horses.

Once they reached the stone barricade, Torvald bowed low and Aderes curtsied, spreading her divided skirt as if it were a proper lady's garment. She had specifically designed her clothing for riding. The appearance of the skirt adhered to her father's and brother's view of what was proper for a well-bred woman to wear, while the modification into two billowing legs suited her own needs. It allowed her to ride in a saddle like a man, without having to fuss with the nonsense of a sidesaddle.

"My lord, to what do we owe this honor?" Torvald asked.

"Tav Arawn wishes to see the herds," Lord Kuval replied. "He is looking for a suitable gift for King Bohdan when he visits the capital this summer, and he thought that a golden stallion of Carwyn would be a fitting choice."

"Of course, tavek," Torvald said with a bow to the stranger.

He is a khafyri, Aderes realized, recognizing the honorific used by her father. She took a second look at the stranger, glancing away when she met his bright green gaze.

"There are many fine studs for you to choose from," Torvald said. "Would you prefer an older stallion or a colt? All have carefully selected bloodlines and come from the finest stock."

"A colt, but one that is broken to the bit," Arawn replied. His voice was smooth, sleek as the black hair that fell to his shoulders. Aderes chanced a glance at him and saw that he was studying Sahnden. "Tell me, surely that is not one of your stock. He is so odd-looking. Such pale eyes and pink skin. I have never seen such a strange-looking creature."

Aderes did not have to look to see her father bristle.

"Sahnden may be an unusual color, it is true," he replied in a tight, barely controlled anger. "But only the cream can guarantee a pure gold offspring. It's the breed trait: two odd horses make the beautiful gold. It's why nobody's been able to replicate our successful breeding program, tavek, and why the Carwyn Gold is so renowned. Everyone throws away the bad, not realizing it is necessary for the good. Tavek." He bowed stiffly.

"I see." Arawn's hard emerald eyes studied the horse once more, taking in both animal and handler. "He certainly has fine lines; there can be no doubt about that, once you look past the unsightly coloring. But I am looking for one of the renowned golds that you speak of. What do you have available that is worthy of a visiting monarch?"

"All of our stock are worthy of kings, aye, even the ones who don't have the color. But let me show you the ones you may be interested in." Torvald hobbled toward the gate.

Aderes quickly tied Sahnden to the oak tree and then caught up with her father.

"The three-year-olds are an especially fine crop," Torvald continued as he walked toward the next pasture. "My cream stud is from their age group, but if you are looking for the golden color, then it's Kulta you'll be wanting. He's a fine colt. Aderes, go catch him for me, will you?"

Aderes ran out into the pasture and haltered Kulta from amongst his small herd and then jogged toward her father so the golden stallion's beautiful trot could be seen by the observers.

"Aye, he's a fine beast, that's to be sure," Torvald said. "Out of my best mare, and the same sire as Sahnden, who you just saw. There's no fairer gift that you could give a king."

"Very well," Arawn replied. His crimson cloak fluttered as his horse pranced underneath him. "See to it that he's ready in two days' time."

Aderes smiled broadly; a horse for a king! Who could've thought that someone would come to such a small fief to choose a mount for a visiting monarch? Her heart nearly burst with pride when she thought of what this must mean to her father, who had devoted his life to breeding the finest, most beautiful horses in the realm. Sahnden may be her father's special favorite, but it would be Kulta who made him famous.

"Of course, the girl will have to come as well."

Chapter Four
Jarond

"TAV ARAWN, WHAT do you mean?" Torvald sputtered.

Only years of training and discipline kept Jarond from making a similar outburst.

"What do you want with my daughter? She is my trusted right hand; without her here, I fear that the quality of the Carwyn Gold will die with me. She is needed here."

"Have no fear, Horse Master," the khafyri replied in an unruffled, unconcerned voice. "I merely require the services of your daughter for my return journey. None of the ham-fisted knights that I brought could be trusted with such a fine, spirited animal. She will aid me where they cannot. Once we arrive at Menai, she will be free to go home. With a proper escort to assure her safety, of course. Although, if she chooses to remain in my service, I would put her to good use; my household is sadly lacking when it comes to talent in the stables."

Jarond listened to the khafyri's words with the inbred suspicion of a warrior. On the surface, the request seemed harmless. But Jarond couldn't help but remember the way his sister looked as she ran through the pasture, leading Kulta: her dark golden hair flowing freely behind her, an unconscious, innocent smile of pure joy on her face as she showed off the stallion, unwittingly showing off her own womanly charms at the same time. And what of the tales he'd heard, the ones that cast the khafyri into a sinister light? Brotherly concern broke through Jarond's warrior discipline.

"Tavek, I request the honor of forming part of Aderes's guard," he said.

The khafyri wheeled his horse to look at him, an expression of surprise, quickly masked, on his face. "Who are you, to speak out of turn?"

"Jarond, tavek," he replied respectfully. For once, the khafyri's eyes held no power to cow him. He met the cold gaze with a hard look if his own "Aderes is my sister."

The khafyri frowned, thoughtful, then said in an offhand manner, "There is no need for that. My own guards are more than suitable to protect your sister from any bandits or brigands. Your duty is here." He turned his horse away from Jarond in clear dismissal.

Jarond opened his mouth to protest.

"I am honored by your attention, tavek," Aderes said, with a small curtsy.

Jarond scowled—it was just like his sister to do whatever she could to keep him out of trouble.

"It would be my pleasure to bring Kulta to Menai." Aderes rubbed the stallion's muzzle. "My brother is very protective of me, but I know that I will be in safe company with your knights. I appreciate your consideration in offering an escort to return me safely home, once my task is complete."

The khafyri nodded. "Very well; we will leave the day after tomorrow at first light. See that you and the horse are set to travel by then." He put his heels into his mount and cantered back toward the castle. After one last look of frustration and exasperation at his sister, Jarond had no choice but to follow with the rest of the guard.

"MUST YOU LEAVE so soon, Tav Arawn?" Lord Kuval asked as soon as they stopped in the castle's courtyard. The khafyri had set too fast a pace for talking while they rode. "We would be honored if you stayed longer; it is such a long road between here and Menai. Surely you did not make such a long journey to only stay two nights."

"I didn't," the khafyri—*Tav Arawn,* Jarond amended in his thoughts—replied as he swung down from his horse and tossed the reins to an approaching groomsman. "I have business at the mines of Tynda that required my immediate attention. Otherwise, I would have sent my head hostler to come choose a horse for King Bohdan. Since Carwyn is on the way, I decided to do the errand myself. I will leave for Tynda early tomorrow and return here in the evening. My business will not take long."

Jarond handed his mount's reins to a stable hand and headed toward the armory to finally drop off his heavy mail and sword. Instead of crossing the walled yard directly, he walked nonchalantly in the direction of the keep's main door, in order to catch as much of the lords' conversation as possible as they returned to the main hall.

"You won't regret coming here yourself, tavek," Lord Kuval replied. "I have ordered the cooks to prepare a fine feast in your honor. You will enjoy it, I am confident. Our horses may have made us known throughout the realm, but if it weren't for them, then surely our chef's fine preparation of suckling pig would have brought us glory . . ." Mercifully, his recitation and embellishment of Carwyn's limited honors was cut off from Jarond's hearing as the entrance door swung closed behind the lords.

"Suckling pig!" Jarond laughed to himself. Nothing so clearly showed the unimportance of the small fief as naming suckling pig as one of its finest achievements. But then, Lord Kuval had always acted as if Carwyn was the most important castle in the realm—second only to the capital, of course. Even in the presence of a khafyri, the lord didn't see the absurdity of his claims.

After shedding his mail at the armory, Jarond stopped by the barracks to change out of his uniform. He then went to the practice yard, intending to work out his frustration by pounding on one of his fellow guardsmen under the guise of sword practice.

The dirt area bordering the barracks, set aside for weapons practice, was empty when Jarond arrived. He picked up a wooden sword, weighted by a lead core, and moved to the center of the yard. He held the sword in a ready position and closed his eyes, trying to focus on the blade and nothing else, hoping to channel his emotions through the carved wood.

Jarond opened his eyes and attacked, swinging the blade in a complex pattern of strikes, parries, and counter strikes. His body moved in a natural rhythm with the blade as he lunged and pivoted, partnered with an invisible foe in the dance of death. His world shrank to encompass nothing but his straining muscles, the swishing sword, and the hard-packed earth beneath his boots. He came to a stop with a flourish at the end of his routine, his breathing even despite the exertion.

"Looks like you could use an opponent," an unfamiliar voice said.

Jarond spun around and saw that he had gathered an audience. Tav Arawn's knights, he realized, dressed in padded sparring clothing instead of their flashing armor.

"I'm Sir Kayden," the man at their forefront said.

Like the rest of them, he had the muscular build of a swordsman accustomed to wearing and fighting in heavy armor. Sir Kayden appeared to be of mixed Haseri and Sermundi descent, giving him an oddly monochromatic look: brown hair, brown eyes, and brown skin. That impression was accentuated with his brown tunic, pants, and boots. He ran through names of his companions, too quickly for Jarond to keep them all straight.

"And you are, Sir . . ." Kayden prompted.

"Just Jarond," he replied. "I'm a guard, not a knight. Sorry for taking up the whole space."

"No worries, Just Jarond," Sir Kayden said with a friendly grin. "We were enjoying watching you work. But what do you say to a sparring partner?"

"Sure," Jarond said, sizing up his opponent as Kayden came toward him, wooden sword in hand.

He appeared to be a few years older than Jarond—likely more experienced, but Jarond often found that knights didn't practice with the same religious intensity that he did. His friend Kamin often joked that Jarond had never found a woman to court because he was already married to his sword. Kayden was more heavily muscled than Jarond, although they were evenly matched in height and reach. *I'll have to be quick—wear him down with speed instead of strength.*

They faced each other, crossing their swords in preparation for the duel.

"Ready?" Kayden asked.

"Always."

"Very well. Begin!"

Jarond struck, the hilt of his sword jolting in his hand as Kayden blocked the descending blade. He spun aside from Kayden's return strike, then darted back with a series of quick thrusts, all of which were turned aside, then shifted to defense as Kayden attacked with a volley of his own hammering overhand blows.

They broke apart; Jarond saw his newfound respect mirrored in Sir Kayden's eyes as they studied each other for a weakness. Kayden took a stumbling step on a stray stone, and Jarond leapt forward to take advantage of the misstep. Another flurry of blows passed, neither gaining an edge, until they stepped back again, both breathing heavily.

Jarond waited for his foe to come to him. It was a short wait. Sir Kayden lunged forward, sword held in both hands, and rained a series of chopping blows at Jarond's head. Jarond parried them, his hands aching with each forceful strike, then saw his opportunity and ducked away, his sword coming under Kayden's guard in a lightning-fast strike that should have ended at the knight's heart—only Kayden was no longer there. In a quickness that belied his size, Kayden dodged the attack and spun away, his own sword coming to rest on the base of Jarond's neck.

Jarond froze, panting, then lowered his sword with a rueful laugh. "Well fought. It's been a while since I've had an opponent best me."

Sir Kayden took his sword from the side of Jarond's neck. "You almost had me there at the end. A month ago, you would have won. But I've had to learn to be quicker in Tav Arawn's service. Khafyri are so damned fast. I doubt I'll ever be able to beat him, but at least now I come away from practice sessions with fewer bruises to show for it."

"You spar with Tav Arawn?" Jarond asked, determined to learn more about the mysterious khafyri.

"Not often," Kayden replied. "And when we do, it's usually three or four of us against him. His daughter joins our practice more often, but she's just as quick as he is. What human can stand against one of the khafyri?"

"What's he like?" Jarond asked.

"You thinking about joining his guard? You're a good enough swordsman, but, no offense, Tav Arawn only takes highborns into his personal service. The khafyri are only interested in people who can strengthen their political ties."

"No, that's not why I asked." Jarond hesitated, reluctant to trust a stranger in the khafyri's service, even one as friendly as Kayden. In the end, the need to protect his sister won out. "Arawn commanded my sister to come with him to Menai, to deliver the horse he wants. I'm just worried. I don't know anything about khafyri; this is a small fief, and I've never seen one before. I need to know she'll be safe."

Jarond watched Kayden's face closely, searching for any evidence of falsehood as the knight responded.

"Tav Arawn is true to his word," Kayden said. "If he has promised your sister's safety, then nothing will harm her."

Jarond saw an unspoken sentence in Kayden's eyes. "What aren't you telling me?" he asked, his unease spiking.

Kayden shook his head. "Nothing. It's nothing. I can't talk about it." He turned and walked away, leaving Jarond with more questions than he'd started with.

Chapter Five
Aderes

"ADERES, I AM worried for you," Torvald said, his concern etched in the weathered lines of his face and filling his warm brown eyes.

She smiled reassuringly and hugged him. "I'll be fine, Father. It's just a short trip to Menai. Five days to get there, and another five to return. At the very most, I'll be gone a fortnight. You'll be able to manage everything while I'm gone. And just *think* about what this will mean for you. Kulta will be a gift for a king, and everyone will see the beautiful golden stallion and know that he is the finest of Horse Master Torvald's famed Carwyn Gold. People already come from around Sermund to buy Carwyn horses; now they'll come from other countries too." She released Torvald so she could see his face, expecting to see her enthusiasm catching.

"Aderes, the horses do not matter to me."

Shock hit her like the blow of frigid snowmelt during a springtime swim. "What do you mean? The horses have always been your life."

"No, Aderes. The horses have been my job; one I have been very passionate about, it's true. But my life is my family: you and Jarond. And your mother, when she was still with us. I would give away every single horse if it meant keeping you and your brother safe from harm. And right now, I am worried about your safety."

"But Tav Arawn promised I'd be safe. Surely one as powerful as he can guarantee it."

"Addie, there's safe, and there's *safe*. Khafyri aren't human; we can't expect them to think the way that we do. I've heard rumors, when I've spoken to traders at fairs, about strange things that go on in their strongholds. Things that people won't talk about, because they are afraid, or because the things are unspeakable. But I've heard enough to know that the khafyri are dangerous."

"I will be fine, Father. I promise," Aderes said, hoping the confidence in her voice quelled his unnecessary fears. Torvald was putting too much belief in traders' tales spoken from the bottom of wine cups. Tav Arawn's contingent of knights would be well able to keep her from harm. "Now I need to go unsaddle Sahnden. Poor fellow must be getting impatient about being tied to the tree for so long."

AS THE SUN caressed the horizon that evening, Aderes herded the band of broodmares back to the castle in order to protect their young foals from nocturnal predators. She rode Kulta, taking him back to the stables in preparation for his departure to Menai. The mares, with frisking colts and fillies scampering close to their sides, trotted ahead of them eagerly, knowing that their nightly ration of oats awaited them in their courtyard corral.

Torvald had made his slow, hobbling way back to the keep hours before, after Aderes had finished with Sahnden. Their disagreement over her safety was still unsettled when he left, so Aderes had been glad of an afternoon free from his worried gaze.

After securing the mares and foals in the pen adjacent to the stables, Aderes untacked Kulta, taking extra care to brush his coat to its magnificent metallic sheen, and then put him in a clean stall with plenty of fresh bedding and hay. The gold stallion immediately rooted through the dried grasses for the choicest morsels.

Aderes stroked his soft coat, imagining the glory that he'd bring to Carwyn. She was pulled out of her daydream when her brother entered the stable, jaw set in a hard line as he walked to her.

"Aderes, you can't go," Jarond said brusquely.

Indignation flared. His tone was far beyond the brotherly concern that she expected from him. He had no right to speak to her in that manner. "Who are you to stop me? Tav Arawn has commanded me to go, so I'm going. You don't have any power to challenge him."

"Someone else can take the damn horse to his damned castle," Jarond snapped. "It doesn't have to be you. He can find someone else."

"Are you jealous that you can't come too?"

Jarond blinked, a frown creasing the corners of his eyes.

"Of course not. I'm just worried about you."

"Well, don't. You're not in charge of me. I'll be fine. You don't always need to be protecting me. I can take care of myself."

"Like that time with the brewer's son?" he asked.

She felt herself flush as heat rose in her. "Am I never going to be able to get past that? You throw one drunken idiot who won't hear 'no' through a door, and so you think that for the rest of my life you need to hover over me like a mother hen. I'm tired of it, Jare. Any time I talk to a man, you act like it's the end of the world. You need to stop it."

"Addie, this is different," he pleaded.

"I don't think it is," she snapped back. "Now leave me alone. I need to get ready for the feast." Without waiting for a response, she slammed the stall door behind her and marched out of the stables, leaving Jarond behind.

Chapter Six
Asho

THE CLATTER OF hooves on cobblestones called Asho out of the stables in time to see a small party of nobles ride into the yard of the Prancing Stag, Aldorn's largest inn. There were three lords, mounted on elegant palfreys sweat-soaked from a hard ride but still full of energy, heads held high and prancing lightly on their hooves. Asho always appreciated fine horseflesh, despite their noble owners.

He kept his eyes lowered as he approached the nobility and gave a short bow. "Will my lords be wanting rooms tonight?"

"Yes, and stable our horses for us too, boy," the one nearest Asho replied, swinging from the saddle and thrusting the reins at him without a second glance.

"Master Hayden will see to your rooms in the Stag," Asho replied, then turned to collect the reins of the other riders.

"Please rub them down well; they've worked hard today."

He nearly dropped the reins in shock at the feminine voice. He looked up, the manners that Master Hayden had beaten into him forgotten in his surprise.

"And give them some extra oats; I'll make sure there is something extra for you too," the woman continued.

He stared, slack-jawed at the hand wearing an elegant kidskin glove extending toward him, not sure what he was supposed to do—bow and kiss it? Then he noticed the reins held in the thin hand, and he quickly took them from the lady.

He had been mistaken on his cursory evaluation of the nobles; she was clearly a lady, although dressed like no other woman he'd ever seen. What sort of lady wore a man's pants and tunic, even if the tunic was beautifully embroidered with vines and flowers? And those *legs*. The close-fitting breeches revealed shapely calves snugly enclosed in tooled leather boots. When he managed to lift his gaze, the lady's brilliant blue eyes looked at him expectantly, and he jerked his eyes away, bowing low to her to hide his flushing face.

"Yes, m'lady. I will see to it that they receive the finest care."

"Thank you," she said, then followed the men into the Prancing Stag.

Asho watched, mouth agape, until the door closed, then turned and led the three horses into the stables.

Once the horses had been fed, watered, and their coats brushed to a soft sheen, Asho entered the inn through the kitchen door and dished up stew from the pot simmering over the fire. Farica caught him peeking through the door into the common room as she returned to refill empty stew bowls from patrons.

"It's no use, lad," she said. "They requested the private parlor. You won't get a chance to see her now. Besides, it's not good to associate with their sort. Dangerous."

Asho opened his mouth to ask her what she meant when the door to the common room swung open again, and Master Hayden entered. He scowled at Asho. "What are you doing in from the stable, boy?"

"Just getting supper," Asho said.

"Well, hurry up about it. I can't have anything happen to those expensive horses. Go keep watch."

"Devlin won't let anyone mess with them," Asho said.

Hayden purpled at his show of defiance. "Do I pay the damn dog, or do I pay you? Maybe he should get the coin, and you should get the meat scraps, for all the good you're doing me right now. Get out!"

Asho scowled, rage burning through him like never before. He always did what Hayden told him, and what did he have to show for it? A hayloft to sleep in and barely enough coin to repay Hayden for the meals he took at the inn.

He took a step forward, but suddenly Farica was between them, smiling too widely and thrusting a warm chunk of bread into his hand. "Here, Asho, go eat in the stables. I'll bring out the bones for Devlin later."

Still smiling, she grabbed his arms with hands strong from kneading bread and churning butter, and deftly turned him around and out the door to the yard. "I'll see you later, dear," she said, closing the door and leaving him in the dark with his bread, half-eaten bowl of stew, and simmering rage. He kicked a small rock in frustration, listening to the sound of it skittering across the ground as he stalked back to the stable.

Shadows filled the cavernous building. A single lantern hung from the wall, illuminating the center of the stable. Asho sat down underneath the lantern hook and leaned back against a sack of grain. He tore angrily at his bread as he ate. Rage pounded in his temples; his temper had always been thoroughly beaten down by Master Hayden, but it was as if floodgates had been unlocked, and once opened, there was no stemming the tide of pent-up rage. His pulse throbbed behind his eyes, and he could feel the pressure of a growing headache.

Devlin approached from the dim back corner of the stable, the light illuminating his blocky head and powerful haunches, jet-black with russet markings on his chest and face. His tail waved gently as he approached Asho.

"Hi, Devlin," Asho said. Even in his anger, he couldn't ignore or rage against his best friend.

Devlin whined softly, apparently hearing the undercurrent of tension in Asho's voice, and lowered his head to lick Asho's face.

"Here, this is what you really want," Asho said, putting his empty bowl on the ground in front of Devlin.

Devlin licked up the remaining scraps from the sides of the bowl with his broad tongue, and then flopped by Asho's side, leaning against him.

The furry bulk of Devlin had always calmed him before, but it couldn't completely banish his temper tonight. Asho felt the rage recede, but it simmered in the back of his mind. Why was he so angry? The confrontation with Master Hayden was stupid, nothing compared to some of the beatings he had received growing up. So why could he put those behind him but not what had happened tonight? He buried his fingers in the thick ruff, scratching. Devlin sighed, head resting on his paws and eyes closed contentedly, but the same peace still eluded Asho.

After a long while of sitting in silence, Asho's anger finally subsided enough to leave him exhausted. He climbed to the hayloft and retreated to the corner he had claimed as his own. It contained all his worldly possessions: a change of clothes, a ragged wool cloak for when the weather grew cold, and his treasure—a small signet ring. It was the only thing that remained of his parents, whom he could barely remember.

The ring was delicately wrought silver, and in the center was a swirled rune of graceful curves. Asho had once taken it to the local monks to see what it meant, but they told him it didn't look like any rune they had seen before. It was too small for even his littlest finger, so he had woven a leather thong to hang it around his neck. He never wore it though; he didn't want Master Hayden to be reminded of the fact that he owned something of value. The ring was far too precious to sell, even if some nights Asho went to sleep with a painfully empty stomach.

Next to his things was his bed, a small nest in the hay adorned with a pair of patched blankets. Asho climbed in and curled up, closing his eyes in an attempt to banish the fully formed headache pounding behind them. Despite the cooling evening air, the loft felt hot, and he tossed and turned, kicking off his upper blanket in an attempt to get comfortable. It was no good. The heat only built up in defiance of the long-set sun, and a thin sheen of sweat soon covered Asho's face and made his rough-spun cotton shirt cling to his back. He pulled it off angrily, but the wool blanket beneath him was no better comfort. He stretched out on his stomach, limbs splayed haphazardly around him, trying to cool down. It was no good, and sleep remained elusive.

Finally, he stood and opened the shutters of the hay door, allowing a refreshing spring breeze to fill the loft and dry the sweat on his bare chest. He stood in the opening for a long minute, watching the scattered clouds scud across the face of the moon, until a shiver shook him and he returned to the comfort of his bed. Master Hayden would be angry if he knew Asho had left the doors open all night. A sudden shower could blow rain into the loft, ruining hay, but Asho took the gamble that he would wake before Master Hayden and be able to close the doors before the innkeeper noticed.

The fresh air cooled him enough that he finally drifted off to sleep, his dreams filled with a twisting rage and overpowering impotence.

A HOWL RESOUNDING in the deep night woke Asho from his dreams of smoldering bloodlust. He bolted upright, recognizing Devlin's bass warning cry. Red light filled the air, twisting and flickering, and in horror, Asho saw flames racing up the sides of the dry fuel filling the hayloft. His blankets smoked under him, and he leapt to his feet with a yelp of fear, miraculously unburnt. The low whicker of horses in the stable below joined Devlin's warbling howl, which continued unbroken.

Asho raced for the ladder, then paused. He sprinted to his meager possessions and grabbed the ring, which he shoved into his pocket for safekeeping. He turned and nearly fell down the ladder in his haste. In the stable below, the deadly red glow shone through the cracks in the loft floorboards, and the horses paced restlessly in their stalls, snorting and blowing in fright.

Asho reached the first stall and grabbed the halter hanging on the hook outside. When he opened the stout timber gate, the mare inside crowded close to him for comfort. She tossed her head in panic, making it difficult to get the halter on, and his efforts were further hindered by the terrified fumbling of his fingers. When at last he had the mare secure, he tried to lead her out of the stables, but she refused to leave the perceived safety of her stall.

"Come on!" he shouted, but the mare planted her feet, leaning back against the pressure of the lead rope.

"Dammit! Somebody help me! Help!" Asho cried out, drawing Devlin's attention.

The guard dog broke off his howl and trotted into the stall. He snapped at the mare's heels, making her leap forward, nearly running Asho over as she bolted from the burning stable.

Asho clung to the rope and managed to regain control once they entered the inn's yard. He ran to one of the hitching rails against the front of the inn and secured her there, then pounded on the front door, which had been locked for the night.

"Fire!" he bellowed.

The shutters above the main door swung open. Master Hayden's suite was set so that he could keep an eye on all the comings and goings of the inn. He leaned out to shout at whoever was rousing him in the middle of the night and saw the blaze across the yard, which had completely engulfed the hayloft.

"Fire!" he echoed.

Asho ignored him, racing back toward the burning structure. With no time to lead the horses out one by one, he ran down the barn aisle, opening the gates to occupied stalls as he went. None of the horses left their stalls. Frustrated, Asho ran into a stall and yelled wordlessly at the gelding within, waving his arms to chase the horse out though the gate, assisted by Devlin's barking and snapping.

The big bay finally bolted toward safety and a relieved Asho ran to the next stall, followed by Devlin. A bell started ringing frantically in the distance, summoning the fire brigade. Help would come too late to save the barn; the best the brigade could hope to do was to stop the inferno from spreading to the surrounding structures.

Smoke filled the air as Asho and Devlin continued to herd the terrified horses out of the barn. The thick gray haze stung Asho's eyes and he stooped over from wracking coughs. At last he and Devlin reached the front of the barn—and the final horse—and broke free into the cleaner air of the yard, coughing and hacking together.

The yard was a scene of chaos. In the time that it had taken for Asho to free the horses, the area had filled with the fire brigade and onlookers from the inn. A few of the recently released horses were milling together in a corner between the inn and the houses on its far side, trapped by the crowd of people between them and the street in front of the inn. The other horses had vanished, no doubt stampeding through the dark streets as they fled from the fire.

Asho collapsed against the wall of the inn, exhausted, and wrapped his arms around Devlin.

"Is this your first time burning something down?" a quiet, feminine voice asked.

Chapter Seven
Jarond

JAROND SAT SULLENLY on the bench next to his fellow guardsmen, unable to join the mirth and laughter that surrounded him. At the other end of the great hall, he watched Tav Arawn, sitting next to Lord Kuval at the high table. The khafyri ate sparingly and rarely spoke to Kuval; his attention seemed to be preoccupied by the servants bringing the different courses. His piercing green eyes studied them as they approached, but he never said a word to them.

"Thanks for saving me a seat," Kamin said sarcastically, wedging himself between Jarond and the soldier to his right to create a space for himself. He piled a trencher high with food. "The captain wouldn't let us off early for the feast."

Jarond barely heard the words, fixated on finding a way to keep watch over his sister.

Kamin paused as he lifted a hunk of coarse brown bread to his mouth. "What's wrong?"

"Tav Arawn wants Addie to go with him to Menai," Jarond said. "He said he needs her to help with the horse he chose."

"So?" Kamin asked around a mouthful of bread. "She'll be coming back, right?"

"That's what he says, but something just doesn't seem right to me." Jarond frowned up at the high table. "Kamin, what do we really know about the khafyri?"

Kamin shrugged as he stabbed a chunk of boiled salt beef. There may have been prime suckling pig at the high table, but none ever made its appearance in front of the guards. "Not much; they've been ruling ever since they showed up in Sermund a few hundred years ago. They left the monarchy in place, although the king bows to them. Who knows what they do? I mean, supposedly they protect us from dangerous enemies, but nobody I know has seen any danger."

"Don't be so skeptical," their fellow guardsman, Xander, interjected from his seat across from them. "The khafyri protect us from the beastly changelings."

Kamin laughed. "Changelings are just myths. Stories for children. Nobody's ever seen a changeling."

"Aye, nobody's seen one," Xander agreed. "But that's because the khafyri drove them off. I spoke to a sailor in Bracken once. Fellow had just come from Juven in the far north. Said that they have to go far out to sea to get around the coast of Varnstad because of all the devilfish in the waters there. He saw them once. Huge, with big white eyes that will steal your soul."

"What do devilfish have to do with changelings?"

"They serve the changelings. Sink ships and drag the drowning sailors back to shore, where the changelings sacrifice them in an unholy ritual. It's how they grow their power. Killing everyone, leaving no survivors. If it weren't for the khafyri fighting them and driving them from Sermund, they'd still be here, with plenty of innocent victims for their sacrifices."

"But how do you know that's even true?" Jarond asked impatiently. "If there are no survivors, then how does anyone know what happens?"

"Some lucky sailor escaped, I suppose."

"But that still doesn't give us any answers as to what the khafyri are. And whether it's safe for my sister to go with one of them."

"Calm down," Xander said. "No need to get so worked up. Haven't you been listening? The khafyri aren't anything to be feared."

"You still don't know what they are. If changelings are as dangerous as you claim, and if the khafyri did manage to force changelings out of Sermund, then how did they do it? What can they do that we can't? It still doesn't mean that they aren't dangerous too. I can't let Aderes go with Arawn."

Kamin laughed. "You're just a protective brother; you and Addie may be twins, but you've always acted like you're her older brother. It's only natural for you to be suspicious of a handsome, mysterious stranger that shows any interest in her."

Jarond looked at Aderes, seated across the room with their father. She hadn't glanced at him once during the course of the feast, no doubt still angry at him over their earlier argument. "It's more than that, Kamin. But Aderes doesn't see it. There's something odd, something *wrong*, about Tav Arawn. Ever since I first saw him, I felt it. Not just from hearing stories—the ones where khafyri aren't the heroes that Xander claims they are. It's something about *him*. I sensed it when I first saw him. And he hadn't been anywhere near Addie then. I feel like I'm going crazy, trying to figure it out. But I know that I'm right."

Kamin paused in lifting another bite of salt beef to his mouth. "You sure?"

"Yes," Jarond said, relieved that his longtime comrade was willing to believe him. Kamin had always followed Jarond's lead, and he needed his friend's faith in him now more than ever.

"Okay, so what do we do about it?"

"You'd better not be including me when you say 'we,'" Xander said. "I don't want to be part of whatever craziness you concoct."

"Fine, stay out of it," Jarond said. He blew out a breath, frustrated, and turned back to Kamin. "I don't know. I don't see that there's anything we can do. I already tried to join Arawn's party for the trip to Menai, but he refused me."

"What about his knights? I saw you sparring with them. What did you think of them?"

Jarond shrugged. "Sir Kayden was a great fighter, but I don't know about him. He knew something about Tav Arawn that he wouldn't tell me."

"Do you think he'd help protect Addie?"

"From outside threats? Sure. But what about from Arawn himself?" Jarond frowned as he thought about it. "I doubt it."

"And you're sure that Arawn is a threat?"

"I can't prove it. But I feel it with every speck of my being."

"So talk to Addie. Reason with her. Maybe you can convince her to stay," Kamin counseled. "Just don't order her to do anything. She's as bad as you in that way." He grinned then shoved the next bite of meat into his mouth.

Jarond nodded, stood, and worked his way around the trestle table to the other side of the hall, where Aderes and their father sat. He squeezed himself on the bench across from them, displacing two clerks. They grumbled in annoyance, then quieted when they saw it was him.

Aderes scowled, but Torvald looked hopeful. "Jarond, maybe you can help me convince your sister to stay here."

Jarond couldn't stop himself from smiling. "So you also think it's odd for Tav Arawn to want her to accompany them? Addie, you have to see it. You'd be foolish to go with Arawn with your eyes closed."

As soon as the words left his mouth, he realized his mistake. Nothing could've guaranteed his sister's obstinacy more than his insistence that she was wrong. A flash of anger flared in her brown eyes, normally warm and gentle.

"I don't need to *see* anything. You're being ridiculous. I'm leaving for Menai the day after tomorrow. That is final." She thrust herself back from the bench and stalked out of the hall.

Jarond and Torvald watched her go.

Torvald turned back to Jarond. "My son, you must find a way for your sister to see reason."

"How?" Jarond asked. "Aderes only listens to my advice when it suits her."

"Do whatever it takes," Torvald said.

Jarond frowned, looking around the hall as he thought of how to best approach his stubborn sister. He realized the high table was missing an occupant. "Where's Tav Arawn?"

Torvald shot a look at the high seat. "He's gone."

Jarond stood. "Stay here, Father, in case Aderes returns. I'll try to find her to make sure she's all right."

As he walked toward the door, he passed close enough to the guards' bench for Kamin to call out to him. "Everything okay?"

"It's fine," Jarond said, distracted as he continued out the hall and turned down an empty corridor toward the stables that were Aderes's safe haven.

Perhaps it was not too late to convince Aderes to not go to Menai. If only he could get her to feel what he felt. His steps quickened, an irrational urgency filling him.

"I have a service that I require of you," a smooth voice said.

Fear jolted through him as he wheeled around, searching for the source of the unmistakable voice of the khafyri.

"This will not hurt; many seem to actually enjoy it. And there will be no lasting harm done." The quiet voice floated on the air, echoing down the stone passage, and Jarond realized that it was coming from around the next corner.

Jarond froze, heart thundering in his ears. He didn't understand what Tav Arawn referred to, but it sounded nefarious. He crept forward slowly, his footsteps muffled in the rushes, straining to catch Arawn's quiet voice.

A soft sigh whispered through the air. "My knights are untouchable, as per their contract. It is a price I must pay for the loyalty of their houses. But this journey has been long, and I have been without sustenance throughout it. I cannot wait until my return to Menai."

"I don't know what you are talking about, tavek," Aderes said, her voice filled with confusion and uncertainty.

Jarond charged forward, hand reaching for his sword hilt. Fury knotted around his chest. Whatever was going on, he was going to stop it.

"What—?" Aderes gasped as he rounded the corner.

She stood passively against the wall, not protesting or fighting back, and Jarond knew from personal experience that his sister had a wicked right hook. Tav Arawn stood before her, head bent with his face pressed against her neck.

He gripped Aderes's shoulders as she stood immobile with an expression of euphoria that Jarond couldn't understand.

"Let go of my sister!" he demanded, stopping in an aggressive stance.

Arawn turned to him. His mouth twisted in a snarl, revealing a pair of sharp fangs dripping blood. His eyes shone in the flickering light from a nearby torch, reflecting and magnifying its brightness in the darkness like a cat's eyes.

Jarond stumbled back a step.

Blood leaked from Aderes's neck from two small holes. Jarond stepped forward, drawing his sword. "Get away from her!"

"This doesn't concern you, boy," Arawn said. "Leave now if you want to live."

Jarond raised his sword. "Let her go."

Arawn stepped forward sinuously, drawing his own bejeweled sword in one smooth movement. Behind him, Aderes slid to the rush-covered floor, a glassy look of shock glazing her eyes. Jarond pulled his gaze from Aderes and lifted his sword.

The khafyri struck, and the clash of steel rang through the corridor. Jarond grunted with the effort of turning Arawn's blade aside; Arawn was much stronger than a normal man his size.

Jarond slashed, but Arawn blocked his attack with contemptuous ease and swung his blade in a high arc toward Jarond's head. Jarond lifted his sword with both hands and caught the blow; with a scream of tortured metal, his blade snapped in half. Arawn smiled, revealing gleaming fangs, and thrust his glittering sword at Jarond's heart.

Jarond twisted away, slamming against the rock wall of the narrow corridor. He stumbled, off balance. Arawn gave him a hard shove, sending him to his knees next to Aderes, who was slumped against the stone wall. Jarond gazed up at the khafyri standing over him, fangs no longer visible.

"You have fought well, young warrior," Arawn said. "But this is a battle you cannot hope to win. You should have walked away while you had the chance."

"Never!" Jarond spat a mouthful of blood onto Arawn's high leather boots. "I would die to protect my sister."

Arawn studied him for a moment with hard emerald eyes. "But would you live to protect her?" he asked softly.

A shout rang through the corridor. "No!" Kamin cried out. He raced down the corridor behind Arawn, bared sword in hand.

Arawn turned to meet the new attacker.

"Kamin, don't!" Jarond yelled.

His friend was a mediocre swordsman at best, no match for the speed and strength of the khafyri. Jarond watched in horror as Arawn blocked Kamin's blade and spun it aside with the force of his parry. Arawn lunged forward, thrusting his gleaming blade through Kamin's chest as easily as a needle through cloth.

As Kamin fell, Jarond pushed himself to his feet with a scream, stabbing recklessly with his sheared-off sword. The jagged end of metal found a gap between the khafyri's ribs, and Jarond shoved it forward until it burst from Arawn's chest.

"Remarkable," Arawn whispered, and then fell forward in a lifeless sprawl.

Chapter Eight
Asho

"I DIDN'T DO anything," Asho protested. How could this woman accuse him of arson? "The lantern must've fallen or something. It wasn't me. Why would you say I burned down the stable?"

"Is this the one?" One of the woman's noble companions strode up to her. He looked to be about forty, although his hair contained a premature amount of salt in its pepper. His black eyes matched what remained of his black hair.

She nodded, her piercing blue eyes fixed on Asho.

"No!" Asho exclaimed.

"I know you didn't mean to do anything," she replied in a gentle voice. "It was an accident. But it was you who did it. You're a first-degree pyromancer."

"I'm a—what did you call me?" Asho spluttered.

"This isn't the place to explain, Damali," the man said, ignoring Asho. "There are too many humans around."

"You're right." She turned back to Asho. "Come with us, and we'll explain." She held out a hand to help him to his feet.

The gesture was a friendly one, but Asho resisted the lure of her captivating looks. Normally he would've leapt at any chance of contact with a beautiful woman, but her words aroused the depths of his mistrust. "I'm not going anywhere with you."

The woman's companion sighed, a look of annoyance crossing his face. "Damned human ignorance. Look at me." Asho flicked his gaze at him. The man's black eyes were captivating inky pools; Asho found himself drawn to them, unable to escape. "*Come with us and don't make a fuss about it. We don't want to attract any unnecessary attention.*"

Why had he refused them before? They meant him no harm. Of course he should go with them. He took the offered hand and stood.

"That really wasn't necessary, Makani," the woman said, irritation coloring her voice.

Makani waved a dismissive hand. "Makes everything easier though."

From his place by Asho's side, Devlin snarled. He took a step toward Makani, eyes intently focused on him, growling menacingly in an unmistakable threat. That wasn't good. If Devlin did anything, it would cause a scene, and he didn't want to draw any attention to his new friends. Makani had said he shouldn't make a fuss.

"Devlin, stop," he ordered. "Sit here and stay put."

Devlin's growl turned into a worried whine; he looked up at Asho, uncertainty filling his warm brown eyes, and licked Asho's hand.

"I mean it," Asho said, and Devlin obediently sat.

Damali and Makani walked toward the door of the Prancing Stag, and Asho followed, looking around the yard. The fire brigade was still furiously pumping water in an attempt to contain the fire; Master Hayden was running around, shouting for everyone to work faster, harder, better. The orange glare from the raging fire showed a lone figure at the edge of the crowd, staring intently at the flames. Asho realized it was the third member of the noble party.

"*Come on, boy,*" Makani ordered.

Asho turned and followed him into the inn.

They went upstairs to what had to be the finest suite of rooms in the Stag. The elegantly furnished sitting room, with its carved cedar chairs and richly colored tapestries, was the finest chamber Asho had ever seen. He looked down at his naked, soot-streaked chest, ragged pants, and callused bare feet, acutely aware that he didn't belong here.

Damali turned to him, her finely woven garb emphasizing his own bedraggled state. Her sapphire-blue eyes studied him with an intense scrutiny that was at odds with her small, delicate face. Auburn hair, woven into an intricate braid, fell over her shoulder. Asho jerked his gaze away when he realized that by looking at the braid, he was staring at her small bosom.

"I probably should've started with this, but what is your name?" she asked.

"Asho," he replied, then remembered his manners. "M'lady."

"There's no need for that," she said. "I'm not a lady. You may call me Damali. It is a pleasure to meet you, Asho. As you may have gathered, my tactless companion over there is Makani. Tycen is our other comrade. He's outside, monitoring the fire."

"What's taking him so long?" Makani complained from the seat he had thrown himself into. "He should be able to take care of a fire like that in seconds."

Damali shot him a look of annoyance. "You know he can't do that here. We're *trying* to be discreet and not attract notice."

He snorted. "Yeah, a great big barn fire is exactly what I think of when I hear the word 'discretion.'"

"There's no reason for any of the humans to think it was anything more than an accidental fire."

"No reason for the *humans* to think that, maybe, but it isn't humans we're worried about, now is it?"

"Even a khafyri would have to be nearby to sense that power. If one were that close, I'd be able to sense them too. We're safe, as long as we don't do anything rash."

Makani grunted. "As you say."

The door opened, and Tycen sauntered in, brushing his hand through wild, reddish-blond hair. He looked to be about thirty, same as Damali.

"All contained; the fire is still smoldering in the ruins of the stable, but it won't spread any farther," he announced, then stuck out his hand.

Asho stared at the hand and shook it.

"Impressive little blaze you started there; must've been quite exciting to be in the middle of it." Tycen winked a mischievous brown eye.

"I didn't," Asho said. "Why do you people keep accusing me of fire-starting?"

It felt like a burning fist was tightening around his heart. Beads of sweat broke out on his chest as he took a labored breath, forcing air into his lungs.

"Easy now," Tycen said, not letting go as Asho tried to pull away. "You're safe, there's nothing to fear. Calm down."

The grip on Asho's chest loosened.

"That's it; let it go. Good. Feel better?"

Asho nodded weakly. "What did you do to me?"

"I just helped you manage your emotions," Tycen replied. "Strong emotion, especially fear or anger, are a pyro's greatest weakness. They can make you lose control. With training, you'll learn to master them. For now, though, I can help you keep them in check."

"In the name of all that is holy, what is a pyro?" Asho asked in frustration.

"One who has the ability to create and control fire," Damali said. "It is a rare gift, especially as a first power. Tycen is the only other first-degree pyromancer alive. He can help you master your command of fire."

"I still don't know what you are talking about," Asho said.

"How much clearer do we have to make it?" Makani grumbled. "You aren't human. You're a changeling."

Chapter Nine
Aderes

ADERES STARED AT the bodies in numb disbelief, trying to comprehend the horror of the last bloody moments. Arawn's corpse was face down on the rushes, the hilt of Jarond's broken sword jutting from his back. Next to Arawn lay Kamin in a pool of his own blood, a red stain on the front of his tunic where Arawn's blade had pierced his heart.

"What do we do?" She fought against the thick fog that enveloped her mind, brought on when Arawn's teeth pierced her neck. She touched her skin and stared at the blood on her fingers.

"Here." Jarond knelt at her side, ripped a section of cloth from his tunic, and pressed it against her wound to stanch the trickling blood. "Are you all right?"

She emitted a mirthless laugh. She felt on the verge of hysteria. "What do you think?"

"Addie, we have to hide them." Jarond's usually calm and rational voice was tight with fear and unshed tears. "We must flee. We're dead if we stay."

Aderes gazed into Jarond's blue eyes, normally so bright and confident, and saw an expression of overwhelming despair. "What? Why?" She frowned. "*He* attacked *me*. You were just defending me. So was Kamin. Why would we have to leave?"

"Khafyri are more powerful than the king. And we just killed one. Do you really think that it will matter that it was in self-defense?"

"But he's a monster."

"Yes. A fact that the khafyri have clearly managed to keep hidden in a web of lies and myths for the last three hundred years. After what I've seen tonight, I imagine that they are more than willing to kill in order to protect that secret from general knowledge."

"But nobody knows we were involved. Kamin and Arawn are both dead— why don't we make it look like they killed each other?"

"Those bite marks on your neck tell a different story. Anyone who knows what a khafyri is would know that you were involved somehow."

Jarond was right. The wounds directly linked her to the dead khafyri. But if they could escape before anyone else realized that something was wrong, they might just have a chance.

"What do we do?" she asked.

"I'll hide the bodies in the moat," Jarond said. "If I weigh them down, they won't be discovered. Then we need to get as far away from Carwyn as we can. Clean yourself up, then go to the stables and saddle some horses. We can leave at first light, when the drawbridge is lowered. The guards expect you to take the mares out to pasture. We'll do just that, only then we'll keep going. If we can get enough distance before they start chasing us, we might be able to make it to a city and get lost among the crowd."

He checked her neck. "You've stopped bleeding, but put a bandage on it, then make sure it's hidden by a scarf or something. We don't want anyone asking questions."

Aderes nodded, wiping away her tears. The matter-of-fact plan laid down by Jarond gave her something to focus on. She pushed aside her confusion from the attack and sorrow for her brother's friend, and then she stood and picked up Arawn's jeweled sword.

"What are you doing?" Jarond asked as she wiped the blade on Arawn's cloak.

"You need a sword, and we need money. I'll wrap the hilt and scabbard in leather to cover the jewels so you can wear the sword without arousing suspicion. Then we can pry out the stones and sell them as needed."

Jarond helped roll Arawn to the side so she could unbuckle the scabbard. Arawn's head flopped sideways, revealing the gleaming points of fangs.

Aderes shuddered, remembering the sharp pain of those teeth cutting her skin. That pain had been overwhelmed by a sudden feeling of euphoria that clouded her mind and impaired her thinking.

"He's venomous," she realized.

"What?"

"When he attacked me, I couldn't fight back. I was completely powerless; it didn't even occur to me to resist, once he bit me. I think he must have some sort of venom that makes it easier to feed on people. But why does he need to drink blood?"

"I don't know, but now is not the time to discuss it," Jarond said. "We need to take care of this mess, before someone comes by and discovers us. Go get ready; I'll deal with the bodies. If someone catches me, I'll take the blame. Pretend that you don't know anything about this."

"But—"

"Go."

With a last worried look at Jarond, Aderes ran down the corridor. If they could get through the night without getting caught, they might be able to escape. Dawn couldn't come fast enough.

Chapter Ten
Asho

"CHANGELINGS ARE MYTHS," Asho said. "Stories for children. There's no such thing."

"No?" Tycen asked. He released Asho's hand and held up his open palm. "Then how do you explain this?" A ball of fire floated between his fingertips, orange and yellow flames twisting and bending in a mesmerizing sphere.

Asho stumbled a step backward, staring in wonder and fear at the burning orb. "How . . . how are you doing that?"

"I am a master pyromancer," Tycen replied. "One of my gifts ties me to fire. It allows me to summon and control fire. You also have that talent. In time, you'll be able to do the same." He flicked his wrist, and the fireball spun around the room, circling the walls before returning to his hand.

"I can do that?" Asho asked, his fear melting into awe.

"Not yet. But you'll learn."

"How?"

Tycen smiled at his eagerness. "Close your eyes."

Asho narrowed his eyes in suspicion. "Why?"

"If you listen to me, you'll find out."

Asho closed his eyes, feeling vulnerable now that he couldn't see what was happening.

"Good. Now, feel with your mind. What do you sense? Look for the fire, but not with your eyes."

Asho focused, feeling foolish as he stood with his eyes closed for several long moments. At last, he felt it—a flickering at the edge of his mind, a burning point of light in the darkness. It called to him, and he took a step forward.

"Don't move," Tycen cautioned. "And don't open your eyes. Lift up your hand, palm up, and call the light to you."

Asho held up his right hand, frowning with concentration as he reached with his mind toward the glowing sphere. It rocked slightly, hesitantly, and rolled toward him, then stopped halfway. Asho could feel sweat beading on his brow as he redoubled his efforts, and the orb slowly floated to him. He felt it shimmering before him, bathing him in a welcoming, warm light.

"Excellent!" Tycen exclaimed.

Startled, Asho opened his eyes.

Fire burned in his outstretched hand, jagged orange flames that bore little resemblance to the sleek sphere Tycen had conjured. Instead of hovering above his skin, the fire danced directly on his palm. Asho yelped in shock, afraid of being burned, and the flames roared toward the ceiling, creating a blazing tower of intertwined blue and orange fiery ropes.

The streaking inferno seemed to smash into something before it reached the wood. The fire broke on what looked like a smooth surface, rolling to the sides to reveal a curved dome above Asho, and then the flames fizzled into nothingness.

Asho stood in shock, trying to comprehend what had happened. He lifted his hand to check the burns to his skin. His callused palm was pale and cool, untouched by the fire. He clenched a fist and felt no pain.

"You aren't burned," Tycen told him. "One of the advantages of being a pyro. Flames won't hurt you. Smoke can still kill you, so you'll need to be careful when firewalking, unless you have a smoke shield."

Asho stared at him, mouth agape.

"Very well done, though," Tycen continued. "Some apprentices take hours to learn to call fire to them. Excellent job."

"I could've burned down the inn," Asho said with growing realization. "Oh gods. I *did* burn down the barn. It *was* my fault."

"No, it's our fault," Damali said. "We didn't realize that you were the one we were searching for. Most changelings get their first power when they are much younger than you—about twelve or thirteen years old. But you've been living among humans, and it apparently kept your power dormant."

"No. I don't know what's going on here, but I'm not a changeling. I can't be. Changelings are—" Asho gulped, a lifetime of stories from inn patrons flashing through his mind.

"Forget everything you think you know about changelings," Damali said. "Most of what you've heard are tall tales, or perhaps even rumors spread by the khafyri to vilify us. They want the human populace to think we are evil, so that the khafyri can more easily acquire power. But the fact is you are a changeling. And when you met us, your changeling nature was triggered, awakening your fire abilities. Unfortunately, I wasn't able to sense that in you until you accidentally used them for the first time. It wasn't your fault, Asho. We should have been more cautious and prepared. As for burning down the inn, don't you think one big fire is enough for one night?" She grinned. "You're safe with us. I put a shield around you so that you could practice. The flames can't pass my barrier."

Asho stared at her, the words sinking in. Clearly the three people before him had powers beyond the ordinary, and if the stories about changelings being myths were lies, then it wasn't a stretch to assume that stories about them being evil could also be lies. "Shield? What does that mean?"

"It's one of my abilities," she replied. "I can conjure a barrier that prevents energy from passing through. It works against changeling powers, like your fire or Makani's mind persuasion, but it doesn't work against physical things. I haven't developed that ability yet."

"What do you mean 'yet'?"Asho asked.

"When a changeling comes of age and their powers are awakened, they take the form of a specific ability," she replied. "Nobody has any control over what that ability will be, although sometimes it's possible to guess a child's first gift based on their heritage, their personality, or their interests. That ability is referred to as a 'first-degree' power. Like how you and Tycen are both first-degree pyros. There are other changelings who've mastered pyromancy, but for them, it is a secondary power. Once a changeling has mastered their first power, they are able to choose another power to learn."

"How many can someone learn?" Asho asked.

"There isn't a limit," Damali said, rolling up her sleeve. "But abilities take months, if not years, to master completely. Each changeling has skriva to show the abilities they have mastered and the one they are currently learning."

She showed her arm to him, sleeve pushed up to near her shoulder. A couple of inches above her elbow was a line of marks on her skin. The runes were about an inch square and jet black, each a distinct shape: a circle bisected by a lightning bolt, a series of jagged circles inside one another, and two curves coming together into a point. She pointed to them each in turn. "Shielding. Power detection. Shape-shifting." The last mark was steel gray instead of black.

"Shape-shifting?" Asho asked.

She glanced away, embarrassment coloring her face.

"I'm sorry," he said, unsure why his words caused her discomfort. "I didn't mean to be rude or anything."

Makani laughed from his seat behind him. "She's just embarrassed because she only developed that one because of her lover." He smirked. "The Council of Masters wasn't pleased that a changeling warrior would develop an unnecessary ability. They saw it as a wasted chance."

"That's none of your business, Makani." Damali's eyes flashed, emotion filling her voice for the first time.

"So when do I get my tattoo?" Asho asked.

"It's not a tattoo," Tycen replied. "When a changeling is marked with the skriva, each individual mark appears and takes its own shape based on that person's abilities. The runes start out gray, then turn black when that power is mastered. Each changeling's skriva are a unique representation of their achievements. No two marks are exactly alike, although similar talents have similar marks. So if you are familiar with the basic skriva shapes, you could see the general abilities that someone has."

A flash of inspiration hit Asho, and he pulled the ring out of his pocket. "Is this one?"

He showed the rune on the ring to them. Disappointment filled him as they each shook their heads.

"May I see it?" Damali asked. She frowned as he handed it to her and studied the rune intently. "I think I know what this is."

"Really?" Asho asked in excitement. "What does it mean?"

"Can you read?" she asked.

He nodded. "Master Hayden insisted, so I could do business for him and not get cheated by tradesmen."

"Look here." She traced one half of the double-looped line with her finger. "If you see this as two symbols, rather than one, it looks like stylized initials. They're lowercase for some reason, but I think this says 'e' and 'l.'"

"Esme Linwood!" Makani exclaimed, shooting Asho an inscrutable look. "How is this possible? Where did you get that?"

"Who?" Asho asked, surprised by Makani's sudden enthusiasm.

"Esme," Damali replied. "Makani's lost sister."

Asho goggled at Makani. "This was my mother's."

Chapter Eleven
Jarond

JAROND RAN DOWN the corridor toward the armory, praying he wouldn't encounter anyone. Splatters of blood speckled his tunic, undeniable proof that something was seriously wrong. But the halls were empty, all the servants undoubtably working hard to carry food from the kitchens to the feast, and everyone else in attendance of the feast in the great hall.

The iron-bound door was unlocked; Carwyn was such a small keep that the captain of the guard had little concern about thievery. Jarond slipped inside and lifted two chainmail shirts from a rack of armor; they would ensure that the corpses wouldn't be discovered for a long time, if ever. He hurriedly retraced his steps to the secluded back corridor, which was still empty, save for the gruesome evidence of the fight.

Jarond reached Kamin first and dropped one of the hauberks in a rattling heap. He knelt next to Kamin and struggled to put the other armored shirt on the heavy and limp body. He pushed his grief over Kamin's unnecessary death aside; he had to be strong. He'd mourn when Aderes was safe.

He dragged Kamin's body to the nearest arrow-slit. He looked through the slit at the deep, murky moat about ten feet down. Jarond maneuvered the body through the narrow sloped slit, the chainmail scraping against the stone edges. Jarond pushed down his panic that Kamin wouldn't fit, then the lifeless body slipped through.

"I'm sorry, my friend," he whispered as he released Kamin and watched him hit the water with a loud splash. "I hope there will be a grand feast waiting for you in the afterlife."

After wiping tears away, Jarond ran back down the corridor to fetch the khafyri's body. He pulled his broken sword from Arawn's back with a sickening wet sliding sound and tossed it through the arrow-slit into the moat; it made a much smaller splash.

As Jarond yanked the chainmail down Arawn's torso, he spotted a coin purse hanging from his belt. *That will come in handy.* He tied it to his own belt, and then pushed the thinner Arawn through the arrow-slit. When the body splashed into the moat, Jarond spat into the dark water.

"I hope there's a special place of eternal flame and torture for people like you."

Jarond quickly bundled the blood-soaked rushes through the arrow-slit; they would float away in the steady current from the diverted river, taking away all evidence of the deaths. He used his cloak to wipe blood splatters from the stones and then spread fresh rushes on the floor, concealing all evidence.

He strode back to the barracks, but not in a hurried manner that would attract the notice of one of his fellow guardsmen if they happened to look down from their wall-top posts. He was grateful for the cover of darkness; only a few torches burned at the edges of the courtyard, and he easily skirted the pools of light they cast, without appearing to be intentionally avoiding them. Once in the barracks—empty, since all guards were either on duty or attending the feast—Jarond stripped out of his bloodstained clothes and put on fresh garb. He bundled his old clothes down the privy and headed toward the storeroom near the kitchens, where he filled a small sack with salt pork, hard cheese, and loaves of bread, then went to the stables.

Aderes was busy saddling two horses when he arrived. She gestured to the wall, where a plain sword with a leather-wrapped hilt was sheathed in a brown leather scabbard.

"That's for you," she said, fingers busy tightening the girth around the belly of one chestnut gelding. A brown scarf wound around her neck, covering the bandaged wounds.

Jarond picked up the sword. Aderes had done a masterful job disguising the jeweled weapon. Her even stitches marched down the side of the leather covering the scabbard, evidence of the hours she spent learning to maintain and repair tack with their father. He buckled the sword to his belt; the familiar weight of a weapon at his side erased his fears and made him feel like he could face whatever challenges came at them.

"Take the sword into the tack room and cut all the girths," Aderes said.

"What?" he asked, confused.

"Armored knights can't ride without saddles; saddles can't stay on a horse without a girth," she said, with the ghost of a grin. "Just don't make it too obvious. We don't want the sabotage noticed until someone tries to actually tack up a horse. It will buy us some time, at least, before they can start pursuing us."

"Good idea." Jarond smiled at her cleverness and trotted to the tack room.

He pulled the sword from the scabbard in a smooth arc, ringing softly. The blade shimmered in the light of the tack room's single lantern, ripples of blue weaving their way down its razor-sharp edge. Jarond drew it across the backsides of the leather straps, scoring their surfaces so only a thin membrane on the front held them together. Hanging on the wall, they appeared undamaged, but Jarond knew that as soon as any pressure was applied they would split like blades of grass.

He hurried back to the main part of the stables, where Aderes was finishing filling saddlebags with the food he'd pilfered, then tying rolled-up blankets on top of each horse's load.

"We can't risk taking a pack horse or too much stuff, because it will look suspicious," she said as she finished tying the last knot. "The only thing left to do is to say goodbye to Father."

"Addie, we can't," Jarond said softly.

Aderes faced him, eyes red but empty of tears for the moment. "Why not?"

"It will only put him in more danger. The only way he'll be safe is if he doesn't know anything about what happened to us. He can claim innocence if questioned. That still might not be enough to protect him completely, but with his bad leg, he can't ride. If he were caught leaving with us, they'd assume he had something to do with the fight. We can't risk it."

Aderes stared at him for a long moment, her eyes filling with tears. He took her into an embrace. Though they were twins, Aderes was five inches shorter than him, allowing her to bury her face in his chest as she sobbed.

"Jare, what is going to happen to us? What will we do?"

He rubbed her back, not letting her hear or see the same uncertainty and fear that was filling him. "It's going to be all right. We'll ride hard as soon as the portcullis opens. If we push the horses, we'll make it to Bracken, where we can sell them, get new mounts, and ride through the night. If we are careful, and lucky, our pursuers won't be able to figure out which road we leave on—you've seen how busy Bracken is, Addie, when you've taken horses to the faire with Father. At the very least, trying to figure out where we went will slow them down."

He paused. Where would they go next? From Bracken, they couldn't go west; that road led to Menai, which was Tav Arawn's own domain. Sir Kayden had mentioned that Arawn had a daughter, and Jarond recoiled at the thought of encountering a khafyri related to the one he had just slain. Who knew what sort of vengeance she might take for the death of her father.

East wasn't an option; the capital city, Serif, lay down that road, and Jarond didn't want to go anywhere near the center of power for other khafyri. He repressed a shudder at the memory of Arawn, teeth bared to reveal sharp fangs dripping Aderes's blood.

Continue north? There were other cities on the Northern Road. Perhaps they could lose themselves among the crowds in one of them. Or even ride all the way to the border. Harondor wasn't under khafyri rule. Maybe they could be safe there.

"We'll keep riding north until we are safe," Jarond said. "I'll protect you, Addie. I promise."

"I trust you," she replied, her voice no longer thick with tears. "If you say we can do it, then I believe you."

Jarond didn't answer, lest his voice betray his fear. He wished he could have as much faith in himself as his twin did. He hadn't been able to save Kamin; what if he couldn't save Aderes either?

As they stood, locked in a comforting embrace, the castle's rooster heralded the coming of dawn. Footsteps tramped across the yard outside as new guardsmen headed to their posts to relieve the night watch.

"At least I don't have guard duty today," Jarond tried to joke. "Imagine our great escape being postponed because the captain saw me trying to shirk duties. I'd be cleaning latrines for a month."

Aderes gave a weak chuckle, untied the two horses she'd prepared, and handed the reins of one to Jarond.

As they rode out of the stable, the sound of clanking chains echoed through the stone-walled yard, ending with a muffled *thump* as the drawbridge came to rest on the far bank of the moat. Aderes leaned from the saddle to open the gate to a large corral set in the corner of the yard, releasing Carwyn's prized broodmares and their gangly spring foals. The dams knew the routine, and the lead mare led the way across the drawbridge, the rest of the herd following, each mother with a golden foal traveling closely at her side.

Aderes and Jarond rode behind, keeping the stragglers moving, as the herd galloped down the Northern Road toward the lush green fields. Once Aderes secured the horses in their pasture, she faced Jarond, her brown eyes meeting his own blue ones.

"Ready?" he asked.

She took a deep breath, then nodded.

"Everything will be fine; I swear it," he lied, and together they turned and raced down the road.

No turning back now, Jarond thought. *If they catch us, we're dead. I don't know if I can keep us ahead of them. But I will do anything to make sure Addie gets away. Even if it means that I don't escape; I'd die for her.*

Chapter Twelve
Asho

ASHO AND MAKANI stared at each other, studying each other's faces. Asho had only seen his own face in a mirror a handful of times, but he recognized the slight arch of his nose, the squareness of his jaw, and the upswept peak of his hair in Makani's features.

"You have my sister's coloring." Makani gruffly broke the stretched silence. "Hazel eyes, like our mother, and brown hair. I always took after Father more."

"How is this possible?" Damali broke in. "Why wasn't Asho raised in Lyndell? Why was he left with humans?"

Makani glanced at his companions. "The two of you are probably too young to remember, but maybe not. About twenty years ago, Esme disappeared while on a scouting mission along the border of Sermund and Harondor. She was alone. When the day passed that she was supposed to return to Lyndell and there was no sign of her, Cirocco scried for her. He found nothing; like you, Damali, she was a strong shielder, so Cirocco didn't know if he couldn't sense her because she was hidden or because she had been killed, or worse, captured. The Council sent out search parties, but nobody ever found anything."

"I remember that," Tycen said. "All the masters were in an uproar. Lyndell was nearly deserted, except for the too-young and too-old. Even the apprentices went out with the squads. It lasted for weeks before they finally gave her up as lost."

"That sounds vaguely familiar," Damali said. "But I grew up in Stenberg. We were less affected by Council-related events there."

"Asho, what do you know about Esme?" Makani asked.

Asho shook his head. "Almost nothing; I barely remember her, or my father. I had no idea what her name was, until now. Most of my memories of them are sitting in the saddle in front of my mother, her arms wrapped around me as we rode. It seemed like we were always riding, always on the move. Then there was the scary day. Mother told me to hide in the stables and that she'd come back for me. I was maybe six. I crawled under one of the horses and held onto his legs. Master Hayden found me there. He told me my parents were dead. He and Farica let me stay here; they gave me a job of tending the stables after a couple of years. Whenever I asked, though, they said they didn't know anything about my parents, other than the fact that they were lawbreakers who finally got caught. Master Hayden didn't like it when I asked questions."

"I want to speak to this innkeeper," Makani said as he rose from his chair.

"Yes, but wait a moment," Damali said.

"Why?" he asked impatiently.

"Asho deserves to be there too."

"Of course he can come," Makani said, heading toward the door.

"Makani," she warned.

"What?"

"Look at Asho."

He turned back toward them. "Oh. Forgot about his clothes. Or lack thereof. Fine, I'll wait." He threw himself back in the chair, one leg slung over the arm.

"I don't have anything else," Asho muttered, flushing with embarrassment. "Everything was in the loft."

"No problem," Tycen said. "You're about my height and build. I'm sure I can find something for you to wear. Makani's clothes would probably fall off your skinny bones. First, though, you need a bath. Come with me."

Asho followed him into an adjacent room, where a large copper tub stood, half-full of water.

"It's not fresh, but it's a good deal cleaner than you are." Tycen summoned a fireball in his palm and then plunged his hand underwater. "Here's a little trick that you'll find handy." The water glowed with the flickering of the orange flames as Tycen maintained the underwater blaze.

"The water doesn't extinguish it?" Asho asked, mesmerized by the bubbling lights.

"It tries to. It's more effort to maintain an underwater flame. I'll show you how to do it later on, once you've gotten the hang of basic control." Tycen pulled his hand out of the water, which steamed slightly, and closed his fist around the flame. "There. All warmed up. Go ahead and get cleaned up. I'll toss some clothes through the doorway for you."

As soon as the door closed behind Tycen, Asho stripped off his soot-stained pants and sank gratefully into the tub, the heat from the water easing the tension in his stress-filled muscles. He scrubbed away the dirt and sweat from his skin, the water turning a murky gray around him. He barely noticed when the door opened a crack and a pile of clothing was dumped on the floor.

When the water cooled, Asho stood, dirty water rolling off him. He spied a ewer on a nearby stand, grabbed it, and used the clean water to sluice off the remainder of the grime, then climbed out of the tub and dried himself off.

Asho nervously picked up the clothing by the door; the soft fabric was finer than anything he'd owned in his life. He pulled on a light gray cotton shirt with long, loose sleeves, a pair of black wool pants, and a dark blue, sleeveless tunic with silver embroidery along the hems. A pair of socks was stuffed into calf-length leather boots. Asho put them on and then tried on the boots, surprised at how well they fit.

He looked down at himself, feeling foolish in the finery. He was a stable boy, not a lord. He felt like an imposter. He mustered all his courage and walked back into the main room.

Makani glanced up. "Finally ready? Let's go." He stood and strode out the door.

Damali smiled at Asho as they followed. "You're looking a lot better."

Asho felt his cheeks warm. "Thanks," he muttered.

The eastern sky was a faint blush when they reached the yard, the remnants of the stables a jumbled heap of scorched beams and warped metal.

Master Hayden was still there, hassling the last of the fire brigade as they left. "Are you sure it's all out? Don't leave! I need help rounding up all these loose horses. Where's that useless boy got himself to?"

Hayden glanced at Asho and his new friends as they left the inn and turned away dismissively, then whipped back around, recognition in his eyes.

"There you are! Where have you been? And what on earth are you wearing? You look like a fool, all dressed above your station. Come over here and get to work," he hollered, striding toward Asho.

Asho flinched, his confidence in his new friends shattered.

Devlin got between them, growling menacingly, teeth bared at the innkeeper.

Hayden skidded to a stop. "What the . . . *paska*! Call the damn dog off, boy, or you'll both get a beating!"

Damali touched Asho's arm. Sudden warmth filled him.

"Make the dog stop, Asho," she said quietly, her eyes twinkling. "After all, we will have a hard time getting answers from Hayden if he gets mauled first." Her smile gave him the courage to return it.

"Devlin, come here," Asho said.

With a final snarl at Hayden, Devlin trotted to Asho's side.

"Good boy," Asho murmured, scratching Devlin's blocky head behind his tiny ears.

"Innkeeper, we need to speak with you," Makani said.

"Not now," Hayden barked. "I'm busy. The boy and I need to work."

"*Asho* is going nowhere with you," Makani said in a deep menacing rumble. "Ever. And we need to talk now. *Come*."

He turned to walk back into the inn. Asho couldn't help but grin that the order had the same effect on Hayden as it had on him earlier. He gave Devlin another scratch while Hayden meekly followed Makani into The Prancing Stag.

Asho looked up to see Damali studying him and Devlin.

"What?" he asked.

She shook her head. "Nothing. Devlin seems unusually attached to you, that's all."

"I raised him from a pup after his mother abandoned him. He's lived in the stables with me his whole life. He's just loyal is all."

"That probably explains it. Come, we won't want to miss out on this conversation."

"Stay, Devlin," Asho ordered, and then followed her inside.

The common room was empty, but Damali led the way to the private dining room where the changelings had eaten earlier. The other three were already seated, Hayden on one side of the long table, the changelings on the other. Damali joined her companions, then gestured for Asho to sit next to her. Hayden shifted in his seat, clearly uncomfortable about having all four of them arrayed opposite him in a distinctly interrogative manner.

"What do you know of Asho's parents?" Makani began.

"His parents? Nothing. They got themselves arrested and executed for some reason or another. Found their whelp in the stables, and in the generosity of my heart, I raised him."

Tycen snorted. "Yes, we can all see you've been quite generous."

"I could've thrown him out on the street," Hayden bristled. "What's he to you, anyways?"

"He's my nephew," Makani said.

Hayden stared, mouth gaping. "What? How? *Him*? How the hell do you know?"

"It doesn't matter how we know," Damali said quietly. "But we are certain. So please, tell us what you know about his parents."

Hayden scratched his head. "Like I said, not much. Never even found out what they did to get themselves killed. Must've been pretty bad though. At least two score knights and a dozen or so khafyri showed up to arrest them."

"Khafyri?" Makani demanded, fists clenched on the table. "Are you sure?"

"Yes, it was a big deal; I remember because several of the khafyri were killed. The rest were furious about that; anyone with half a brain stayed indoors or well clear of them until they left. That's why I didn't find the boy until after they were long gone."

"And you're certain that Asho's parents were killed?"

"There was a massive explosion where the fight happened. Anyone in the center was killed."

"That's not enough proof."

"I saw the survivors leave the next day. They rode past the Stag, and I peeked through the shutters. A half dozen khafyri and a dozen knights. Nobody else." He shuddered. "Haven't seen a khafyri since then. Gods willing, it will stay that way."

Damali looked at the others. "I think that's all we can learn here."

Makani drummed his fingers on the table with a sigh, then nodded slowly.

"We'll spend the day here and leave early tomorrow morning. Asho looks exhausted. He needs to recover from last night before we travel. That is, Asho, do you want to come with us?"

Asho blinked at her through an exhausted haze. Leave Aldorn? Never be bullied by Hayden? Not have to work all day with barely a glint of coin to show for his efforts? There was hardly a choice to be made.

"Yes, I want to go with you," he said.

"Wait just a minute," Hayden protested. "I need the boy here."

"Too bad," Makani growled. "We didn't cross two countries and into enemy territory only to be thwarted by the likes of you. Asho belongs with us."

"But—"

"*Silence!*"

Hayden's mouth snapped shut.

"Find a room for Asho to stay in," Makani ordered. "And tell nobody of our conversation here. Or anything about us."

Master Hayden scurried out through the doorway. Not long after, Asho was ushered to his own room, a modestly furnished chamber down the hall from the changelings' suite. Despite the sun climbing up from the eastern horizon, he collapsed into the bed, luxuriating in its softness before his fatigue claimed him. *I have family.*

Chapter Thirteen
Jarond

THE SUN WAS reaching its zenith when Jarond and Aderes left the road and followed a short side trail to a small creek that wound through the shade of a copse of cottonwoods, where they stopped to water their horses. The clear water tumbled over smooth, mossy stones, and the horses lowered their muzzles to drink from a shallow pool between the rocks. Jarond swung his stiff leg over his horse's back and landed on the ground harder than expected. After giving himself a shake to loosen tight muscles, he unslung his waterskin from his saddle and crouched upstream of the horses to fill it.

"Toss me your waterskin," Jarond told Aderes, who had dismounted with considerably more grace than he had. She complied, then rummaged in her saddlebags and pulled out bread and cheese for their midday meal.

How much has changed in one day, Jarond thought as he capped his own waterskin and began filling Aderes's. *Just yesterday, I was counting down the minutes until the end of a boring guard shift. Now look where we are. On the run, and Kamin is—*

Couldn't dwell on Kamin's death. Couldn't mourn. He had to stay focused on the present, remain vigilant, and plan their next move. His grief would have to wait until Addie was safe.

Aderes handed him food, and he methodically tore the bread apart, alternating bites between the gritty, coarse bread and mild, nutty cheese. The horses, their thirst satiated, grazed the lush green grass covering the stream bank.

"How much farther to Bracken?" Jarond asked. He'd been to the city a handful of times, but Aderes went a twice a year, in the spring and fall, to buy and sell horses with their father.

"I think we're about halfway," Aderes said. "It's usually a two-day trip, and we camp not much farther from here, but at the pace we're going today, we should make it by nightfall."

Their horses lifted their heads from grazing and looked toward the road, ears pricked forward. Jarond's horse whinnied, and an answering nicker came through the trees.

Jarond tensed and put his hand on the sword hilt. "Get back on your horse," he whispered. Who was coming? Had guardsmen already been dispatched to search for them? If only they'd continued riding immediately after watering the horses. Nobody was in sight, but their presence had been betrayed by his mount.

Jarond swung into the saddle, looking around for an alternate route to escape detection. Away from the road, the ground was covered with scraggly bushes and trees with low, whippy branches. Their horses wouldn't be able to pass through without breaking foliage, easily giving their location away to anyone nearby. He spun his horse back toward the road.

"Get ready to make a break for it," he whispered. "If they try to take us, I'll hold them off. You ride as fast as possible, and don't look back." He fingered the leather-wrapped hilt of his sword, ready to draw in an instant.

Another whinny sounded from the road, and Aderes's horse answered.

"Paska," Jarond muttered. How had pursuit caught up with them so quickly? The sound of hoofbeats was soon audible, accompanied by a strange, rhythmic creaking sound. Jarond's mount fidgeted under him, sensing his tension.

But a moment later, a large, gaudily painted wagon came into view, pulled by two spotted black-and-white draft horses. One nickered when it saw Aderes and Jarond's horses. A man sat on the driver's bench, wearing clothes of bright blue and yellow that matched the wagon, while two men and a woman walked behind, each in matching motley.

"Whoa, there," the driver said when he spotted Jarond and Aderes on the side of the road.

The big horses lumbered to a halt, close enough for Jarond to see the words "Lucke's Lamborous Lacklanders" painted in eye-smarting yellow on the side of the peacock-blue wagon. He released the hilt of his sword.

"Hullo, there," the man called. "Where're you two off to on this fine spring day?"

"Bracken," Jarond said warily.

"Ach, a pity," the man replied, shaking his head. "We wouldn't a minded a bit o' company on the road south. Lucky Kell's the name, and this here's my troupe of travelin' troubadours."

"What does your sign mean?" Aderes asked.

Jarond stifled a sigh of annoyance—they needed to be moving again, but Aderes's curiosity was always insatiable.

"Well, we're lacklanders acoz we don't own nothin' other than our wagon here, just roam from town to town and entertain folks. Best troupe south o' the Telnor River. Best troupe north o' the river too, but we ain't north o' the river right now. As for lamborous—" Lucky Kell laughed. "That word means whatever we want it to mean. I tells the fancy folk that it means we're amusing t' watch. But truth be told, there's a diff'rent meaning amongst ourselves—the road gets awful lonely sometimes, if y'know what I mean." He winked and gave a lewd smile to Aderes.

Jarond scowled, and he put his hand back on his sword hilt.

Kell laughed. "Easy there, youngster. No need t' draw steel over a bit o' friendly conversation."

Jarond gritted his teeth.

Aderes threw him a warning glance. "We'd best be going now. No use holding you up."

"How much farther to the next town?" Kell asked.

"Carwyn's about thirty miles south of here."

"Thirty miles? Damn. Gonna be 'nuther couple a' cold nights on the road for us. Best be on our way." Kell clucked at his team, and the wagon resumed its ponderous drive south.

Jarond and Aderes turned their mounts in the opposite direction and trotted down the rutted dirt road. Sunlight filtered through the trees, warming their backs. Jarond settled himself into the rhythm of his horse's movements, rejuvenated by the meal and break, ready for the remainder of the long miles to Bracken.

Chapter Fouteen
Asho

ASHO JERKED AWAKE to unfamiliar surroundings. The mattress beneath him was soft, without the prickly ends of straw he was accustomed to sleeping in. Light streamed through a window, too bright for the normal soft glow of dawn that usually awakened him. Slowly the memories of the previous night trickled into his mind. The fire in the stables. The revelation that he was a changeling. The discovery that he had family, an uncle.

Can this be real? Surely he imagined the events of the night before, the fireball spinning around the room at Tycen's command, the flames flickering on his own palm without burning his skin. But why else would he be sleeping in a room at the inn? He got up and walked to the window. Late afternoon sunlight filled the inn's yard, and across from his window lay the blackened, burned husk of the stable. It hadn't been a dream.

Then that means my parents are really dead. The realization hit him harder than he expected. He'd always known that his parents were dead—despite Master Hayden's refusal to answer any of his questions, he knew deep down that they wouldn't have abandoned him as a child. But some small part of him had clung to a sliver of hope that they were alive, that something other than the ultimate finality of death had caused them to be separated from him. But they were gone, dead a dozen years, killed by khafyri for crimes unknown.

No, not for any crime, Asho realized. *They were killed because my mother was a changeling.* A bolt of fear jolted through him. *Makani and Damali were concerned about being discovered by khafyri last night. What if I go with them and the khafyri hunt me down because of it?*

He paced the small room, feeling trapped. Should he tell the changelings that he didn't want to leave with them? But then what would he do? He couldn't stay at the inn and continue to live a normal, human life. He might start another fire, and someone could get hurt. He was lucky that it was just the barn that burned down—if Tycen hadn't been there to put out the flames, they might have spread to the thatch roofs of the neighboring houses, and the whole of Aldorn might have gone up in smoke.

No, he needed to go with the changelings. At least until he had control over this strange new ability. Tycen was the only one who could help him. And he could learn more about Makani. Was he the only living relative Asho had left, or were there more? A whole unknown family? Makani was gruff, but he had warmed up a bit toward Asho once he'd learned Asho was his nephew.

Decision made, Asho left the room and walked downstairs to the common room. It was empty; too early for the local patrons to be in for supper and ale. Master Hayden was likely outside, supervising the cleanup of the stables. Asho was grateful that he didn't have to see the innkeeper, unsure of how Hayden would treat him after the events of the night before. The scent of roasting meat wafted from the kitchens, and Asho followed his nose through the swinging door, his stomach rumbling with awakening hunger.

In the kitchen, a half-dozen chickens were skewered on a spit over the fire next to a large pot of simmering vegetables in broth. Farica was pulling fresh bread out of the oven. She turned and smiled at him, but Asho noticed lines of worry tugging at the corners of her eyes.

"It's good to see you're unharmed," she said. "When I saw the fire, I feared the worst for you. How did it start?"

"Um," Asho gulped, the falsehood he knew he should say sticking in his throat. He stared down at the floor. He knew he should tell her that the lantern must have fallen, but he couldn't bring himself to lie to the woman who was the closest thing he'd had to a mother for most of his life. But telling her the truth would be even worse—that he'd started it. That he wasn't even human.

"It's true, then," Farica said.

Asho looked up and saw sorrowful acceptance in her sharp eyes.

"You're leaving with the—" She hesitated. "With your people."

"Yes." It felt strange to say aloud, as if that one word changed everything, set his course in stone.

She nodded sadly. "When Hayden told me, I didn't want to believe it. Didn't want my suspicions, my fears, to be true. Hayden never suspected anything about you, but from the moment we found you, part of me knew what you were. And the rest of me hoped you'd never find out."

"Why didn't you tell me?" Asho asked.

Farica sliced the loaves of bread, then went to the pantry and returned with a block of cheese. She cut off a thick slab and handed it to Asho along with a piece of bread.

"Because you're the son I never had, and I wanted to protect you." Her voice cracked as tears formed in her eyes. "I wanted you to have a safe, normal life. I know it hasn't been easy for you, living under Hayden's thumb, but at least you were safe here. From the day we found you in the stables, motherless, I only wanted to guard you from the evils of the world. And what those people are is dangerous. I—"

The kitchen door swung open, and Makani entered. He was dressed more casually than he had been the night before, with a sleeveless green tunic. His black skriva marks stood out boldly on his muscular left bicep.

Farica looked at the runes for several seconds, then turned her gaze to Makani's face.

"What can I do for you, Master?" she asked. "Supper will be ready in an hour, but there's bread and cheese if you need something to hold you over."

Reminded of his hunger and the food sitting before him, Asho began to eat. He had always known Farica was the guiding force that kept the inn running, not Hayden, but he had never considered what she might know of the world beyond the small, walled town of Aldorn. She had never volunteered any information about her past—everything was focused on the present for her.

Makani studied her for a long minute. "How do you know my title? It's been centuries since we've had any public presence south of the Harondor border."

"Maybe so, but I've seen your kind before. And I know well enough to keep my head down and not say what I know where unwanted ears are listening. I don't want anything to do with what's going on between you and the khafyri. I only wish there was some way to keep Asho out of all this."

"So do I."

Farica cocked an eyebrow at him, an expression of disbelief on her face.

"It's true." Makani drummed his fingers on the table, then sighed as if making up his mind. "Asho is my sister's son. He's the only family that I have. I'll look after him as if he were my own son. Have no fear on that account."

"Your nephew? Family or no, I love that boy like my own," she said in a fierce tone Asho had never heard before. "And if anything happens to him, so help me, I will make you wish you were never born. Understand?" She shook her ladle under his nose.

"Yes, ma'am," Makani replied quietly.

Asho stared. He would never have expected anyone to be able to chastise Makani so thoroughly, let alone quiet, gentle Farica, who always seemed to be overshadowed by Hayden.

"Very good." Farica gave a brisk nod and then turned back to the hearth to stir the simmering pot of vegetables and rotate the chickens.

Makani glanced at Asho, who looked down, embarrassed to be the subject of their conversation but filled with warmth from the way Farica had spoken of him.

"How are you feeling today?" Makani asked Asho. "Are you recovered from your—" He paused, then clearly changed what he had been planning to say. "From escaping the fire?"

"I'm tired," Asho admitted. "Even though I've been sleeping all day. I don't know why I should still feel exhausted."

"You should go to bed early tonight," Makani told him. "It's expected that . . . everything . . . would take a lot out of you. Especially since you weren't prepared. We'll be leaving early tomorrow and riding all day, so you'll want to keep your strength up."

Asho nodded and yawned, feeling the weight of the events the night before catching up to him. The last bite of bread was difficult to chew, as sleepiness overcame his appetite. When he finished, he left the kitchen to return to the comfort of his bed.

As he crossed the floor of the empty common room, Master Hayden entered from the yard. Asho made eye contact with him, and Hayden scowled fiercely. Asho wasn't sure if it was his exhaustion or his knowledge of his new family that kept him from flinching like usual under Hayden's angry gaze. He returned the look with a level stare, then turned his back on Hayden and climbed the stairs, leaving behind his former overseer.

Chapter Fifteen
Aderes

ADERES STOOD IN her stirrups as her horse trotted up another long, gentle slope. They reached the crest of the hill and Bracken came into view below. The city owed its existence to sitting on the crossroads of the Northern Road and the King's Road, which connected the capital of Serif to the coastal city of Menai. Aderes was always amazed by the number of people living in and passing through Bracken, but she knew it wasn't even considered a large city by traders' standards.

The last light from the setting sun illuminated a stone wall surrounding Bracken, punctuated by the occasional guard tower. Farmsteads to the south, east, and west abutted the city's walls, while the northern edge was filled with riverfront quays. A castle sat at the northwestern corner, ready to defend the civilian populace against sea raiders who made it past Menai to raid up the mighty Telnor River.

Aderes slowed her horse to a walk, Jarond following suit. She had pushed their horses hard, alternating between long stretches of brisk trotting and short walks where she and Jarond dismounted to allow their mounts to regain their wind. Both horses were lathered with sweat, white foam dripping from their chests and back legs as they breathed heavily from the exertion. Aderes patted her horse's neck, grateful for its unfaltering effort throughout the ride; although the two animals were regularly used as fast couriers, even they had to struggle to complete the sixty-mile journey to Bracken in one long day.

"The horses are spent," she told Jarond. "We'll kill them if we keep pushing them this hard."

"They made it to Bracken—that's the important part," he said. "We can get fresh mounts here. You know the horse traders. Who's the most likely to have animals fast and fit enough to keep us ahead of any pursuit?"

"Nestor," she said. She had thought about that question throughout the long, grueling day. "He's a fierce haggler, but he always has good stock. He and Father have always admired each other's horses, although it would be like pulling teeth from a chicken to get either of them to admit it. The problem is, Nestor won't take our horses in an outright trade for fresh mounts. We'll need to use one of those jewels from Arawn's sword."

"No need to use the gems yet," Jarond said with a triumphant grin. "I took Arawn's coin purse before I dumped his corpse. We have a fair bit of coin to get by. I think it will be safer if we don't leave a trail of jewels for any potential pursuers to follow."

"Are you sure we'll be followed?"

"As sure as I was that Arawn was a danger."

She shot Jarond a glare. "I swear, if I hear 'I told you so' one more time, I'll make your horse buck you off."

"I didn't say 'I told you so.'" An impish grin undermined Jarond's protest, which only furthered her ire. She hated it when Jarond was proven right. Victory made him insufferable for days afterward.

NESTOR'S BUSINESS WAS on the far side of Bracken, near the gate that led to the bridge spanning the Telnor River. A small building that served as both his home and office sat next to a large corral, which contained a small herd of horses that Nestor had for sale. Aderes looked them over with a critical eye as she and Jarond rode up. A few heavy draft horses, a spotted pony, a pair of colts chewing on the wooden fence. The rest were difficult to discern in the fading light. She hoped at least two of them would be suitable for fast distance riding.

She hitched her horse to the rail in front of Nestor's and pounded on the locked door. A few minutes later, it swung open, revealing Nestor's hooked nose and desert-brown skin.

"We're closed for the day," he grumped, then recognition sparked in his black eyes. "Torvald's girl. But not Torvald. What can I do for you? Your father all right?"

"We need fresh horses."

"Heh! Those pretty horses your father breeds aren't good enough, eh?"

"Do you have anything decent?"

"Decent? Heh! I always have fine stock," he said. "As it so happens, though, I recently acquired a pair of Kochi desert horses. They're finer than anything you'll find in Torvald's stables."

"A swaybacked old horse is still a swaybacked horse, Kochi or not."

"Swaybacked? Heh!" He drew himself up. "I'll show you what real well-bred horses are. My father's people breed the finest horses in the world."

Nestor rummaged around for leads and then entered the corral. He returned with a pair of gray horses. Both had the finely dished faces, proudly arched necks, and light, quick steps of Kochi desert mounts. Aderes ran a hand over their legs, checking for any swellings or hot spots, fighting hard to keep the interest from showing in her eyes. A quick look in their mouths revealed the strong, straight incisors of animals in their prime.

"They'll do, I suppose," she finally said. "We'll trade our two horses for these."

"Heh! Two worn-out horses for the finest Kochi steeds? I think not."

"These horses are from Carwyn stock. They're far more valuable than your flea-bitten desert nags."

"I see two disheveled, exhausted horses. Why should I trade my best mounts for them?"

"All they need is a night's rest; they traveled nearly sixty miles today."

Aderes saw the flash of greed in Nestor's eyes, and she knew she had him.

Nestor quickly tried to downplay his interest. "Heh. So you say. But what proof do I have? For all I know, you are trying to unload a couple of lamed coursers on a poor, honest trader."

She laughed. "Give it a rest, Nestor. I know all your tricks, and I know exactly how much the horses are worth. But to save myself some hassle, I'll throw in two silver pieces to sweeten the deal for you."

"And the tack."

"How are we supposed to ride then? Two silver pieces, and two of the finest Carwyn mounts, or I'll take our horses to Mercer."

"Mercer? Heh! That halfwit? He doesn't have anything that can match my stock."

"Last chance," Aderes said.

Nestor rubbed his chin.

She turned to Jarond. "Let's go. This old fool can't help us."

"Wait!" Nestor cried as they turned to leave. "The two horses and two silver pieces. Deal."

He held out a hand, which Aderes took with a firm grip of her own. "Deal."

Jarond fished the money out of the pilfered coin purse as Aderes untacked their own weary mounts and transferred their gear to the fresh horses.

"You're leaving so soon? Where are you in a rush to?" Nestor asked.

"The capital." Aderes looked at Nestor in an unblinking gaze. "We have urgent business for Lord Kuval there."

"Maybe you'll visit me again on your return," Nestor replied. "If I still have these horses, I will generously offer you the same deal: two tired horses and two silver pieces for two fresh steeds."

Aderes rolled her eyes. "Brigand."

"Heh. Safe travels."

"Thanks."

Aderes and Jarond swung into the saddles and rode east down the street toward the King's Road; once they were out of sight of Nestor's, they turned left, and circled back around to the Northern Road.

As they passed through the town's gate, Aderes nudged her horse into a fast trot, reveling in the long, fluid strides of the Kochi desert horse. In the darkness next to her, Jarond's horse was an elegant wraith keeping pace. She smiled; as long as they were together, nothing could harm them.

Chapter Sixteen
Jarond

JAROND BOUNCED ON his mount's back, jarred with every beat of the long-striding trot. Exhaustion weighed him down, threatening to drag him off his horse the same way it dragged his eyelids lower with every blink. The road stretched endless before him: a pale, moonlit strip of dirt that rose and fell continuously over gently rolling hills, occasionally shadowed as they passed through groves of oak trees.

The bulbous moon hung over his left shoulder, flirting with the mountaintops as they continued their unrelenting northward trek. Despite the punishing pace for half the night, Jarond's horse moved easily under him, hooves lightly tapping the earth in an unwavering beat. He desperately wished he felt the same energy as his steed.

Slightly ahead of him, Aderes whooped in joy as they descended the final slope of a hill to the level plains of a broad valley, urging her horse faster. The lithe animal, shining ghostly gray in the moonlight, leapt forward into a gallop. Jarond's own horse followed suit without any urging from him; instead he clung to its mane as the desert horse charged after his sister. He didn't understand how riding a horse could be so invigorating for Aderes. It sapped his stamina, whereas she almost seemed to draw strength from her mount.

At last she reined her horse back to a walk. Jarond sighed in relief as the jarring motion slowed; his thigh muscles screamed in agony from the unaccustomed work of riding, and he was afraid to find out what the skin between his legs looked like. Between the chafing and the periodically mistimed bounce in the saddle, his manhood was in constant agony. Hopefully he would survive this grueling escape while retaining the ability to sire children.

"How much longer should we ride tonight?" Aderes asked. "These desert horses are used to nightlong rides, but even they can't run forever. We'll need to conserve their strength. I doubt we'll be able to find replacements any time soon; just plow horses and heavy chargers, and they won't be much use for a long journey. Besides, I'm tired."

"It's about time. I was beginning to think you would never tire atop that horse. Let's make camp in that little grove of trees up there."

They heard the low chuckle of a small stream as they reached the shadows of the looming oak trees. Jarond slithered gratefully to the ground, clutching the saddle to keep his knees from buckling as he landed. He staggered to the water's edge, where his horse began sucking up long gulps of water. He knelt upstream of the animal, cupping water in his hands to first wash the road grit off his face and then take a drink of his own.

The moonlight filtered through the trees enough for him to see Aderes approaching with her own horse. It was hard to be sure in the uncertain light, but Jarond thought Aderes was walking with considerably greater ease than he had. He felt a brief spike of envy as she gracefully knelt and splashed water on her face. When she finished, they stood quietly for a moment, the silence only broken by the wet sounds of the horses drinking.

Once the horses were satiated, Jarond and Aderes untacked them and picketed them in the long grass near the trees. The animals began devouring the foliage, and the twins searched the saddlebags for their own meal of dried meat and hard cheese, which they ate in a weary silence, then wrapped themselves in their blankets on a level patch of ground.

Despite his bone-deep exhaustion, sleep eluded Jarond. Had they gotten enough of a lead to shake off any pursuit? How long would it take for the alarm to be raised, for Arawn's knights to realize he wasn't just missing, he was dead? What if messenger birds reached the northern towns before them, and guards were expecting them when they finally arrived?

Jarond rolled over, hoping that a new sleeping position would banish his worries. A knobby root dug into his shoulder, and he scooted sideways to get away from it. Nearby, Aderes's steady, quiet breathing informed him that she'd had no such difficulties falling asleep. He focused on that sound, forcing himself to think about the positives. Aderes was alive. They were free. He was alive to protect her. Somehow, someway, he would ensure her safety. He had to believe that.

Chapter Seventeen
Asho

ASHO BROKE HIS fast at dawn with the three changelings in the private dining room. Accustomed as he was to a simple morning fare of bread and perhaps a boiled egg or two, he regarded the plate of poached eggs, fried tomatoes, spicy sausages, and bread slathered with butter as a feast for kings, although Makani grumbled that there was no coffee available.

"What's coffee?" Asho asked.

"The only thing that makes Makani bearable in the morning," Tycen said, grinning at Makani's scowl.

"It helps wake me up enough to deal with all the overly perky people around me," Makani said.

"It *is* the perfect drink for you," Tycen agreed affably. "Black and bitter, like your soul."

Makani shot him another look of annoyance and then pointedly turned his attention back to his food.

"Leave him be," Damali said when Tycen opened his mouth, clearly prepared to give Makani another verbal jab.

Tycen sighed, but lifted a forkful of egg to his mouth. They finished the meal in silence.

"Makani, you and I will get our belongings from our room," Damali said, once the plates were empty. "Tycen, you and Asho can go get our horses ready."

Asho and Tycen went out into the yard, and Devlin's tail wagged in greeting as he fell in at Asho's side. No workmen were around yet to continue the monumental task of clearing the wreckage from the fire.

"But all the tack is destroyed," Asho said as Tycen strode toward the blackened remains of the stable.

Tycen winked at him. "Trust me; nobody spends time with pyromancers unless their belongings are thoroughly fire proofed. There are strong wards laid on all our gear." He picked his way through the rubble and stopped at a charred door near the edge of the largest pile of timber. With a grunt of effort, he dragged the door open.

Asho's mouth fell open in surprise. The stable's small tack room was intact, with no signs of fire damage. Charred beams surrounded the outside, but inside was unharmed. He helped Tycen carry the changelings' gear back to the yard, picking another saddle from tack room for himself at Tycen's direction.

Tycen went to the corner of the yard, where several horses from the inn were enclosed in a makeshift pen made of ropes and slightly singed timber. He whistled, and the three horses belonging to the changelings came to him.

"Good, none of them escaped," Tycen said. "Is there a horse that Hayden would be willing to sell?"

"That one." Asho pointed at a tall bay gelding. "Hayden took him in payment and has been trying to sell him ever since. He's overpriced though."

"Money isn't an issue," Tycen said. "Take him and saddle him up."

As Asho was tightening the gelding's girth, Farica appeared in the yard. She handed him a small bag, heavy with coins.

"I've been saving this for you," she said, her voice choked and eyes bright with unshed tears. "I'd hoped one day you might meet a special girl, start a new life somewhere else. Well, you're starting a new life, to be sure, and I want you to know that you have all my love and support."

"Thank—" The words stuck in Asho's suddenly tight throat. "Thank you, Farica."

She swept him into a tight embrace, her arms sheltering him as though he were a little boy, not nearly a man and a head taller than her. He blinked back tears, determined to not cry in front of the changelings.

Far too soon, Farica released him. "Take care of yourself, Asho," she said, then looked down as Devlin nuzzled her hand. "You look after my boy, won't you, Devlin?"

Devlin gave a quiet *wuff* in response.

Farica gave a sharp nod, returning to her usual practical self. "I need to go back to the kitchen before the bread burns."

"Goodbye," Asho said, the word feeling completely inadequate, but not knowing what else he could say.

Farica passed Damali and Makani as they exited the inn, carrying three sets of bulging packs. Damali gave her bag to Asho to put on her horse while she returned to the inn to pay Hayden for Asho's gelding. When she came back, they mounted up.

Devlin trotted next to Asho's horse as they rode away from the only home Asho had ever known.

"The road is a tough place for a dog," Tycen cautioned him. "Perhaps you should make him stay."

Asho shook his head. "I can't."

"As you wish."

The small group rode out through the gate of Aldorn's walls. Asho turned back to look at the town for a brief moment. He was leaving nothing behind; his past was in ashes. He looked forward: the Northern Road stretched before him, leading to an unknown future. He smiled and kicked his mount to catch up to the changelings. There was no reason to look back again.

"C'mon, Devlin!" he called.

The dog's long tail waved as he followed his master.

Chapter Eighteen
Jarond

DESPITE A SHORT night of sleep, Jarond and Aderes were up with the dawn. They ate a quick cold breakfast and tacked their horses. Swinging into the saddle was even more painful than Jarond had anticipated, despite moving as gingerly as possible. It seemed like the few hours of rest he had gotten had only served to increase his pain and stiffness. He winced as he settled on the saddle. He opened his eyes and noticed Aderes looking at him with concern.

"What's wrong?" she asked.

"Nothing," he said. There was no way that he'd confess the nature and location of his saddle-sores to his sister. "Let's go."

They set out at a steady walk, giving their horses a chance to warm their muscles up before increasing speed to a brisk trot. Soon they settled into the pace of the previous day: long segments of swift trotting, followed by a walk on foot for their horses to recover their breath. Jarond gritted his teeth against the pain; nothing would prevent him from continuing down the road.

Three hours of hard riding brought them to a small, unwalled village. Jarond intended to ride straight through, but Aderes stopped at an herbalist shop.

"What are you doing?" Jarond asked.

"I'll just be a minute."

Jarond contemplated dismounting and following her, but the throbbing pain in his nether regions made him reluctant to perform any unnecessary movements. He sat as still as possible, trying to ignore the discomfort. Aderes returned quickly with a small parcel.

"What's that?"

"I'll tell you later." Aderes swung back into the saddle with an ease that Jarond envied. "Let's go."

They reached a small stand of trees just out of view from the town, and Aderes stopped and dismounted. With a repressed groan, Jarond followed suit.

Aderes handed him the parcel, a tinge of red in her cheeks. Jarond saw that it contained a roll of bandages and a small jar of salve. "Here. Go behind the bushes and, ah . . . take care of yourself."

Mortification warred with gratitude as he took the package and did as she said. He returned to the horse and was able to remount without any additional pain.

"Thanks," he muttered, his cheeks burning.

"Don't mention it," Aderes said. "Ever."

They set out again at a fast trot. Jarond's tired muscles protested, but he could handle that pain. Against his better judgement, a hint of optimism crept into him. Maybe he could protect Aderes after all.

Chapter Nineteen
Aderes

AFTER MILE UPON mile of farmlands and wood-and-thatch cottages, the low gray walls of the large town before them loomed like a scar in the lush green landscape. The Northern Road led through the iron-bound doors that pierced the southern wall. Aderes and Jarond slowed their horses to a walk as they passed through the ten-foot stone expanse. The cobbled streets of the town were busy with pedestrians, street vendors, and ox carts.

"We should resupply. But we need to make it quick; I don't want anything to delay us too much." Jarond swung down from his horse and handed the reins to Aderes, who stayed mounted. "I'll buy; you take care of the animals."

They made their way through the town, Jarond stopping frequently to purchase food and load it into their saddlebags—fresh bread from a baker, dried apples and peaches from a fruit-seller's cart, a sack of beans from the back of a farmer's wagon.

He went into the butcher's shop to buy meat as Aderes patiently sat on her horse and held Jarond's. She looked around. Across the street was a mound of blackened timber, the gutted remnants of a large building. Workmen were beginning to clear the scorched beams, hounded by a stout man who scurried around, shouting orders at everyone. An inn stood near the burned building; between the two structures was a small dirt yard, with a makeshift pen containing a half dozen horses. Aderes realized that the destroyed structure was the inn's stable.

She rode over to look at the horses—perhaps they could purchase a pack horse so they could carry more supplies. A quick glance quashed any hope. The horses were heavy drafts and past-prime riding horses. None of them would be able to keep up with their Kochi desert steeds.

The man supervising the workers walked over to her. "Are you interested in taking a room at the Prancing Stag?"

"No, I was just looking at your horses."

"Some of them are for sale. Are you interested in buying one? Perhaps something more sturdy than that skinny horse you're riding?"

She shook her head.

The man peered at her suspiciously. "Is there anything you want? No? Then go away. I have no time to waste on gawkers."

"Nice to meet you too," Aderes muttered as she rode back across the street to the butcher's shop.

Jarond walked out of the shop shortly and packed the last of their new supplies in his saddlebags. She noticed he was able to swing back into the saddle with considerably more ease than he had that morning.

"I found out what the roads look like farther north," Jarond said as they wound their way through the foot traffic, carts, and wagons. "There're only small towns on the Northern Road between here and the border. There's a large crossroads before the border though. The eastern road goes into the mountains, and the passes are still snowed in this time of year. We might want to take the road to the coast; if we get to Port Deren, we can book passage on a ship there and head north a lot quicker. Who knows, maybe we can go as far as Juven, or even Evlar."

"What will we do in those countries, though, Jare?" Aderes asked. "We left our entire lives behind us."

"Don't think like that; there's plenty of possibilities open to us. I can get hired on as a guard somewhere, and I'm sure you'll be able to find a job as a hostler or something. We have enough coin to last us for a while, and when we sell the gems from the sword, we'll have no concern for money. We'll be fine; you'll see."

"What about Father? I'm worried that something will happen to him."

Jarond's eyes darkened. "I'm sure he'll be fine too."

"If you say so." Aderes didn't tell him that she knew he was lying; some lies were better left unchallenged. If only she could believe him.

They passed through the thick wall of the northern gate, the sound of their horses' shoes on cobblestones echoing off the stone walls. As they reemerged into sunlight, the footing changed to hard-packed dirt, and the hoofbeats quieted.

Aderes pasted a smile on her face. "Onward again!"

She nudged her horse into a trot. The animal leapt forward smoothly, its long legs striding fluidly. If only it would be so easy to run away from her inner turmoil.

Chapter Twenty
Asho

"SOMETHING'S COMING," DAMALI said, stopping her horse and turning to look south down the road.

Makani and Tycen put their hands on the hilts of their swords. Asho wished he had a sword, although he was probably more likely to behead his own horse than he was to impale a foe.

"A khafyri?" Makani asked.

Damali shook her head slowly. "No. It feels almost like changeling power."

"Nobody else is this far south."

"I know."

As Asho shielded his eyes and squinted down the road, a pair of horses appeared over the southern rise, their riders pushing them hard. "There!" he said, pointing.

The three masters looked.

"Is that where you feel the power?" Makani asked.

"Yes," Damali said.

"Let's wait and see," Tycen suggested. "There's only two of them. We should be able to defend ourselves if it turns out they're enemies."

A surge of hope filled Asho, although he tried to quash it. Two riders, with the power of a changeling. Could it possibly be his parents? *No, it's impossible.* His parents were long dead. They wouldn't have abandoned him if they were alive all these years. Still, a flicker of hope burned in him.

As the horses drew nearer, Asho saw that they were ridden by two youths near his own age. One was a girl, wearing a sturdy, practical brown dress with skirts divided for riding, with a tumble of dark golden hair blowing over her shoulders. Despite the warm day, a brown scarf wrapped around her neck. Her companion had short brown hair and wore a dark green tunic. A sword was belted at his waist.

As the two riders approached the small group on the edge of the road, they slowed to a walk. The boy shifted his horse so that he was between the girl and Asho's party, resting his hand on his sword hilt.

"Where are you headed?" Damali asked.

The pair reined in their horses.

"Port Deren," the girl replied, at the same time the boy said, "North." He turned and shot a look of warning at her.

"We're headed north too," Damali said. "It can be dangerous to travel in small groups, though."

"We'll be fine," the boy said.

"One sword won't matter much against bandits," she said. "Where did you get it?"

Alarm flashed over the boy's face, although he made a visible effort to hide it. "None of your business. C'mon, let's go, Addie."

Before they could put their heels into their mounts, Makani growled, "*Stop.*"

Asho heard the compulsion woven into the order and felt a brief flash of empathy for the two strangers.

The girl halted. The boy got a couple strides away from her before he turned and saw that she wasn't following.

He tugged his horse to a stop. "Addie, let's go."

"I can't," she replied.

Confusion filled his face, soon replaced by anger. "What did you do to her?"

Makani was frowning at him. "Why didn't it work on you?"

"What did you do?" the boy snapped, drawing his sword. It came out of the sheath with a clear ringing sound. The blade was elegantly rippled with blue and gray layers that shimmered in the bright sunlight.

"Strieborna!" Tycen exclaimed.

"Where did you get that, boy? *Answer me,*" Makani ordered.

"What did you do to my sister?" The boy kicked his horse toward Makani, eyes filled with deadly intent.

Damali put herself between Makani and the strangers. "Makani, let the girl go," she commanded with a hint of exasperation, and then turned to the strangers. "I'm sorry, we mean you no harm. But that is a strieborna blade; only changelings make them. We need to know how you came about it."

"Who are you?" the boy asked instead.

"I am Damali; my companions are Makani, Tycen, and Asho." She pointed to them each in turn. "And Devlin." The big dog had flopped in the shade cast by Asho's mount, tongue lolling out as he panted. "We are changelings."

"Really?" the girl exclaimed, eyes bright with curiosity. "I thought changelings were just stories."

Damali shook her head with a small smile. "No, I assure you, we are very much real. And *that,*" she pointed at the boy's sword, "is one of our weapons. Where did you get it? And who are you?"

The girl hesitated, her enthusiasm visibly dimming. "I'm Aderes. This is my twin brother, Jarond."

"And the sword?"

"It's mine," Jarond said stubbornly. "It's none of your business where I got it."

Tycen laughed. "You can't even use it properly. You have no business bearing it."

Jarond's blue eyes flashed with anger as he looked at Tycen. "Do you want to bet on that?"

"Sure," came the cocky response, and fire blazed from the sword blade, flames licking up and down its length, turning the gray ripples into a pattern of flickering red.

Jarond jerked his arm in alarm, but to Asho's surprise, he didn't drop the burning sword. The horse he rode snorted, prancing to the side, but Jarond forcefully reined it back under control. He lifted the blade, eyes fixed on Tycen, who smirked.

"Enough!" Damali roared.

Asho was amazed at the volume she was able to project.

"Tycen, put it out!" The flames immediately disappeared. "Jarond, put it away."

Jarond kept the sword at the ready.

Damali raised one elegantly arched eyebrow. "Any one of us could channel far more power through that sword than the little trick Tycen just did. I'll only say it once more. Put. It. Away."

"Jarond, listen to her," Aderes said.

With a disgruntled look at Aderes, Jarond slammed the sword back into its sheath.

"Thank you," Damali said. "I know you're afraid, but we're not going to hurt you. We need to know where you got that, though. Strieborna blades are only wielded by changelings, unless they are stolen when a changeling is killed. We try to recover any that we can. They are incredibly powerful, and extremely difficult to forge."

"It was Tav Arawn's," Aderes blurted out. "We took it after Jarond killed him."

"*You* killed a khafyri?" Tycen asked, respect filling his eyes. "But you're human. What possessed you to fight him in the first place?"

"He attacked Aderes. I was protecting her."

"Did he bite you?" Makani asked Aderes.

She nodded, tugging her scarf down to reveal a white bandage.

"Let me see," he said in a gentler tone.

She pulled off the bandage. A pair of small, round wounds were scabbed on the side of her neck.

Makani rode closer to her. "Hold still," he commanded, but without the force of compulsion, and stretched a hand out to her neck. He covered the wounds with the palm of his hand, eyes closed in concentration. He pulled his hand away, and the injuries had vanished; only the faintest scar remained.

Aderes fingered her neck. "Thank you," she said, a look of awe on her face.

Tycen gazed at Jarond. "How did you manage to kill him? That's impressive. Not many humans have ever killed a khafyri. They're too fast and strong for your kind."

"He was beating me—easily, I hate to admit—but he got distracted when my friend attacked him from behind," Jarond replied, the admiration in Tycen's voice clearly thawing his anger. "He killed Kamin, but I stabbed him through the heart when he was turned."

"With that sword?" Tycen gestured.

"No, with what was left of my own sword," Jarond replied. "Arawn still had this one. Mine was broken in the fight, so I took this one after Arawn was dead."

"Did you burn the body?"

"No, I weighed it down and threw it in the moat."

"*Paska*," Tycen cursed, turning pale.

Makani and Damali looked at each other, worry filling their faces.

"What?" Jarond demanded.

"You can't kill a khafyri by stabbing it with steel," Damali said finally. "You have to burn the remains. Sometimes a strieborna blade will do it, if it's spelled correctly. Or use an olkar blade." She drew her dagger and showed it to them. The blade was a shimmering bluish-white, nearly translucent. It had a single edge and a slight curve, ending in a razor-sharp point.

"But he was dead," Jarond exclaimed. "I saw him die."

She shook her head. "No. He was in a death-state, but he wasn't dead. He would have recovered quickly from the wound. Throwing him in the moat probably delayed his reawakening, but I assure you, he is not dead."

"*Paska!*" Jarond cast a fear-filled glance at his sister.

"What do we do?" she asked, her own face terror-stricken.

"Come with us," Damali said. "We'll be able to protect you from the khafyri. We'll take you to Varnstad. You'll be safe there."

"Damali, are you sure?" Makani objected. "Varnstad is our refuge; outsiders are rarely allowed."

"Thwarting the khafyris' revenge on these two is worth the risk," she said with quiet authority. "But we need to get out of Sermund before we are discovered. No doubt they will pick up our trail in Aldorn as they pursue Jarond and Aderes. And if the khafyri catch us, we'll all wish we were dead."

Chapter Twenty-One
Arawn

ARAWN'S FIRST BREATH took in a lungful of vile, sewage-laced water. His eyes snapped open to a murky green gloom; polluted water surrounded hum, the sunlight streaming in weakly from above. He fought the urge to breathe, not wanting to take in any more of the filth. A fish nibbled at his fingertip, then fled to the shadowy weeds when he angrily shook it off.

As he pushed himself off the rocky bottom of the moat, he noticed an unexpected weight resting on his chest; his hands felt the cold, smooth links of a chainmail hauberk over his clothes. *Clever.* Admiration warred with irritation. *If the boy had succeeded in killing me, my body would never have been discovered.*

He dragged the heavy armor off over his head, allowing it to fall to the riverbed in a softly shimmering heap of steel links. Another body lay nearby: the young guard, the one he had slain. Arawn left him there, pushing off hard against the stony bottom, breaking the surface of the water in great choking gasps. The gray wall of the castle rose above him, the smooth stones offering no handhold; he kicked away from it and swam toward the opposite shore.

A peasant farmer, paused in the act of plowing a field, stared at him as he dragged himself through the mud and reeds, the filthy water of the moat dripping from his once-fine clothes. Arawn heard the man's racing heartbeat pounding through the air, pulsing in his neck.

Arawn's throat burned with thirst. Healing from his wounds, plus however long he had spent at the bottom of the moat, had drained him. He felt his fangs extend in response to his need. Before the peasant could react, Arawn had him in a firm grasp, the man's lifeblood flowing through puncture wounds into Arawn's greedily sucking mouth.

When he heard the man's heartbeat falter, Arawn forced himself to pull away. No need to kill, even if it was only a peasant. He drew back, his strong grip now holding the man upright rather than restraining him.

He used a fang to pierce the skin on his own index finger and dabbed a drop of blood on each of the fang marks. They sealed, even as the wound on his finger healed itself.

He lowered the peasant to the ground. "Take the rest of the day off." He reached for his coin purse to pay the man—he still retained some civility—but discovered it was missing. He scowled. *Damn boy must've stolen it. My sword too. He will have a lot to answer for when I finally catch him.*

Arawn stalked to the front of the castle. The drawbridge was lowered, so he didn't have to deal with any foolish human sentries—in his bedraggled state, he would have had a hard time convincing them of who he was.

He passed under the raised portcullis and spotted a few of his knights sparring in the practice yard. Sir Kayden, the head of his honor guard, saw him and stilled his sword, giving a short bow.

"Tavek?" Sir Kayden frowned, confused. "What happened to you? Nobody has seen you since the feast. We thought that maybe you rode to Tynda without us."

"How long ago was the feast?" Arawn fought to keep the snarl out of his voice.

Sir Kayden took a slight step backward. "Two nights, tavek."

"What happened to the boy?"

"The boy?"

"The guard. The one with the sister."

"There's two guards missing, tavek. One had a sister, though. Jarond. He and his sister Aderes haven't been seen since the feast."

"That's him; he tried to kill me. The other guard is dead."

"Tried to kill you, tavek? What happened? Where have you been?"

"At the bottom of the moat, with the guard I killed." Arawn decided he'd had enough of the human's questions. "Find the lordling of this castle and bring him to me; I'll be in my chambers, getting cleaned up. Then saddle our horses for immediate departure."

Without waiting for a response, he turned and stormed into the keep, brusquely ordering the first maid he encountered to draw him a hot bath. She scurried to do his bidding.

He bathed and dressed in clean clothes—black breeches and tunic, matching his foul mood—then entered the antechamber of his suite to find Lord Kuval awaiting him.

Lord Kuval bowed low. "Tav Arawn, we've been concerned about you. Nobody knew where you had gone. What happened?"

Arawn ignored the question. "Do you have messenger birds here?"

"Of course, tavek. For the capital."

"None others?"

"No, tavek. There has never been need. We use mounted couriers if we need to send a message elsewhere."

Arawn sat at the side desk, scrawled out a hasty message, and copied it on another sheet. He thrust the completed missives at Kuval. "Send these with your fastest birds. With any luck, we'll still be able to catch the miscreants."

"Tavek?"

"Go. Now."

Kuval scuttled out of the room.

Arawn paced the small chamber. *When was the last time someone bested me? A hundred years? No, that was when I won my sword off that changeling apprentice.* He gave a rueful laugh. *I'll have to admit, the boy was quick. Not many could've taken advantage of such a slight distraction. It's too bad. He might've proved useful. Now I'll have to make an example of him.*

When he deemed that enough time had passed for his knights to be ready, he strode down to the courtyard. Their horses were hitched to rails, but none were saddled.

"Why aren't our mounts ready?" He snarled at the closest hostler, resisting the urge to bare his fangs in rage.

The hostler stumbled backward, pale-faced. Arawn smelled the fear rolling off him. "All . . . all the g . . . girths have been cut, t . . . tavek."

"What? Fix them. Immediately."

"Y . . . yes, tavek. We're working as fast as we can."

The man gave a jerky bow and rushed back into the protection of the stables.

Arawn paced away, needing space between himself and the incompetent humans. His fangs poked into his lower lip as he ground his teeth; with a great deal of effort, he forced them to retract. His kind hadn't spent centuries hiding their darker nature from general knowledge for him to reveal the truth and slaughter the entire garrison.

As he stalked about the yard, he remembered the castle's master of horse was the father of the two he sought. He saw Sir Kayden near the walls, warily watching him.

"Find the horse master," Arawn ordered.

Sir Kayden bowed and rushed toward the main keep.

A few minutes later, the man limped across the yard to him. Around the stables, grooms were finally beginning to saddle the horses.

"The runaways. Jarond and Aderes. They are your offspring, no?"

The man hesitated. "Yes, tavek."

"Where did they go?"

"I don't know, tavek."

"*Tell me the truth!*" Arawn snarled, tensed to attack.

The man's heartbeat leapt in response, but he stood his ground, meeting Arawn's eye. "I am, tavek. The last time I saw my son and daughter was at the feast two nights ago. They had a fight; Jarond didn't want Aderes to ride to Menai with you. If you kill me or not, my answer will not change."

Arawn contemplated him for a moment, debating. Clearly the boy inherited his spirit from his father; a quality Arawn normally found admirable, but in this case had caused him a great deal of nuisance. It would give him a great deal of satisfaction to kill the man and vent some of his anger, but it would raise questions.

Sir Kayden approached. "The horses are ready, tavek." He bowed.

"We'll leave immediately."

As Arawn cantered away from Carwyn, the clattering group of armored knights following, he contemplated the upcoming chase. *Once my message arrives at Serif, Naresh will send out more birds to Menai, Port Deren, and Learen. All the main roads will be watched, and tracking parties sent out. Those two will be caught like rats in a trap. And then, I'll have my revenge.* He smiled, fangs extending in anticipation, and spurred his horse to greater speed.

Chapter Twenty-Two
Aderes

"IF THE BORDER is on alert, how will we get back to Varnstad? We won't even be able to cross into Harondor," Makani asked.

Aderes sat next to Jarond at the night's campfire as Makani and Damali argued about their route. A stewpot hung over the dancing flames, which drove away the cool evening chill. Aderes had been fascinated at the way Tycen had snapped his fingers and caused flames to instantly spring up among the green wood he'd stacked in the middle of a small clearing. She wondered what it would be like to have such power so readily available. At the very least, she wouldn't have been so pathetically helpless when Arawn attacked her. She didn't want to be forced to always rely on someone else for her defense.

"What about Port Deren?" Damali said. "We could take a ship."

"If the border has been alerted, I can guarantee that the khafyri at Port Deren will be on the lookout for us too," Makani countered.

"Ride east? Cross the mountains and head north when we reach the desert?"

"The passes aren't open yet. Even our two flamethrowers won't be able to melt their way through all that snow."

"Why are you only talking about running and escaping?" Tycen broke in. "We should head for the border. I'll scorch any khafyri who tries to stop us." He juggled three fireballs in the air for emphasis.

A small smile crept across Aderes's face as she watched the flames spinning through the air. With a last flourish, Tycen flipped them into the flickering tongues of the campfire, where they merged seamlessly with the rest of the flames.

Makani rolled his eyes. "Ah, right. I'd forgotten that we brought the invincible Master Tycen with us. I'll sleep soundly as a babe, despite the fact that every khafyri in the country is probably hunting us down by now."

"Why did you come here, if it's so dangerous for you?" Jarond asked.

"We were looking for Asho," Damali replied.

"You told me that, but how did you know to look for me?" Asho asked from a stump next to a drowsy Devlin. "You were surprised when you learned that I was the one you were searching for, but you never explained why you were looking in the first place."

"We were following a prophecy," Damali said.

Asho's eyes narrowed. "What sort of prophecy? Why didn't you follow it before, when I was younger?"

"Because the prophecy wasn't made yet."

"I thought prophecies were really old."

Damali shook her head. "Some are. But one of our youngest apprentices is a new prophet. Most of what she says doesn't make much sense, since she's still refining her abilities. But a month ago, she spoke a prophecy that had some unmistakable facts in it."

"What facts? What was the prophecy?"

"'The lost boy, the unknown son, lives in the south, amongst the blood-soaked streets of the aged town. Unless he is found, hunters will capture him as they pursue a different quarry. A forked path lies before him, reflecting his duality. Down one road lies the utter destruction of his parents' legacy. Down the other is salvation, both for him and his kind. For any hope of reconciliation, he must be found. His past is fire and blood, and so shall be his future. He is the instrument of change, for he is the forgotten key, and change is in his blood.'"

"That doesn't sound very informative," Asho said, a touch of fear in his hazel eyes.

"Anaya's instructor, Master Tacchi, is experienced in unraveling prophecy. He took it to mean that a young pyro was living in Aldorn—which means aged—so we came looking for Asho. We couldn't risk taking a larger group across the border, since it would have increased the likelihood of being spotted by khafyri. We originally assumed the prophecy was referring to a child that one of our men unknowingly fathered. The offspring of a changeling and a human sometimes end up with a changeling's abilities, and it wouldn't be the first time that a child was born without his changeling father's knowledge. Prophecies have helped us find such children before."

"But who was my father then?" Asho asked. "Did any other changelings go missing at the same time?"

"No," Makani replied. "Your father must've been a human that Esme met in the south."

"But why didn't Esme come back to Varnstad?" Tycen asked.

Makani winced slightly. "Our parents believed that changelings needed to keep the bloodlines undiluted. They thought that having children with humans weakened the offsprings' abilities. I'm not surprised that my sister would choose self-exile if she fell in love with a human. She and our parents had sharp disagreements, and our father was particularly adamant in his beliefs. Esme probably thought life would be more peaceful away from Varnstad."

"But what about the rest of the prophecy?" Jarond asked.

"I don't know. Master Tacchi is still trying to decipher it. Perhaps he'll have figured it out by the time we get back to Lyndell," Damali said.

"The question remains then: How *do* we get back to Lyndell safely?" Makani interjected.

"I say we head for the northern border. We can leave the road, cut across country, and then slip across between outposts."

"And the river gorge? The Napier River is impassible without a bridge or sturdy boat."

"Tycen, do you think you can carry us across?"

"Sure, I should be able to manage everybody one at a time. We'll have to leave the horses on the south bank though."

"How can Tycen carry us?" Jarond asked.

A mischievous smile crossed Tycen's face. He stood up, a look of concentration on his face. The next moment, feathery brown wings burst from between his shoulder blades, spreading ten feet to either side of him. Jarond, Aderes, and Asho all jumped.

"How did you do that?" Aderes asked. "Where did those come from?"

"From manakore," Tycen said.

"From what?"

"Manakore. It's where changelings draw power from. It surrounds us all, but there is a veil that separates it from what you can see and feel. When changelings use their abilities, they pierce that veil, and draw matter or energy from manakore into the physical world and shape it to their will. For example, when I summon fire, I am actually drawing energy from manakore and making it manifest itself as flames. The matter necessary for my wings comes from there too. And when I want to get rid of them"—the wings on his back withered to nothing—"then I'm sending that matter back into manakore. There are countless ways a changeling could choose to use the power from there, but each takes time to master completely, so there is a limit to what each individual can do."

"What about the khafyri?" Aderes asked. "Why do they drink blood? Is that connected to manakore?"

Surprise showed in Tycen's eyes. "Most don't make that connection so quick. Given your history with khafyri, I shouldn't be surprised. Yes, their need to drink blood is tied to manakore. You see, everyone—human, changeling, or khafyri—has a life force. Some people call it a soul. It is an individualized energy that resides in manakore. When khafyri feed on blood, they are able to draw some of that life force into themselves. It is part of what makes them immortal."

"So Addie's soul is diminished now?" Jarond broke in, casting a worried look at her.

"No, don't be afraid, the soul is much more difficult to destroy than that. It is able to heal and replenish, much the same as her blood levels were restored. If the khafyri had bled her out, she would have died, but khafyri generally prefer to let their food source renew itself. Keep the supply from running dry, so to speak."

"What happens if they feed on a changeling?" Jarond asked. "You all have been acting like they would want to catch you, but you haven't explained why."

"When a khafyri feeds on a changeling, they are able to access not only the life force, but also whatever abilities that changeling is capable of. It's not permanent—a few weeks, at most. It depends on how much they drink and how much they use the powers. That's why they try to capture changelings and keep us prisoner as their own personal power sources."

"Sounds awful." Aderes shuddered, remembering the violation and helplessness she had felt when Arawn bit her. To be a prisoner, fed on by khafyri whenever they chose—it was a prospect she didn't want to consider.

"Food's ready," Makani announced.

The group was quiet as they ate. Aderes guessed that their thoughts, like hers, were focused on the difficult journey ahead, and the monumental task of evading the powerful khafyri. The hot stew, rich with beans, root vegetables, and a rabbit that Devlin had killed that afternoon, was a comfort to her, a far more pleasant meal than the dried meat and hard cheese that she and Jarond had been subsiding on the last days. Perhaps the food was a sign that their luck was on the rise, now they'd met the changelings. She could only hope that were true.

"Asho, it's time for another lesson," Tycen said, once they'd finished eating. "Come sit with me."

The two changelings sat cross-legged, facing each other, as Damali raised a protective shield around them to keep any flames from straying.

"Okay, remember what I said about the manakore?"

Asho nodded.

"I'm going to teach you how to summon fire from there. Hold out your hand, palm up. Good. Now concentrate on the area just above your palm; imagine you are placing all your anger in your hand."

"But I'm not mad right now."

"Doesn't matter; focus all of your energy and emotion on your palm. Rage often brings out fire; think about something that makes you angry and put it there."

Asho's brow furrowed in concentration, but nothing happened. Tycen didn't seem perturbed. He kept Asho working at it for nearly an hour. Aderes saw Jarond glancing around the small camp, clearly bored, but she found the lesson fascinating to watch.

"I can't." Asho slammed his fist into the ground in frustration.

Across the fire from him, Devlin whined softly. It gave Aderes an idea.

"The khafyri will kill Devlin," she said, not knowing or caring if her words were true—it only mattered if Asho believed them.

"What?"

"They'll kill him, and there will be nothing you can do to stop them."

"I won't let them!" Asho cried, fists clenched. Fire sprouted between his balled fingers.

"Excellent!" Tycen exclaimed.

Asho looked down, clearly stunned to see the flames now licking up his forearms. As he stared in shock, the flames died down and vanished.

"Good thinking, Aderes," Tycen said. "Asho, wonderful job. Did you feel the surge of power?"

Asho nodded.

"I think that's enough for tonight," Damali said. "We'll have another long day tomorrow. There are still many miles to cover before we reach the safety of the border. Get some sleep; tomorrow will bring its own challenges soon enough."

Chapter Twenty-Three
Arawn

ON THE SECOND day after leaving Carwyn, Arawn and his contingent of knights reached the river city of Bracken. The heavy armor and massive horses of his honor guard had slowed down his progress considerably, so he ordered the knights to ride west to Menai, his own domain. He would continue the pursuit along the Northern Road, unhindered by the slow pace of the ceremonial human guard. Arawn didn't want to rely on other search parties to find the two he pursued, since it would deprive him of the pleasure of catching them himself.

He knew they were on the right track so far: a small group of troupers they had encountered near Carwyn had confirmed seeing the two humans that matched the descriptions of the ones he was pursuing. Arawn ground his teeth in frustration. Those two had unwittingly gotten lucky when they had sunk him to the bottom of the moat, delaying his reawakening.

There was one small benefit to their slow progress to the crossroads at the river: it had given time for his message to reach Serif and Menai, and for responses to be waiting for him when he entered the chambers of Bracken's steward. He picked up the first one and scanned it.

> I am riding to Bracken with a small party of scouts. If the perpetrators head for the coast, we will find them. I will save their punishment for your pleasure. — Reka

Arawn put aside the missive from his daughter and picked up the other, scowling as he read the thinly disguised scorn in the letter from the capital.

> A villain that defeated the mighty Arawn? Surely he can't be a mere human. Did a changeling slip past our guard, or is Arawn not as quick as he used to be? I will send appropriate responders and take all measures necessary to track down these heinous criminals. — Naresh

Arawn crumpled the letters and threw them in the fire, realizing he had erred in the message he'd sent from Carwyn. He never should have written why he was seeking the two humans, but in his anger, he hadn't exercised good judgment.

"Would you like to send a return message, tavek?" the castle's steward asked.

"No need," Arawn replied, striding from the room.

A fresh horse was waiting for him in the castle's yard. Arawn took the reins from the groom and was about to swing into the saddle when a clatter of steel-shod hooves caused him to look toward the castle's main gate. His fangs extended in anger as he saw the new arrivals, and he struggled to retract them before the newcomers saw his lack of control.

Five khafyri rode into the yard, girded in breastplates that rippled with the elegant gray and blue of strieborna. Each bore a round shield, the multi-colored layers of strieborna expanding outward from the center boss, which was studded with gemstones of various hues.

"Arawn!" their leader called in greeting, a malicious smile on his face. "Good to see you back in the land of the living."

"Naresh," Arawn replied stiffly, nodding a greeting to the other khafyri.

Naresh's smile widened. "No sign of the villains on the King's Road. Of course, if they were quick enough to best you, perhaps they were clever enough to give us the slip."

"If they were clever, they went north." Arawn ignored the jab. "Once they get past Aldorn, there are several different routes that branch off the Northern Road before the border. The longer they remain free, the smaller chance we have to catch them."

"Then by all means, we should leave immediately," Naresh said.

"That won't be necessary. I can handle the pursuit from the south myself. You did send messages to the northern cities, yes?"

"Of course. Anything to bring these dangerous renegades to justice."

"Then your job is done." Arawn swung into the saddle and turned to depart.

"Wait, Arawn."

He glanced back over his shoulder, resisting the urge to scowl at the mocking grin on Naresh's face.

"I would hate for anything to happen to you, especially now that these villains are armed—with your own blade, no less. Take a shield before you go." He snapped his fingers and beckoned. One of the other khafyri held out his shield in Arawn's direction.

Arawn was torn—the gesture was a mocking one, and he knew if he accepted the shield, it might make him appear weak. But strieborna artifacts were rare, and priceless in a fight against a changeling.

He doesn't think I'll actually take it, Arawn suddenly realized, and he smirked at the look of surprise on Naresh's face when he took the proffered shield.

"Thank you for your generosity," Arawn said, the mocking edge now in his voice. He turned, trotted out through the castle's gate, and rode through the city to the Telnor Bridge and the Northern Road. His quarry wouldn't be able to outrun him for long.

AFTER A HARD day's ride, Arawn arrived in Aldorn. He rode down the main street, looking for a place to exchange his horse for a fresh mount. A whiff of charred timber floated on the breeze, carrying with it the hint of a greater power. Arawn followed the scent until he came across a large inn and the remnants of a burned stable. The smell of ash and fire was strong, but the feeling of power was unmistakable. *Changeling.*

Arawn unslung the shield from his saddle and strapped it to his arm before dismounting. He doubted that any changelings were still in the area, but it was impossible to take too many precautions against their powerful abilities. He looped his horse's reins around a hitching rail in front of the inn, then strode to the blackened ruins to examine them more thoroughly. A few men were working on clearing the rubble, but Arawn ignored them, studying the wreckage.

There was no doubt this was the work of a pyromancer, although Arawn was puzzled as to why a changeling would risk exposure by using such a substantial amount of power so deep within Sermund's borders. Naresh would have told him of any confrontation between his kind and a changeling.

Arawn smiled as he contemplated the possibilities. It had been years since he had tasted the power of a changeling's blood. *If I wasn't chasing that boy, this would have gone unnoticed, written off as a human accident, unless another khafyri happened to ride through this town.*

A man approached him from behind and bowed as Arawn turned toward him. "Would you care to take a room at the Prancing Stag, my lord? Our stables are under repair, as you can see, but we'll still be able to care for your mount."

"You are the innkeeper?" Arawn asked as the man straightened.

"Yes, my lord." Comprehension and fear filled the man's face, and Arawn heard his heartbeat increase in reaction to that fear. "F . . . forgive me, tavek, I didn't realize . . ."

Arawn ignored the reaction. He was used to seeing it when humans recognized him for what he was. "How did this fire start? And when?"

"Four nights ago, tavek. The stableboy knocked over a lantern."

Wrong. "Where is this stableboy now?"

"Gone, tavek."

"Gone!" Arawn barked.

The innkeeper recoiled, his heartbeat spiking even higher. "Yes, tavek."

"Where did he go?"

"I don't know, tavek. He and his companions did not say."

"Companions?"

"Yes, tavek. Two lords and a lady. They arrived the evening the stable burned and left the next day, taking the boy with them."

Arawn contemplated for a moment. Could he have picked up the trail of three—maybe even four—changelings? What were their kind doing so far south of the heavily guarded border? They knew the khafyri were all too eager to sink fangs into them. The right captives might even be enough to change the tide of the subtle, centuries-long war their two species had been engaged in.

"Did you see any black marks on their arms?"

"They wore long sleeves, tavek."

"And the boy? Who is he?"

"An orphan, tavek. Showed up in my stables twelve years ago. I took him in and raised him. Name's Asho."

Twelve years ago in Aldorn. How did we not sense the child? To think that a changeling has been living under our noses, hiding in plain sight in this insignificant town.

Ignoring the innkeeper, Arawn remounted his horse and rode to the small tower that was the residence of Aldorn's lord. A hostler rushed out to greet him and took his reins.

"Get me a fresh, fast horse. Immediately."

The hostler bowed as Arawn strode through the large oak doorway of the three-story tower.

"Who is in charge of the messenger birds?" he asked the first servant he saw, and was led to a scribe's small room behind the tower. It was dimly lit and overflowing with musty old parchments, cracked leather-bound books, and a wall of small wood cages filled with a score of messenger pigeons.

The small man sitting behind the cluttered desk rose and bowed. "How may I be of service, tavek?"

"I need to send urgent messages to the capital and the northern border. Where are your birds trained to fly?"

"Serif, Learen, and Port Deren, tavek," the scribe replied, pulling a blank sheet of parchment from a tottering stack of papers.

"Get me two birds for each." Arawn sat and scrawled out his message.

> Signs of four changelings in Aldorn. At least one pyro. Riding
> north. Do not allow them to escape. I am pursuing from the
> south. — Arawn

He copied the message three times, then tore off the strips, rolled them tightly, and slid them into the tiny message tubes.

"Send two copies to Learen and Port Deren," he ordered.

As the scribe began attaching the small tubes to the pigeons' legs, Arawn composed his message to Tav Naresh in Serif.

> Signs of four changelings in Aldorn. At least one pyro. Riding
> north. Have alerted Learen and Port Deren. They will not escape.
> Too bad you won't get a share of the prize. — Arawn

He smiled as he copied the words and placed the two missives in message tubes. The scribe had already released the first group of birds. Arawn waited until the final pair was thrown into the air, their blue-gray wings pumping furiously as they rose toward the clear sky, circling once above the rooftops before winging their way south.

A new horse was saddled and waiting for him when he returned to the front of the tower. Arawn leapt into the saddle and charged down the road, in pursuit of a new—and far more rewarding—quarry.

Chapter Twenty-Four
Asho

ASHO WAS RIDING at the end of the group, Devlin pacing at his horse's side, when Damali pulled her horse to a stop, holding up one hand to halt the others.

"What is it?" Tycen asked.

She wheeled to face them, a touch of fear visible in her sapphire eyes. "Khafyri."

"How many?" Makani demanded.

Damali's eyes closed, and a frown pulled at her forehead as she concentrated. "Just one."

"What do we do?" Asho asked, flushing with embarrassment as his voice broke. "Do we run?"

The three masters looked at one another, thoughtfully.

"Are you sure it's just one?" Makani asked.

"Yes."

"We can take it." Tycen's voice was filled with nonchalant confidence. He summoned a fireball into one hand and twirled it lazily between his fingertips.

Out of the corner of his eye, Asho saw Jarond twitch when the fire appeared, hand darting to his sword. He heard Jarond breathe out "Arawn" in a whisper, his voice a mixture of fear, anger, and hate.

"Not Arawn," Damali corrected. "This one is coming from the north. It might have been put on alert by Arawn though. There may be human guardsmen with it. I don't know. I can't sense humans."

"What's the plan?" Tycen asked. "We don't want it escaping and letting others know where we are."

Damali cast a look around; their journey that morning had brought them to a series of low, pine-crowned hills. She pointed to a nearby jumble of rocks. "Asho, you and the humans go hide behind those rocks. Keep out of the way. Take Tycen's horse with you. Tycen—go airborne. The tree cover is thick enough that you shouldn't be spotted. Land behind the group and cut off their retreat. If there are any humans, try to capture them instead of killing them. If it comes down to it, make sure none escape. Makani and I will remain here."

Tycen dismounted, and Aderes took the reins of his horse. Wings sprouted from his back the moment his feet hit the ground.

A gust of wind blew through Asho's hair as Tycen pushed off powerfully, wings sweeping down to propel him up through the tree canopy. In a moment, he was gone from sight.

"Come on, Asho, over here," Aderes called. She and Jarond were already guiding their horses behind the protective mound of boulders. Asho followed, Devlin at his horse's heels.

An ancient, twisted pine tree grew on the far side of the rock pile. The three secured the horses to a low limb, then scrambled up the rocks so they could peek over the top.

"Stay out of sight," Damali warned them, and they lowered their heads. Asho found a gap between two of the uppermost boulders that allowed him to see the road in front of Damali and Makani, who waited patiently atop their steeds. Makani had drawn his sword, and Damali was flipping the opalescent white olkar dagger casually in one hand.

Asho waited for what seemed an interminable time, though the trees' shadows hadn't shifted before the khafyri appeared, a dozen lightly armored men riding behind him.

Asho couldn't pinpoint exactly what it was about the khafyri that made him know that he was looking at something that wasn't human—perhaps it was only because he'd been forewarned, although he doubted that. There was something in the smooth, sinuous movements as the khafyri rode his cantering horse that spoke to a greater-than-human speed and strength. Other than that, the khafyri looked human—sandy hair, blue eyes, and the finely tailored silk clothing of a wealthy lord. Then he rode through a sunbeam that pierced the shadows covering the hills, and his eyes flashed in the light, revealing the reflective gaze of a nocturnal predator.

The khafyri pulled his horse to a skidding halt a dozen paces from Damali and Makani.

"Changelings!" he said in a tone of surprise and—was that fear? The khafyri bared his teeth, revealing sharp fangs, and drew his sword. "Take them alive if you can; if not, kill them both!"

His men drew their swords and prepared to charge.

"Throw down your weapons and your lives will be spared," Tycen called, landing gracefully behind the group. He unsheathed his sword and pointed it at the khafyri. "All except yours, of course."

"Kill them all! Quickly!" the khafyri screamed, panic in his voice now that he realized he had ridden into a trap.

A jagged streak of fire blazed down the length of Tycen's sword; the rubies studding the hilt shone in the reflection—or did they cast a light of their own? The flames streaked through the air like a javelin, striking the khafyri in the chest and billowing out to engulf him. He shrieked in pain; his horse beneath him spun and bucked in a panicked frenzy, desperate to dislodge its fiery passenger. The khafyri was thrown to the ground in a blazing heap— mercifully silent—and the horse bolted for freedom.

Pandemonium engulfed the humans. Most galloped along the road away from Tycen, apparently hoping that Makani and Damali were a lesser threat than the winged man and his burning sword.

One man broke away from the rest and spurred his horse through the underbrush toward the rock pile Asho and the others were hiding behind. The guard veered sharply around the boulders, his horse jumping over a fallen log as they bolted toward freedom.

They need to be stopped, Asho thought.

Devlin lunged from the rock pile. He snapped at the horse's legs, tearing with powerful jaws. Bellowing in pain, the horse stumbled and fell. As it plowed into the ground, out of control, its neck snapped with an audible crack. The horse collapsed, lifeless; neither it nor its rider moved.

"*Stop!*"

The roared command from Makani had the surviving guards yanking their panicked steeds to a halt, dragging cruelly on the horses' tender mouths as the animals fought to flee from the flaming corpse behind them.

"Much better. Dammit, Tycen, you didn't give me a chance to compel the guards first."

Tycen was preoccupied with poking the burning, motionless body of the khafyri with the tip of his sword. A few flakes of ash fluttered in the wind. He glanced up. "You wouldn't have affected this one though. I couldn't see much through the tree canopy, so my timing was guesswork. No sense whining when everything worked out fine in the end." He turned back to the corpse, missing the scowl Makani cast his way.

Makani looked at the guards, his voice carrying the compelling tone that Asho was becoming familiar with. "*Keep riding south. You were sent to find two runaway humans. You haven't seen them. Your group has always been this size; nobody else rode with you. Your journey has been uneventful. You never saw us.*"

Confusion clouded the guards' faces, glazing their eyes. They rode past Makani and Damali without glancing at them, picking up a slow trot once they were back in formation.

Makani watched them disappear from sight, a look of satisfaction on his face. "That takes care of that problem."

Asho scrambled down from his viewpoint in the rocks. Devlin approached him, tail waving proudly, bloody saliva dripping from his mouth.

"That's disgusting, Devlin," Asho said. "Go clean yourself up."

The dog trotted to a small stream nearby and lapped up some water. When he returned, his muzzle dripped clean.

"Good boy." Asho ruffled up Devlin's fur, then turned to see Damali staring at him from the road.

"What?" he asked, feeling his cheeks burn under her studying gaze.

"Did you teach Devlin that command?" she asked.

Asho shrugged. "No. He's a smart dog. He's good at figuring things out."

Damali rode closer so it was easier to speak. "That's more than just being intelligent. Animals don't understand speech, only certain trained commands."

Asho looked away, unsure of how to respond.

"Do me a favor. Tell Devlin to go to Tycen, bark three times at him, and then return to you. Don't use any gestures, just words."

"What?"

"Humor me."

Asho sighed. "Devlin, go bark at Tycen then come back."

The dog cocked his blocky head at him, curiosity in his warm brown eyes.

"Please?"

Devlin trotted past him, unleashing three booming barks when he reached Tycen, who had left the rapidly disintegrating body of the khafyri and was busy burning the dead soldier and horse to ash. Tycen jumped and scowled at Devlin.

Devlin returned to Asho and flopped down at his feet.

Asho stared. How had Devlin known what he meant? He hadn't even said to bark three times—Damali had—and yet the black dog had done exactly that. He looked up at Damali, and saw surprise and puzzlement filling her eyes.

"What does that mean?" he asked.

"He's bonded to you," she replied slowly. "I've suspected it since we first met—he's been unusually responsive to your moods and commands. But I thought it wasn't possible. It *shouldn't* be possible."

"Why not?"

"You're developing two gifts at once. That's never happened before."

"What does it mean? Why can I do it?"

"I don't know. Only the future can tell. It will be interesting to see just what you become."

Chapter Twenty-Five
Jarond

JAROND WATCHED WITH more interest that evening as Tycen instructed Asho in the control of fire. The ease with which Tycen had annihilated the khafyri that afternoon had been impressive. He smiled as he imagined Arawn in the unknown khafyri's position, flames searing his snarling face, smoke rising from a motionless corpse, never able to harm his sister again.

He glanced at Aderes. She was watching the flames flowing between Tycen and Asho, a look of fascination and admiration in her eyes. Jarond's protective instinct flared, but he pushed the feelings aside—what better person for Addie to be interested in than someone who could protect her as efficiently as a changeling? Even though Asho was still untrained, in time, Jarond knew he would be as formidable as Tycen. If Tycen had been in Carwyn when Arawn attacked her, then Kamin wouldn't have had to die.

Jarond flinched at the thought of his friend. During their desperate flight over the past days, he had been forced to put his grief aside. Survival had been his only focus. Now that a feeling of safety was returning to him in the presence of the changelings, his pain of loss came back to him.

Kamin had been his closest friend for three years, since both of them joined the ranks of Carwyn's guardsmen at the age of fifteen. Jarond had been following his passion for physical competition; Kamin was looking for a chance of steady meals. As the youngest of seven sons on a small farm, he stood to inherit nothing and decided that his best option for steady—and relatively low risk—work was employment at the small, peaceful castle. Carwyn was too far from the coast to be threatened by sea raiders, and too far from any land border to have any worry of disputes with neighboring countries.

Jarond felt conflicted. On one hand, he wished Kamin had stayed at the feast, eating and drinking and out of danger. On the other hand, he owed his life—and, possibly, the life of his sister—to Kamin's intervention. It was a debt he could never repay, and guilt over Kamin's sacrifice gnawed at him.

A pillar of fire rose from Asho's hand, flames coiling around one another as they lifted skyward, their upward progress halted by Damali's protective shield.

"Very good," Tycen encouraged. "Now, bring the fire back down and snuff it out."

Asho obeyed, the pillar shrinking in size until only a small flicker remained in his palm. He closed his fist, and the fire disappeared. A thin sheen of sweat covered his face, which was plastered with a triumphant grin.

"I did it," he exulted. "It didn't get away from me that time."

"Excellent work," Tycen said. "But don't get overconfident. Remember, fire—even fire you haven't summoned—will respond to your emotions if you let your control slip. You have to always be on your guard, so you don't accidentally hurt someone. As your training progresses, you will need to learn to disconnect your emotions from your fire-bond, so that they no longer have the power to influence the fire outside of your conscious control."

Asho nodded, his hazel eyes intent. "What about the bond with Devlin though? How can I learn to do more with that?"

Tycen ran a hand through his short, reddish-blond hair. "I'm not sure; it's not something I've learned about." He glanced at his fellow masters. "Any ideas?"

Makani shrugged. "Never paid much attention to the animal folk. Didn't seem all that useful."

"I spent a little time with Arwa in Stenberg," Damali said. "She had an animal bond. For her, it was limited to the olkar, but I know others have been able to exert their will over any number of species. Unfortunately, I don't know much about their training, so I'm not sure how much help I can be. Until we get to Varnstad, you might have to figure out your limits yourself, Asho. See if you can think commands to Devlin, instead of saying them aloud. Or try to order other animals the way you do with Devlin and see if they respond the same way he does."

Asho stared intently at Devlin, who was stretched out a few feet away from him, beyond where Damali's protective shield had been.

Asho's brow furrowed with concentration; Devlin looked back at him, tongue lolling out of his mouth and head cocked to one side.

"Nothing," Asho finally said.

"Try again later; it might just take time to develop."

"Why are changelings afraid of khafyri?" Jarond asked. He had been wondering that ever since he'd seen Tycen's pyromancer abilities used in combat. "It seems like you completely outmatch them."

"Not always," Damali said. "A pyro has a significant advantage, it's true. But khafyri are strong and incredibly quick. Tycen made it look easy today because he caught that one by surprise. Also, the khafyri today was unprotected and had a plain steel sword."

"How does that make a difference? I can't imagine that plate mail would make any difference to being scorched by fire."

"Steel armor wouldn't make a difference. But strieborna armor would."

"Why?"

"Do you know that your sword and scabbard are embedded with gemstones?"

Jarond was surprised. The weapon and sheath had been well-disguised by Aderes. "How did you know that?"

"All strieborna weapons and armor have some sort of gemstones connected to them; the stones are repositories of power. I can sense the power in the weapon you bear. Some gems can hold unrefined energy that can be used by the bearer as power for their own abilities. Others have specific spells embedded in them; those can be used by anyone, regardless of their own abilities."

"So I could learn to use them."

"Sorry, I misspoke. Humans don't have the necessary influence over manakore to use the power and bend it to their will. Some things will work; one of the stones in that sword is clearly designed to protect its wielder. That's why Makani's compulsion didn't work on you when we first met. That power is only a small part of what the sword can do, and most of it is outside of a human's ability. But a changeling—or khafyri—can use it. That's why strieborna is so dangerous in the hands of the khafyri. It allows them to use our power against us."

"Where do the khafyri come from?"

"I don't know. They've been a scourge on our people since they appeared three hundred years ago. Their numbers have been growing ever since. They forced us to retreat north, to the refuge of Varnstad, and have taken over the human government of Sermund."

"Why do we still have a king then? Is he a khafyri?"

"No, but he wants to be. The khafyri used a combination of superior force and promises of immortality to the human rulers when they took over. They mostly aren't interested in the tedium of day-to-day politics and laws, but they want the support of the human's military might for when they need it."

"But why? What could they possibly need a human army for?"

"Us." Damali gave him a small, sad smile. "Varnstad is a protected refuge, and the khafyri have been unable to penetrate our borders so far. Our coast is guarded by tekula, and our land, besides being protected by nearly impassible mountains, has the country of Harondor as a buffer between it and Sermund. Fortunately, the kings of Harondor are an independent, suspicious lot, and they mistrust the khafyri. They won't let an armed force from Sermund cross their lands. We have managed to foster a good relationship with them, however, and changeling units help guard the Harondor-Sermund border against khafyri or human invasion. One of our elders sits on King Bohdan's council."

King Bohdan. The name sounded familiar, but Jarond couldn't remember where he'd heard it before. He'd probably overheard it from a trader or a wandering minstrel. They spent their whole lives on the move, stopping for a few days to earn coin and then following the road wherever it took them next.

"We should get some rest; tomorrow will be another long day," Damali said. "I set a ward border a mile from our camp. It will alert me if any khafyri crosses it, so we don't need to worry about being ambushed in the night."

Long after everyone else had fallen asleep, Jarond lay awake, listening to Makani's rumbling snores. The world had suddenly grown so much bigger than the little castle and small acreage of Carwyn. Amongst his human peers, he was a superb swordsman. But the people he now traveled with—and the creature that hunted him—were beings of legend and myth. What could a simple swordsman like him bring of value to this age-long battle, where kings and monsters commanded the armies?

Chapter Twenty-Six
Aderes

ADERES WOUND THROUGH the fragrant pine trees as she followed the burble of the nearby stream. Jarond was fishing in the small creek, and she wanted to see if he'd had any luck landing a trout. She pushed her way through a wall of ferns, the flowing water at last in sight, and froze in horror.

Arawn stood on the mossy bank before her. As his cold, predatory eyes locked with hers, he smiled, revealing gleaming fangs dripping blood. At his feet was Jarond's pale corpse, still and lifeless.

"No!" Aderes screamed in denial. Her knees collapsed, and she fell to the damp ground.

Arawn took a step toward her, his smile full of malice and anticipation.

ADERES WOKE, JERKING upright in a tangle of blankets as she frantically looked around for her brother. The glowing embers of the fire cast a soft light on the small camp, revealing Jarond sleeping nearby.

Just a dream. Nothing to be afraid of here.

A massive shape materialized in the gloom next to her, eyes glowing in the reflected light of the fire. *Khafyri!* She opened her mouth to scream, then closed it as she recognized the blocky head of Asho's dog.

"You scared me, Devlin," she whispered, letting out her breath in a gusty sigh.

He licked her face, his warm, wet tongue washing away the mixed sweat and tears on her cheeks.

Aderes scratched Devlin's ruff. His hind leg thumped in appreciation as his eyes closed in ecstasy. He lowered himself to the ground and rolled on his back to present his belly to her. She scratched his ribs, avoiding the uncontrollably kicking hind leg as Devlin reveled in her ministrations.

"Devlin?" A quiet whisper came from behind her. "Where'd you go?"

Aderes turned to see another dark shape sitting upright. Asho. "He's over here," she whispered back. Devlin licked her fingers, trying to recapture her attention. "Go back to Asho."

"No, it's okay," Asho said. "I was just worried when I woke up and he wasn't there. I thought maybe something had happened to him."

Aderes felt a pang of guilt when she remembered telling Asho that the khafyri would hurt Devlin. "Sorry about what I said earlier."

"What?" Asho paused. "Oh. About Devlin. No, you shouldn't apologize for that. You helped me."

Aderes was still jumpy from her nightmare and didn't want to go back to sleep.

"What's it like?" Aderes asked, hoping she wasn't prying too much. "To think you are human and then to suddenly find out that you are a changeling?"

Asho hesitated. "Scary. I always wondered about my parents; I remember being on the run with them, and when Master Hayden told me they were executed, I thought they must be bandits or murderers or something. But it didn't make sense from the memories that I had of them—I always felt loved, and safe with them. Now, to find out they were changelings—or, at least my mother was—it's crazy. I just always thought I'd live in Aldorn, maybe take over the inn when Hayden died. He never liked me much, but he and Farica never had any children, and she was always fond of me. Now, I don't know. I don't know what I'm supposed to do. I have this crazy power over fire, which I can barely control, and it seems like I'll be expected to join this war between the changelings and khafyri. I'm just a stableboy. How can they expect me to know what to do?"

He sighed. "Sorry, I didn't mean to dump all that on you at once. It's just that Damali, Tycen, and Makani always seem so confident and self-assured. And I feel lost. I never thought I was meant for great deeds and courageous acts."

"I know what you mean," Aderes said. "I mean, I don't really know what it feels like to have powers like you, but I feel the same about my future. I always thought that I'd spend my life at Carwyn, helping my father breed and train horses, and then take over from him. But now I don't know. Jarond and I are on the run—what future is there for us? Even if the changelings offer us refuge, what will we be able to do? We'll be two powerless humans amongst a whole society of supernatural beings. I don't want to be a burden or a charity case."

"You won't be," Asho protested. "You're so good with the horses—I'm sure that there'll be something that you'll be able to do there."

"Maybe, but I don't have a bond with animals the way you do."

"Just Devlin. And that hasn't brought me much."

"Yeah, but from what Damali said, it seems like there are changelings with other sorts of bonds with animals. Your gift could end up growing."

"It might," Asho said. "But nobody knows for certain. But there's one thing that I do know: no matter what happens, I'm sure you'll be fine."

She smiled at the unbounded optimism in his voice. "And I'm sure you'll be fine." Despite the uncertainty of their future, she knew it to be true. "You have such amazing gifts. The fire control, and the bond with Devlin."

"Maybe," Asho said uncertainly.

"I'll make a deal with you." She projected as much confidence in her voice as she could muster. "We both won't worry about the future, since we are both confident that the other will be fine."

She saw the white flash of Asho's teeth in the firelight as he grinned. "Deal."

As Aderes curled back up to sleep, Devlin tucked close to her side. She sleepily scratched behind his ears. *It will be all right*, she told herself, holding on tight to that thought as she drifted back to sleep.

Chapter Twenty-Seven
Jarond

THEY BROKE THEIR fast in the pre-dawn grayness, eating oatcakes in silence, then packed up their camp and saddled the horses. Jarond moved stiffly; the salve Aderes had bought for him was gone, and his chafed skin rubbed painfully against the inside of his pants.

Makani stood slightly apart from the others, tightening the girth on his sorrel gelding. Jarond approached him, relieved for the opportunity to talk to him in semi-private. It was bad enough that he had to tell anyone—and for it to be Makani, of all people. Even Damali would have been easier to approach. No. A man was better, even if Makani mocked him.

"When you heal someone," Jarond began, keeping his voice low. "Do you—do you need to touch the injury the way you did with Addie?"

Makani's sharp black eyes met his. "No," he said, a small frown tugging down between his eyebrows. "I just need to have physical contact with the person I'm healing. Location helps, but it isn't vital. Why do you ask?"

"I was wondering if you could heal me." Jarond felt his cheeks flush.

"Heal you? What's wrong?"

Jarond couldn't meet his eyes. "Saddle sores," he muttered, waiting for a mocking laugh. He would tolerate ridicule if it meant relief from his pain.

To his surprise, the laugh didn't come.

"Didn't think about that," Makani said. "If you've got them, I'll bet Asho does too. Doubt he's ridden much either. Give me your hand."

Makani's grip was firm and cool around Jarond's callused hand. A tingle raced up his arm into his body. It felt strange, though not unpleasantly so, and as it coursed through him, it erased the ache of sore muscles and the grating of chafed skin. Makani released his hand, and Jarond felt energized and, more importantly, ready to face another long day in the saddle.

"Thanks," he said.

"Don't mention it." Makani left him and went to Asho, apparently to offer healing, since shortly afterward he took Asho's hand in his own.

"What was that all about?" Aderes asked as she rode up to him.

"Makani healed my saddle sores," Jarond replied as he thrust his foot in the stirrup and swung into the saddle. "Need him to help you?"

"Some of us are used to riding and aren't so fragile, brother dear," Aderes replied with a wicked grin. "Glad you're better though."

THE MORNING WAS a blur of trotting interspersed with brief sections of walking. Jarond felt strong again, his body able to tackle the rigors of the ride. They pushed their horses hard, although not quite so hard as he and Aderes had that first, fear-filled night. Their mounts needed to last them all the way to the border if they were going to escape capture by the khafyri.

The member of their party who struggled the most with the pace was Devlin. By early afternoon, the muscular dog was barely able to keep up, panting heavily as he trotted determinedly onward. Every time they stopped at creeks to water their horses, Devlin flopped in the water, lapping up big gulps as the current washed over his heavy-set body, providing cooling relief.

"Is there anything you can do to help him?" Asho asked Makani at one of their hurried rest stops, his voice tight with worry.

Makani shook his head. "Sorry, but I can't heal animals. It's not part of my abilities."

"Maybe he can ride with you," Aderes suggested. "Your horse is strong enough to bear the weight of both of you, and if you tie him down behind the saddle, he won't fall off."

Aderes held the reins of Asho's mount, talking softly to the bay gelding to keep him quiet while they loaded Devlin on his back. It took both Jarond and Asho to lift the huge animal into place.

At least Asho can control Devlin enough to keep him quiet, Jarond thought as they heaved the massive dog atop the horse. *Even a small dog would be difficult to secure on a horse if it squirmed or fought back. And Devlin is only small in relation to the horses.* He eyed Devlin's powerful jaws, which hung open to reveal long, curved canines as he panted. After seeing Devlin take down the fleeing horse and guard, he knew he wouldn't want to be the focus of his temper.

At last, they had Devlin secure, draped across the horse's back behind the saddle and gently bound with ropes to keep him from falling as they moved out. He seemed content to lie there, head lifted to watch their surroundings as they continued their journey northward.

AS DUSK FELL, they reached a crossroads. The Northern Road intersected with the Trader's Road in the middle of a wide, grassy plain, which bore evidence of longtime use by trading caravans. Bare patches of earth and mounded dirt from filled-in latrines showed that the crossroads was a favored camping spot. Trading caravans carried goods across the realm, from the great seaport of Deren, the gold-rich Witroc mountains, and along the length of the fertile central valley of Sermund.

"We should camp out of sight," Damali said. "We don't want any word of our whereabouts getting spread."

They crossed the meadow and continued into the forest, cutting through the underbrush away from the road. Much of the forest floor was cleared, no doubt by traders scavenging for fuel for their campfires. At last, Damali called a halt in a small, secluded meadow. A stream ran close by, and the meadow was filled with lush grasses to feed their horses. Asho and Jarond lifted Devlin down from the horse as the rest of the group set about making camp, all too weary for small talk as they completed their tasks.

After a quiet supper huddled around a small, smokeless fire, Tycen ordered Asho to join him for another lesson in pyromancy.

"Another?" Asho groaned. "Can't it wait? I'm exhausted."

Jarond felt empathy for Asho. He could barely keep his eyelids open, and was already thinking longingly of his warm blanket. He might have envied Asho's power, but he certainly didn't envy his lesson schedule after a hard day's ride.

"Every day," Tycen replied. His voice was unwavering, but it didn't contain the same enthusiasm it usually did. "As long as you are untrained, you are a danger to both yourself and those around you. Once we get to Lyndell, you will have much longer, more rigorous training. But even though we are on the road, we can't afford to skip out on your lessons. I don't want to scare you too much, but your control over your abilities could be the difference between life and death if the khafyri catch us."

With a final grumble of protest, Asho went to sit with Tycen.

Jarond watched as Tycen continued Asho's instruction on how to summon fire. Despite obvious effort, Asho was only able to bring forth a weak, flickering flame. Eventually, Tycen called a halt to their lesson, and Asho stumbled to his bedroll, curled up, and immediately fell asleep.

Jarond yawned. "Do we need to post a guard tonight?" he asked Damali.

She shook her head as a yawn overtook her. "I set a ward that will alert me if any khafyri get close. Get some sleep while you can."

Chapter Twenty-Eight
Arawn

NOT LONG AFTER sunrise, as he continued his northward pursuit, Arawn heard the steady cadence of trotting horses coming down the road. A moment later, he saw the source of the sound: nine mounted guardsmen, wearing the cream-and-brown livery of Learen, riding south in formation. They drew their horses to a halt when they approached him, bowing in unison from the saddle.

"Tavek," their leader said respectfully.

"Report," Arawn replied.

"We have been riding for three days, tavek, searching for the two human fugitives. We haven't seen anything unusual. Perhaps they took a different route."

Arawn frowned. The squad of soldiers should have passed the crossroads for the Trader's Road before the changelings could have made it that far north. This squad was sent out before his message about the changelings arrived in Learen, but the Sermundi soldiers were experienced enough to recognize a changeling and know to use any means necessary to capture any changelings they encountered. Something wasn't right.

"Just nine of you?" he asked. "Where is the tenth man of your squad?"

The soldiers looked uneasily at one another, uncertainty filling their faces.

"It's just us, tavek," the leader replied. "Nobody else left Learen with us."

Arawn considered the khafyri stationed at Learen, and wondered which of them was most likely to lead such a search party. *Elsu,* he decided. Elsu always hated being confined to one place.

"Elsu didn't ride with you?" Arawn asked.

"No, tavek."

"So Elsu stayed at Learen while you rode out on pursuit?"

The leader hesitated, brow furrowing in confusion. "No, tavek."

"He was somewhere else, then?"

"No, tavek."

Someone has altered their memories or compelled them, Arawn decided. The situation was too odd. They must have had an encounter with the changelings, but were forced to forget it. That was the only explanation for the missing tenth member of their group, and the contradictory reports about Elsu's whereabouts.

He debated about whether he should order the soldiers to ride with him in pursuit; extra bodies were always helpful when dealing with changelings. But the risk of having his own soldiers turned against him was too great. A changeling powerful enough to compel the soldiers to forget their companions was likely strong enough to force them to attack him, making the human pawns a detriment rather than a benefit.

"Keep riding south until you reach Aldorn," he ordered. "Then you can return to Learen." The task was pointless, but it would keep the human guardsmen occupied and out of his way.

"Yes, tavek."

The guardsmen bowed again as Arawn rode past, and they continued on their futile southern pursuit.

ARAWN RODE HARD all day, not stopping even when the sun slipped behind the horizon. The blackness of night didn't bother him. His kind were comfortable in the dark, at home in the concealing shadows. The scant moonlight filtering through the tree cover was more than enough for him to push onward, hopefully closing the gap between him and his quarry.

As long as the hunter doesn't become the hunted. But armored khafyri reinforcements, prepared to meet a changeling threat, should already be mustered out from Learen and Port Deren. The changelings would be trapped between them, with no escape. And even though he was alone, Arawn wasn't unprotected. He smirked. Naresh was to thank for that. No doubt the other khafyri would be furious to know that the shield, intended as a mocking gesture, would actually be useful in protecting Arawn's life. Naresh certainly wouldn't mourn if Arawn were killed. *He'd probably throw a celebratory feast.*

Arawn had examined the strieborna shield earlier that day, deciphering the protective runes etched around the cluster of rubies in the center boss. There were powerful wards contained within the shield, including protection against pyromancy. The changelings would have to summon an extraordinary amount of power to break through the wards. Not impossible—especially armed with strieborna blades, which they no doubt bore—but difficult, even more so once Arawn was reinforced by other khafyri.

As the night wore on, his horse began to stumble from exhaustion. Arawn snarled in frustration, but reluctantly stopped to allow the animal to rest and graze. He needed it to recover its strength—he was too far into the wilderness to count on being able to get a remount any time soon. And despite the animal's relative frailty, its endurance was, overall, greater than what he could do on foot. Khafyri were fast, but not equipped for the great distances he still needed to cover.

As the horse rested, Arawn crouched on a rock. Waiting for sunrise.

Chapter Twenty-Nine
Asho

AFTER BREAKING CAMP in the morning, Asho and the others continued their relentless journey northward. Devlin was afoot for the start of their journey; Aderes and Damali had agreed that they needed to conserve as much of their horses' strength as possible, and they wouldn't load Devlin onto the back of Asho's horse until he was too tired to continue under his own power. For the moment, Devlin was clearly reveling in his freedom, his long black tail waving like a proud banner as he trotted at Asho's side.

During their brief rests, Asho practiced his control over Devlin, with mixed results. Any spoken command—no matter how unnatural for a dog to do—was obeyed. Devlin drank water from specific points in streams, brought certain sticks or leaves to Asho, and scent-marked particular trees. But any time Asho attempted to give Devlin a silent command, the dog was unresponsive. After a few hours of practice, frustration filled Asho. He knew he could do it, *knew* Devlin could respond to his thoughts—after all, during their brief skirmish with the khafyri and squad of guards, Devlin had attacked the fleeing rider without a spoken command—but for some reason, he couldn't seem to consciously tap into that part of his bond with Devlin.

They rested their horses at midday, eating dried strips of beef while the horses grazed. Asho concentrated on Devlin. *Go sit next to Aderes. Go keep her company.* Devlin remained where he was, sprawled in the darkest patch of shade near the stream.

Damali jumped to her feet, startling Asho from his focus on Devlin. "We need to get off the road. There are khafyri approaching from the north."

The others scrambled back into their saddles, chewing hastily on the last bites of tough meat.

"How far away are they?" Asho asked.

"Five miles," Damali said. "There's a lot of them. Too many for us to handle."

"Should we go east or west?" Tycen asked.

"West," Makani said. "If we can get through the Coastal Range, we can take the Coast Road north."

"But we'll be hemmed in by the ocean," Damali countered. "Easier to trap. We should head east. The Witrocs are far enough away that we'll have some room to maneuver, and if we get desperate, they're more passable than the ocean would be."

"But—"

"Let's vote," Tycen interjected. "I say we head east."

"Fine," Makani grumbled. "Guess I'm overruled."

Instead of riding through the underbrush, Damali urged her horse into the creek that the animals had just been drinking from. "No tracks to follow," she said, and the others followed her lead, riding single file along the gravelly stream bed.

The horses splashed easily through the water, which was knee-deep for them, but Asho noticed that Devlin was struggling. The water reached past his chest, and he valiantly bounded forward, lunging through the water.

He won't be able to keep up much longer, Asho realized. He knew the others, especially Makani, wouldn't want to take the time to stop and help his dog up on a horse when the khafyri were so close. There was no time to waste. Asho scanned their surroundings, looking for anything to help Devlin get on his horse.

The creek narrowed ahead of them, cutting its way through a rocky outcropping. It crumbled into a series of boulders away from the watercourse and ledges that might be climbable for Devlin, and at the water's edge, it was high enough for the dog to leap onto his horse's back.

Asho turned in the saddle, opening his mouth to give the order to Devlin, but saw the dog already scrambling out of the water toward the rocks ahead. He clambered up the side and reached the flat top just as Asho rode though the narrows.

Smiling in triumph, Asho stopped his horse long enough for Devlin to jump aboard. Instead of getting behind the saddle, Devlin leapt in front of Asho, where Asho could wrap his arms around him and keep him from slipping off. It was a tight fit with such a bulky dog, but Asho hung on, determined to keep Devlin from falling off and falling behind.

After a mile of wading through the creek, Damali rode out of the water. "Speed is more important than stealth now." Once the rest of them were on dry land, she urged her horse into a fast trot, weaving through the trees and underbrush as the others followed.

As his horse bounced underneath him, Asho struggled to keep ahold of both Devlin and his reins. Finally, he dropped the reins, trusting in the herd instinct of the horse to keep up with the others—and praying that the animal wouldn't run his knees into a tree trunk or scrape him off on a low-hanging branch.

Aderes, riding just in front of him, looked back. Worry was written in tight lines across her face, but when she saw him clinging onto Devlin, a brief smile appeared. He smiled back, ignoring the fear-induced churning and knotting of his stomach.

They rode through the trees as twilight fell, turning the forest into a gloomy, gray landscape of monochromatic trees, bushes, and grasses. Instead of slowing their pace, Tycen cast a fireball in the air and floated it in front of their group so they could still see as they trotted eastward, occasionally following game trails when they headed in the right direction, but mostly forging their own path through the trees.

Asho's muscles were screaming in protest by the time they finally stopped to make camp. Jarond helped Devlin down to the ground, and Asho wearily followed.

"The khafyri are out of my range to sense," Damali said. "They must've continued south down the road. We can get a few hours of rest and continue on in the morning."

Arms aching, Asho wearily untacked his horse and picketed him with the others, then crawled into his blanket. Devlin lay down next to him, and Asho draped an arm over the dog, fingers burrowing into the warm, comforting fur as he succumbed to exhaustion.

Chapter Thirty
Arawn

BY MIDMORNING, ARAWN found evidence he was on the right trail: ashes, bearing the distinctive acrid scent of a burned khafyri, were scattered across the road. He briefly dismounted, searching for any evidence of the khafyri's identity or any indication of other abilities possessed by his foes. A short way off the trail, he found another, larger pile of ashes. One whiff told him it wasn't another khafyri—the tenth guard, most likely, trying to escape the changelings through the forest. He remounted his horse and continued north. They wouldn't outrun him for much longer.

ARAWN REACHED THE crossroads at midday and hesitated. Which way did his quarry ride? He dismounted and studied the tracks along the intersection of the Northern Road and Trader's Road. Hoof prints from horses, mules, and oxen marred the tracks in all directions, making it difficult to discern which belonged to his prey.

Arawn snarled in frustration. Reinforcements were coming from Learen and Port Deren, but the eastern Trader's Road had no khafyri outpost along it. If they went in that direction, there would be nobody ahead of them to set a trap. But he doubted they would turn east unless forced to do so. This early in the spring, the Witrocs were an impenetrable barrier except for the truly desperate. He couldn't afford to make a mistake at this point. They were too close to the border. He couldn't let them escape.

As he had ridden, he had noticed large paw prints accompanying the hoof marks of his targets, but they had abruptly disappeared a few miles earlier. Either the dog was left behind, or they put it on a horse. Whatever the cause, there were no paw prints for Arawn to track.

As he debated which way to go, a trio of riders appeared to the west. Arawn smiled as he recognized the three khafyri. Arlen, Ronit, and Giolla. All three had been sired by him, and together they ruled Port Deren, solidifying Arawn's dominion of the coast.

The other khafyri were armored in strieborna breastplates and open-faced conical helms. Arlen and Giolla bore shields as well, and Ronit had his strieborna longbow and a quiver of arrows hanging from his saddle. Arawn broadened his smile at the sight of the bow. He knew each arrow had a strieborna shaft and a diamond arrowhead that was filled with enough power from manakore to punch through nearly any changeling defensive shield. They were priceless, and had been a hard-won prize in the last major encounter between the khafyri and the changelings, just before the changelings retreated to the impenetrable defenses of Varnstad.

Even more valuable than the weapons was the compass Giolla held out as they approached. It had no directional markings on it, but a tiny moonstone was imbedded in the directional arrow. It unerringly pointed toward any nearby fluctuations of manakore. It would lead them directly to their quarry.

"Any sign of changelings?" Arawn asked as his three neophytes bowed to him.

"The compass started picking up readings a few miles back. They're north-northeast from here."

Arawn's fangs extended in anticipation of the upcoming encounter. His grinned as he swung back into the saddle. He kicked his horse into a canter up the Northern Road, the three khafyri following loyally. *So close now. They won't escape.*

TWO HOURS LATER, they encountered four khafyri from Learen. Arawn fought back a scowl. Navati and Kalei were both sired by Naresh. Navati's mate, Zephyra, and his second-in-command, Gerik, were both nearly as loyal to Naresh as if they'd been sired. Arawn didn't like his followers being outnumbered by those whose loyalty he couldn't rely on. Even though Naresh wasn't present, it would take deft maneuvering for Arawn to stay in control of the situation—and of any captives they took.

"Where's Elsu?" Navati demanded without any greeting.

Arawn took a small amount of satisfaction in having guessed the identity of the ashy remains. "Dead. Wasn't prepared for the pyromancer I'm pursuing. Most of his squad survived. The changelings seem to be trying to throw off the trail as much as possible. The humans were compelled."

"*Paska*," Navati cursed. "Which way did they go? We haven't seen any evidence of changelings."

Arawn smirked. "You missed a sign then. They're still northeast of here. They must've left the road and cut through the woods before you came across them."

"How do you know?"

Giolla held up his compass. The moonstone arrow pointed unwaveringly to the northeast.

Navati cast a covetous glance at the compass.

"We'll follow them and then split up to surround them as we get nearer," Navati said.

"This is my hunt," Arawn snapped. "You'll obey me, or you'll have nothing to do with it."

Navati glared, defiance filling his ice-blue eyes, but Arawn bared his fangs and snarled. "Do you wish to challenge me?"

Arawn keep his eyes steady on them, ready for an attack.

Navati lowered his pale eyes and gave a short, stiff bow. "As you wish. Just so long as we receive our share of the prize."

"You'll receive what you deserve," Arawn snapped. "Now let's go. The longer we spend bickering like old women, the farther our prey gets."

"They won't get far enough," Giolla said with a smile. "They can't hide from us."

"Lead the way," Arawn said.

Giolla spun his horse and set off down the road, holding his compass in one hand. The moonstone arrow fixed steadily on their target.

Chapter Thirty-One
Jarond

THE GROUP OF changelings spent the following day riding on a northeast slant toward the Harondor border. Damali said they were still miles away from the Napier River Gorge. Jarond felt like they had been on the run forever, always riding, always afraid of being caught. And just when he began to feel a bit of safety with the changelings, a greater threat arose.

The border was only a few days' ride through difficult terrain away, but it seemed like they'd never reach it. They were riding two miles east for every mile they made to the north, hampered by gradually steepening canyons. The land itself seemed to be fighting them, drawing them ever toward the impassable Witroc Mountains, whose snow-capped peaks rose closer in front of them with every passing hour.

In the early afternoon, they reached a small sunny valley, clear save for a few solitary oak trees. As they trotted across the grassy valley floor, more open than the thick forest they'd been winding through single file, Jarond found himself riding abreast with Damali, who was quiet with brow furrowed in concentration. What she could feel through her mystical powers, Jarond could only guess. But a more pressing thought occupied him, a question that had been fomenting in the back of his mind ever since Aderes and he had joined the changelings.

"Why did you bring me and Aderes with you?" he asked. "Why not just leave us behind?"

Damali looked at him, her stare appraising and thoughtful. "I'm not quite sure. Just an intuition, I suppose. Even though your path crossing ours meant that the khafyri were able to pick up our trail"—Jarond flinched, but her tone held no accusation—"that was through no fault of yours. We all knew the risks of this mission. But between the three of us, our powers give us a decent chance of staying one step ahead of any pursuit."

"I'm sorry that we put you in danger," Jarond said with a twinge of guilt.

"It quite possibly would've happened anyway, after Asho's gifts awakened in such an explosive fashion. Khafyri are adept at sensing our power—they might've picked up the trail."

Her tone was matter-of-fact, but Jarond caught the worried look she cast over her shoulder. Pursuit was miles away, yet he knew all of them felt that the khafyri could appear behind them at any moment.

"Besides," Damali continued, "it's really no extra risk to us to have you along. What's done is done, and there's no use complaining about it. If we'd left you behind, you would've been basically defenseless against the khafyri. Sure, you could kill one with that new sword of yours, but it'd been unlikely you'd get the chance going one-on-one against a khafyri. At least with us, you might be able to help, if it comes to a fight."

Jarond fingered the hilt of his sword. He might not be able to use it to the extent that a changeling might, but at least he was armed and prepared—as much as any human could be. If he came face-to-face with Arawn again, he'd drive the blade through his heart, and then burn the corpse just to ensure the monster was truly dead. Then, maybe, Aderes would be safe.

He ached all over when they finally made camp late in the evening, but he'd been aching for days. At least his saddle sores hadn't returned after Makani had healed him. Even Aderes looked exhausted, and at Carwyn she had spent nearly every waking hour riding one horse or another. With their father's extensive breeding program, there had always been plenty of work breaking the young horses to saddle.

Everyone was quiet as they made camp. The six of them had traveled long enough that it was second nature to unsaddle and picket the horses, spread out their bedrolls and blankets, and collect enough firewood to cook some of their dried rations. The other nights, Tycen had been the one to light the campfire, but this night, he told Asho to do so. After several minutes of staring intently at the thin, dried branches, sparks jumped from between the wood, quickly catching and expanding into a merry blaze.

As Asho smiled in weary triumph, Jarond sank to the ground near the flames, grateful for the warmth rolling across his skin and soothing his tired muscles. He wasn't so exhausted to miss the look that passed between his sister and Asho as they mutually reveled in the young pyromancer's success. Jarond tried to quell his annoyance, reminding himself once again that Asho would be well-equipped to take care of Aderes and protect her against khafyri. Once he was trained, at least.

After a hot supper of beans and dried meat, they all retired to their blankets to sleep. For once, Jarond didn't ask if they needed to post a guard. He was too drained, and besides, Damali would set a ward to alert her if any khafyri got close. And none had. They were fast enough to stay ahead of their pursuers.

Chapter Thirty-Two
Asho

"WAKE UP. NOW." Damali's low, urgent voice jerked Asho from a fitful sleep. As he sat up, he saw that Tycen and Jarond were already on their feet, alternating between studying the surrounding darkness warily and looking at Damali for answers. Jarond's knuckles were white around the hilt of his drawn blade. Asho scrambled to his feet, wishing he had a sword of his own.

"What is it?" Tycen asked.

"Khafyri. A lot of them. We need to leave now."

The next several minutes passed in a flurry of movement, as the six of them broke camp and tacked the horses. Asho's fingers trembled as he tightened his cinch and fumbled to tie his saddlebags in place. As usual, Aderes was the first to swing into the saddle, but the rest of them weren't far behind.

"Where are they?" Makani asked.

"All around. A few miles out. They're trying to surround us. None to the east though."

"Lead the way."

Tycen summoned a fireball to light their way, floating it in front of them to illuminate the uneven, treacherous ground along the dry stream bed they followed eastward. They pushed their horses as fast as the terrain allowed, breaking into canters during the brief flat sections, slowing to a walk to allow their mounts to pick their way amongst scattered rocks and boulders.

Near the end of the line, Asho struggled to retain his balance as his horse reacted to the others, leaping forward in response to their increased speed, skidding to a halt as Jarond's horse in front of him suddenly slowed because of a change of footing that Asho couldn't see.

The surrounding trees thinned, and the light of the waxing moon revealed craggy canyon walls rising high to either side of the stream they followed. The farther they rode, the steeper the slopes became.

"Hurry!" Damali hissed. "They're getting closer."

Asho's heart thundered under his ribs. He readjusted his sweat-dampened grip on his horse's reins and shivered in the cool night air. *Just focus. You can do this. Be like Tycen.* He tried to focus on his fire-bond, but it slipped elusively from his grasp.

A whine sounded over the clacking of his horse's shoes on rocks, and Asho looked down at Devlin, a large black shadow moving through the soft moonlight. A spark of courage filled him; even if he couldn't summon fire, Devlin wouldn't fail him.

At the front of the line of riders, the glowing sphere of Tycen's fireball disappeared around yet another bend, the steep walls of the canyon—now proper cliffs on either side—hiding the light briefly from view until Asho rode around the sharp bend. His stomach plummeted in a twisting ball of horror and fear as he saw what lay ahead.

The sheer walls of the canyon curved together, melding into a seamless, impassible rock face. Tycen's fireball hovered high in the air, bathing the gray rock in a red light and illuminating their predicament. There were no cracks, no dark passages in the rock for them to make an escape. They were trapped.

Makani pushed in behind Asho's stopped horse. "What's the holdup?" he grumbled, then halted next to Asho as he took in the view. "*Paska.*"

"Tycen, can you get us out of here?" Damali asked.

"How far are the khafyri?"

"Quarter mile."

Tycen shook his head. "Not enough time for even one trip. These cliffs are too high."

"Go airborne anyways. See if you can pick any off from above. With luck, they won't have fire shields."

"Can't count on luck," Makani said.

"Got a better idea?"

Makani shook his head; sweat beaded on his face.

Tycen dismounted, unfurled his wings, and pushed off into the sky, disappearing into the blackness above.

"At least they won't see him," Asho said.

"Darkness makes little difference to a khafyri," Damali said. "They have excellent night vision."

Makani drew his sword, wheeling to face the entrance to the blind canyon.

"Get behind us," Damali said, drawing her olkar blade. The white dagger shone in the pale moonlight, capturing each white beam and magnifying it.

Asho complied, nudging his horse into the space next to Aderes, between the two masters and the solid rock wall, but Jarond rode forward, drawing his own sword as he joined the defensive line.

"Stay back, boy," Makani growled. "You'll only get hurt."

"You need all the help you can get," Jarond retorted.

Makani shrugged. "Your funeral."

Asho held out a shaking hand, willing a flame to appear. A spark flickered above his palm. He focused on it, coaxing it to grow. It wavered, trembling like his nerves. Where was his anger when he needed it? All he could feel was a hollow numbness.

He looked up; the sound of steel horseshoes on stone echoed through the canyon, drawing closer with every step. Concentration broken, the spark disappeared. There were too many beats for Asho to guess how many horses were approaching down the dry stream bed.

"What do we do?" he whispered.

"We fight," Damali said without her usual assuredness.

Chapter Thirty-Three
Aderes

EIGHT HORSES MATERIALIZED out of the darkness. Their riders' eyes glowed in the black night, reflecting the flickering fireball suspended in front of them. *Khafyri*. Silver shone from their breastplates and shields, and the soft scrape of metal floated on the air as they drew their swords.

The khafyri spread out in front of them, filling the width of the narrow canyon, and halted. One rode forward half a pace.

"There is no escape. Surrender, and your lives will be spared," Arawn said.

A blinding streak of fire ripped through the air from above in a blaze of whites and blues and reds, roaring its crackling fury as it shot toward Arawn. Elation filled Aderes as she anticipated the inevitable death of the khafyri.

Arawn lifted his shield, and the fire broke and splintered before it touched him. Sparks and tongues of flame fizzled as they skipped and bounced off an invisible wall curving around him, landing harmlessly on the ground.

"Ronit!" Arawn ordered.

One of the other khafyri lifted a strung bow. The metallic bow shone, rippling with the multi-toned pattern of strieborna. The khafyri nocked an arrow with a shimmering barbed arrowhead and drew the bowstring in a fluid motion as he aimed at the sky. Aderes saw that the arrow shaft was also strieborna, with delicate metal fletching.

The khafyri loosed the arrow, which disappeared into the night sky. He must have missed, because another streak of fire descended toward him with a crackling roar.

Three of the khafyri surrounding the bowman lifted their own shields, and Tycen's flames once more harmlessly dissipated.

The archer nocked another arrow, carefully tracking his target across the sky. The bowstring released with a *thwang*, and a scream echoed between the canyon walls above.

Asho yelled, "No!" and Devlin began a mournful howl.

A dark shape spun through the air and tumbled downward with little control. The fireball had extinguished when the arrow met its mark, but the moonlight revealed Tycen crashing into the ground amongst the khafyri, the metallic glint of the arrow visible at the base of one of his wings.

Tycen spun in a circle, flames blazing out from his sword and engulfing two shieldless khafyri in flames. They screamed, collapsing in flaming heaps.

The archer drew another arrow from his quiver, fangs glinting in the firelight as he smiled and sighted on Tycen.

Damali and Makani spurred their horses and raced toward the khafyri. Makani swung his sword as a khafyri rode into his path. The khafyri blocked Makani's blade, but Damali lashed out with her olkar dagger and thrust it toward his heart. The short blade parted the strieborna breastplate as easily as a scythe swathed through dried grass. The khafyri fell from his horse in a dead heap. As the weight of the body pulled free from her dagger, Damali kicked her mount forward.

"Tycen!" she screamed.

A strieborna arrow whistled through the air and punched through Tycen's rib cage with a meaty *thunk*. He lifted one hand, sparks flickering between his fingertips, then fell forward, lifeless.

Damali and Makani battled with fury as they slashed and stabbed at the remaining five khafyri.

Aderes looked at Asho. "Can you help them?"

"I'm trying!" he said in a desperate voice.

The fear in his eyes, hazel saucers on a milk-white face, made Aderes feel even more helpless. A pale orange fireball sputtered in his hand and grew to the size of an apple. Asho threw it at the khafyri who warily circled Damali. The fireball bounced off the khafyri's shield and fizzled out.

Jarond shifted in front of Aderes, sword lifted as he kept himself between her and the fighting khafyri. "Addie, I have a plan. You need to do exactly what I say."

"What?" Terror clutched at her throat.

"The three of us will make a break for it along the edge while the khafyri are distracted. Stay close to me. But don't stop, no matter what. I'll deal with anyone who comes after us. Asho, do whatever you can to help."

Jarond spun his horse around.

"Now!" he yelled, digging his heels into his mount.

Aderes and Asho galloped after him.

They charged toward a small gap between the canyon wall and the three khafyri engaged with Makani. The khafyri closest to the wall swung his horse around to block their escape.

Without slowing down, Jarond aimed his horse at the horse's haunches. The horses collided and staggered to remain upright.

"Addie, go!" Jarond screamed, swinging his sword at his foe.

Aderes jammed her heels into her horse's ribs, sending him bolting forward through the small opening between Jarond and the canyon wall. Jarond swung his sword wildly, parrying the hard, fast blows of the khafyri. Devlin snarled and snapped at the legs of the khafyri's mount, making it prance and frantically kick at the attacking dog, giving Jarond an edge to hold the khafyri at bay.

As Aderes galloped past Jarond, Devlin latched on to a hamstring, and the horse stumbled and fell, bellowing in pain. Aderes glanced over her shoulder to see Asho and Jarond rushing toward her down the twisting, narrow canyon. With a last shake of his massive head, Devlin released the wounded horse and bounded after them.

The moon was still up, giving enough light to illuminate dirt and sand in pale silver and cast uneven shadows from treacherous boulders. Aderes gave her horse its head, trusting in its superior night vision to find a safe path through the darkness.

Hooves pounded behind her, but she couldn't turn to look; she didn't want to upset her horse's balance over the rough terrain. *Three sets of hoofbeats,* she guessed—Asho, Jarond—who else?

A bellow of pain and the thunderous sound of a horse crashing to the ground came out of the darkness. A scream rent the air, piercing her heart. *Jarond!*

She dragged her horse to a stop. The gelding stumbled as Asho's mount slammed into his hindquarters.

"What are you doing?" Asho yelled.

She heard Jarond's horse continuing to thrash in the darkness, whinnying its distress.

"I have to help him!" she cried.

"Addie!" Jarond's voice cracked with pain. "Don't stop! Run!"

Aderes tried to force her way past Asho, but a black shape came rushing and snarling out of the darkness in front of her. Her horse wheeled and bolted toward the canyon entrance. She clung to the panicked horse's mane, tears streaming down her face as they galloped through the darkness, leaving behind all sounds of the fight, and her brother's fall, until all she could hear was the pounding of two sets of hoofbeats as she and Asho raced through the night, not knowing their direction, only knowing that every galloped stride took them closer to freedom.

Chapter Thirty-Four
Arawn

ARAWN PARRIED A cut from the female changeling. She was quick, but her short blade was a marked disadvantage in mounted combat. He circled warily, respectful of the mortal danger the olkar dagger posed, and sent a probing jab toward her leg; he wanted to capture her, not kill her.

Movement at the corner of his eye caught his attention: the two humans and the young changeling were using the distraction of the fight to make a dash for freedom. Giolla engaged the young guard—Jarond—in an effort to stop the escape. Arawn smiled; they wouldn't get away.

A muscular dog bounded into the fight, snapping and tearing at Giolla's mount. When the horse collapsed, Jarond galloped toward the canyon mouth.

"Ronit!" Arawn bellowed, pitching his voice to be heard over the clash of steel. "Stop him!"

The *thwang* of a bowstring quickly followed his command, and an arrow buried into the haunches of Jarond's mount. Bellowing in pain and unable to use its right hind leg, the animal tumbled to the ground in a brutal crash.

Arawn returned his attention to the fight at hand. Arlen had the female changeling engaged in close combat. Her back was turned to him. *Perfect.* He struck the back of her head with the flat of his sword blade and sent her tumbling from the saddle, unconscious.

The male changeling cursed as he watched his companion fall, redoubling his efforts to fight through the three khafyri surrounding him. The khafyri closed in tighter, eyes bright with forthcoming victory. A quick slash from Navati sliced through muscles and tendons in the changeling's sword arm. His weapon fell to the ground with a clatter.

Desperation filled his eyes as he wheeled his mount, searching for a non-existent escape.

"It's over," Arawn called softly. "Surrender."

The man spat bloody phlegm. "I'll never be a prisoner to the likes of you."

Arawn saw the intent in the changeling's eyes as he drew a dagger with his uninjured left hand.

"Stop him!" Arawn ordered.

A red river flowed from the quick slash the changeling made across his own neck. The defiance faded from his eyes as the life left his body, which slid limply to the ground.

Arawn cursed, then dismounted and went to the unconscious female changeling. Her olkar dagger lay next to her, gleaming dangerously in the moonlight. Arawn picked it up, smiling. *What an unexpected prize. But what about her? What powers do we have here?* He used the blade to cut away her left sleeve, revealing her skriva marks.

There were three; the two black marks indicated a master shielder and power detector. Arawn grimaced—not very useful abilities, especially compared to the dead pyromancer. Now *that* would have been a useful ability. A pyromancer would've made a dangerous prisoner, but an immensely valuable one. His kind had always been thwarted in their attempts at capturing a pyro.

The third mark, the unmastered talent, was one that Arawn wasn't familiar with—two curved lines forming a point. Interrogation would have to serve to remedy his lack of knowledge. Arlen approached, strieborna shackles in hand. They would serve to prevent the changeling from using her abilities when she regained consciousness.

"Bind her," Arawn ordered. He took the scabbard for the olkar blade on her belt and sheathed the blade at his hip. That prize was his to determine how to use.

One more thing to check—the fate of the young guard. Navati and Zephyra had beat him to the place where Jarond's mount had fallen. A sword cut bisected the animal's throat from where one of the khafyri had ended the animal's suffering. Jarond was conscious, his right leg trapped under the fallen animal. The two khafyri were feeding on him, Navati drinking from his throat, Zephyra with one of his wrists clutched to her mouth. Jarond's eyes were glazed from the venom of the two khafyri. His heartbeat was a faint pulse in the air, growing weaker with every passing moment.

Arawn studied the boy for a moment, debating. He had a rare opportunity before him—it was a gamble to use it on the boy. Would it be a waste? Arawn admired the boy's spirit and courage, but could he get him to change his way of thinking, to understand the gift he could bestow?

The fingers on Jarond's free right hand twitched, reaching feebly for the sword hilt just beyond his grasp. Even at the brink of death, he would not stop fighting.

"Enough," Arawn ordered. "Let the boy live."

Zephyra dropped Jarond's arm deferentially, but Navati faced him, fangs extended and dripping blood. "Why should we spare the whelp? He's an earned reward for our help in your hunt."

"Are you challenging me?" Arawn asked softly, fixing the other khafyri with a hard gaze. He didn't bother extending his fangs, but let his contempt show on his face.

"Naresh will hear of this," Navati snarled.

"Naresh isn't here. I am."

Navati glared at him, then strode angrily away. Zephyra followed quickly, hunched as if trying to keep from drawing any more of Arawn's attention.

Arawn watched them leave, and then returned his gaze to Jarond, whose eyelids fluttered as he fought to focus through the haze of venom. Moving swiftly, Arawn used his own blood to heal Jarond's wounds—he couldn't do anything about the blood loss, but he could prevent it from continuing.

With a grunt of effort, he lifted the dead horse enough to drag Jarond's trapped leg free. Below the knee, the leg bent in an unnatural angle. Jarond gasped quietly in pain as Arawn moved him, then his eyes rolled back in his head as he lost consciousness. All the better. There wasn't anything Arawn could do with Jarond until the venom of the other khafyri had left his bloodstream. His plan would have to wait.

Arawn retrieved his strieborna sword and scabbard. He stripped off the leather that disguised the gemstones embedded in them and returned the sheath to his own sword belt. Another success of the evening.

He returned to the other khafyri, and was pleased to see that they had loaded their bound captive back onto her horse and tied her prone body across the saddle. The other changeling horses were unharmed. Arawn took one of them, lifted Jarond onto it, and secured his limp body to the saddle in the same fashion.

He saw that Navati and Giolla had claimed the strieborna blades of the two dead changelings. That was fine—he had already taken the most valuable weapon from the woman.

"Mount up," he ordered.

"What about the bodies?" Arlen asked.

"Leave them; they're useless to us now."

"And the two who got away?"

Arawn hesitated. Did he want the hunt to continue for the youth from Aldorn? He glanced around and realized Naresh's followers had been reduced to two, while his had gotten through the fight unscathed. He had a definite upper hand now. Navati would have to obey him. And the last thing he wanted was for the boy to fall into Naresh's control, which might happen if they continued the pursuit now, giving Naresh time to send more reinforcements after them.

"A human and an untrained apprentice," Arawn finally replied. "They aren't worth our time. Better for us to get our captives back."

"But—"

"You heard me," Arawn snarled, baring his fangs.

Navati glared sullenly.

Arawn mounted his horse, grabbed the reins of the horse with Jarond's unconscious body, and turned to the trail they had followed to enter the canyon.

"Naresh will hear of this," Navati muttered again.

I don't doubt it, Arawn thought. But no matter. It was worth bearing Naresh's wrath for this.

Chapter Thirty-Five
Asho

ASHO BENT LOW over his horse's neck, clutching its mane and trusting the animal to see well enough in the pale light of the rising sun to not trip and fall. Sweat soaked the animal's hide, but Asho dug his heels in relentlessly. He didn't dare stop.

His mentor, Tycen. His newfound uncle, Makani. Their fearless leader, Damali. Aderes's twin brother, Jarond. All lost, either dead or captured. From the way the changelings spoke of the khafyri, the former was the preferable fate. He didn't want to experience either for himself. The blind canyon was miles behind them, but not far enough away for his peace of mind.

Devlin barked. Asho glanced behind him. Aderes had stopped her horse and was rummaging in her saddlebags. He pulled his reins to circle back, noticing the laborious breathing of his horse as he halted next to her.

"We need to keep going," Asho said.

"We'll kill the horses if we keep up this pace." Aderes's face was pale. "And I need to stop."

"Why?" Asho asked.

"My leg."

Asho looked down. Aderes held a bright red cloth against her thigh. Bile rose in his throat as he realized that the crimson was her blood.

"*Paska*," he cursed. Nothing had prepared him for dealing with wounds. "Do you have any bandages?"

"No, but I have an idea," Aderes said. "Help me get down."

Asho dismounted, and his horse wandered to the lush green grasses nearby. Aderes swung her leg over her horse's back. Asho hesitated as he reached out to help her down. Where should he support her? Butt? Hips? Armpits? What if he accidentally grabbed a breast? He didn't want her to think he was intentionally fondling her.

Aderes slid down and staggered as her feet touched the ground. Asho grabbed her shoulders—safe—and helped her regain her balance.

"Thanks," she said, then put her free arm around his neck. He supported her to a fallen log nearby, then helped her sit down.

"What's your idea?" he asked.

"I need you to seal this wound so I don't keep losing blood."

"How? I can't heal like Makani." He winced at his uncle's name.

"I know. But fire can stop a wound from bleeding."

"What? Fire? You want me to—I can't. I'll hurt you," Asho protested.

"No more than I'm already injured. I can't keep losing blood like this."

"But I could kill you."

"So could this wound. Please, Asho, I need your help."

Asho stared at her in horror. What if he lost control? He could barely light a campfire, let alone cauterize a wound without letting his power spill out of control. He looked down at the cloth Aderes pressed against the wound. So much blood. How much blood could a person lose and still live?

Asho held out a shaking hand, concentrating on the intangible connection to the fire, willing a flame to appear. A flickering tongue of orange shimmered above his sweaty palm, dancing brightly in the gray light of dawn. He willed more energy into it, coaxing it to grow and get hotter. Sweat beaded on his forehead as the fire rolled in on itself, tumbling in an interwoven ball of reds and blues.

Asho took a deep breath. "Are you sure about this?"

Aderes nodded. Her face was tight with pain, but trust filled her eyes.

Can't break that trust. "Okay, take the cloth away."

Blood seeped from the wound as Aderes lifted the bloody rag. The wound was a long gash across her right thigh, reaching from her knee almost to her hip. Quivering red muscle showed in the gaping slash. Asho swallowed, fighting to keep his stomach from heaving.

Aderes pulled her torn clothes to the side, keeping them as far from the wound as possible. "Do it now," she said, a tremble in her voice.

Before his courage abandoned him, Asho brought his hand down, dragging the fireball along the length of the wound, searing the length of the gash.

Aderes shrieked as her flesh sizzled. The sound cut through Asho's heart, but he didn't stop. As he finished, the flow of blood stanched, and Aderes rolled away from him.

"Addie?" Panic filled Asho as he closed his hand around the fireball, extinguishing it, and scrambled to Aderes's side. Had he killed her?

Devlin beat him to her and was washing her face with his tongue as Asho shook her shoulder frantically. "Addie? Talk to me, Addie. Are you okay?"

Aderes groaned.

Alive. Relief washed through Asho. But not out of danger. Not yet. He didn't know how long it would take for pursuit to catch up to them, but they couldn't stay here, in the open and unprotected. But Aderes couldn't travel far. She needed to rest until her wound healed. They needed a place to hide.

Devlin whined and nudged him. Asho looked around as an idea tickled his mind. It was crazy, but it was the only thing he could think of that might work. After all, his bond with Devlin had changed the dog in ways he had only just begun to discover.

"Devlin, can you find a place for us to hide? Somewhere that we'll be safe for a while?"

Devlin wuffed quietly, licked his face, and trotted away through the underbrush.

Asho looked at Aderes's prone form. No way that he could carry her any distance. He walked to where the two horses were grazing, led Aderes's horse to her, and tied the animal to a nearby tree so it couldn't walk away.

Careful to not touch her injured leg, Asho picked Aderes up and draped her across the horse's back. He lashed her to the saddle with a length of rope, double-checking to make sure she wouldn't slip off. As he tightened the last knot, Devlin reappeared at his side.

"Did you find a place?" he asked.

Devlin barked quietly in reply.

"Take us there," Asho said.

He mounted his own horse and led Aderes's horse behind him as he followed Devlin through the trees. After a few minutes of ducking under branches and winding around bushes, they came across a brook. Instead of crossing, Devlin followed the water upstream, where it curled through a small ravine. He stopped at an overhang and sat down, looking back at Asho.

Asho dismounted and went to the overhang. It was the entrance to a snug little cave, big enough to hide them and their supplies. But hiding wouldn't help them if the khafyri followed their trail. Time to enact the rest of his plan.

He untied Aderes and, ducking at the low entrance, carried her into the cave and laid her gently on the smooth floor. After placing both of their saddlebags in the cave, he remounted his horse.

"We need to go back to where we stopped," he told Devlin.

As he followed the dog back through the woods, Asho paid close attention to their path. It shouldn't be too hard for him to find the cave again. All he had to do was walk in the right direction until he found the brook, then follow it into the ravine.

The bloody cloth on the ground caught his eye. Asho picked it up and tied it to the side of Aderes's saddle. It would brush against foliage as the horse moved through the trees, leaving behind a faint blood trail. From what Tycen had told him about khafyri abilities, their senses were honed to find and track blood trails. He hoped that it would help lure the khafyri after the horses and away from the hidden cave.

Asho tied the reins of Aderes's horse to the back of his saddle, and then knelt next to Devlin. This was the crux of his plan; without it, everything would fall apart. He had to go through with it. No matter how much it hurt him.

"Devlin, I'm sorry, but I have to do this." He used both hands to scratch Devlin's ruff, for both of their comfort. "It's the only way that I know to save Aderes. There's no other option."

Devlin whined, his warm tongue cleaning the tears from Asho's cheeks.

"You need to make a false trail for the khafyri to follow. I'll hide our tracks from here to the cave, but we need to give the khafyri something to chase. I can't leave Aderes; she'll die without someone to help her right now. So it has to be you. Lead the horses far away from here. And you can't come back, not unless you are sure you won't be followed. I'm sorry, Devlin, but I need you to do this for me."

Devlin howled, a mournful cry that echoed through the trees.

Asho hugged him tightly, and then held out the reins. "I'm sorry, Devlin. But the longer we stay here, the more likely it is that we will be caught. You need to go now."

Devlin's anguish filled his warm brown eyes, but he gently took the reins in his mouth. With a last, low whimper, Devlin trotted away, the two horses following.

Asho watched him leave, heart breaking as his loyal friend disappeared into the woods, and then made his way back to the cave, carefully wiping away hoof and foot prints behind him.

Chapter Thirty-Six
Arawn

EVEN THOUGH HE had obtained his prize, Arawn didn't allow for any slackening of the pace as they rode west, back toward the Northern Road. Their two captives remained unconscious—Jarond was still lost in the haze of blood loss and venom, while the changeling woman was kept in a spelled sleep to keep her from resisting.

A day of travel brought them back to the Northern Road. Arawn ordered Navati and Zephyra to return to Learen, while he and the other three rode south.

"Learen is closer," Navati protested. "We should take the prisoners there. Secure them quicker."

Arawn smirked. *And put them in your stronghold, where Naresh can claim them as his own.* "No, they will be going with us."

"To Port Deren?" Navati asked.

"No," Arawn lied, knowing that Navati would report to Naresh the first chance he got. "I'll take the Northern Road south, and then take them to Menai."

"Very well," Navati said. He gave the slightest hint of a bow, and then he and Zephyra turned their horses to the north and set off at a gallop.

"Sire, are you sure you want to take them south?" Arlen asked.

Such a waste it was to turn this one. He may be loyal, but hardly an ounce of intelligence. Still, he brought useful connections from the human nobles.

"I won't be going straight south," Arawn replied. "Hopefully Navati bought my lie as easily as you did. I'll return to Port Deren with you, and then take the prisoners south on the Coast Road. Once we reach Deren, we shouldn't have to worry about Naresh poaching our prizes."

ARAWN FELT SOME of his tension release when they reached the crossroads without encountering any khafyri riding up from the south. He had been concerned that his mocking message to Naresh at the start of the hunt might entice the other khafyri to ride in pursuit. And there were enough khafyri loyal to Naresh who lived in the capital for Naresh to bring a formidable force with him. It had been nearly a decade since the last changeling had been captured, and the dungeons of Serif were running low on changeling prisoners.

The sun was nearing the horizon, shining directly in their faces as they turned toward the coast. Time was essential; he needed to get to the security of Deren before Naresh or his supporters caught up to them. Naresh had the advantage of numbers and political power, but each khafyri was preeminent lord in his own domain. Arawn had sired Giolla, which meant that even though Giolla was the ruler of the port city, ultimately it was under Arawn's control.

He pushed their horses to the limits of their endurance; fresh mounts awaited them in Deren. The road was rutted from wagon tracks and muddy in places as it climbed through the Coastal Range, but the conditions were little hindrance for mounted riders. The springtime storms had finished renewing the land the previous month; otherwise, the roads would have been boggy and slow going.

None of them spoke as they rode. As night fell, the sounds of awakening nocturnal creatures—buzzing insects, hooting owls, and the eerie howling and yipping of a coyote pack—filled the forest around them. The pounding of hooves and the heavy breathing of their steeds were harsh noises against the peacefulness of the night. The moon was more than enough to light the way for the horses, and when they reached the final ridge before Deren, it reflected palely on the endless expanse of ocean stretching to the horizon before them.

The gray walls of Deren shone dully in the weak light. The city gates were closed and barred for the night; insurance against bandits or raiders.

"Open the gates!" Giolla called up to the wall-top guard.

"Gates will open at sunrise," a grumpy voice replied. "You'll have to wait until then."

"Do you know who I am?" Giolla snarled.

"I don't care who you are. The gates stay closed."

"Ronit, take care of it," Giolla said.

"With pleasure." Ronit swung from the saddle and ran to the wall. The blocks of stone had been chiseled into smooth, fitted shapes and the gaps filled with mortar, but there were still enough cracks and finger-holds for a khafyri to scale the walls. Ronit scrabbled up the side like an overgrown spider.

"What the—?" The guard's voice was quiet, but plenty loud for the ears of the khafyri below. "Tavek, forgive me. I didn't realize who you were." Fear filled his voice with tremors.

"Open the gates," Ronit said with soft menace. "Or you will answer to me."

"At once, tavek!" The guard's boots thudded down the inner stairs as he rushed to comply.

Soon the ratcheting of the crank filled the night air, and the heavy bars of the portcullis lifted. The thick wooden gate swung open, pulled by two guardsmen on each side of the two doors. Arawn and his party rode through.

"Leave the gate open," Arawn ordered.

"Yes, tavek." The guard bowed low.

Ronit, already on the other side of the wall, remounted, and they trotted through the streets toward the castle.

The castle was located on the harbor side of the city. Arawn was grateful for the night; the streets were empty of humans, allowing them to trot without hindrance down the cobblestone thoroughfare. They reached the castle's moat and in only a matter of moments, the drawbridge lowered and the gate opened. Giolla's household guard was more accustomed to identifying their inhuman rulers.

"Shall I have a chamber made ready for you, sire?" Giolla asked as they rode across the drawbridge.

"A fresh mount and a carriage for the prisoners," Arawn replied. "I wish to return to Menai as soon as possible."

"Do you want any guardsmen to accompany you?"

"No. I don't want to be slowed down."

While he waited for the carriage to be prepared, Arawn took advantage of the hospitality of Giolla's blood servants. It had been too long since he'd last fed. Once he finished, he returned to the courtyard, where Jarond and the female changeling were being loaded into the carriage, which was hitched to a team of four sleek horses built for speed. A driver already sat in the coach's seat, ready to leave.

"If Naresh shows up, stall him," Arawn told Giolla.

"Yes, sire."

Arawn smiled. "I know I can always count on you."

He briefly clasped arms with all three of his neophytes, then mounted his fresh horse and started back through the city. The creaking coach followed closely as they began their short journey south.

Back home. To see if my gamble will pay off.

Chapter Thirty-Seven
Aderes

ADERES WOKE UP aching and sore. A throbbing pain in her thigh reminded her of the slash she had received—and the way it had been healed. She was curled up on her left side on an uneven rock surface. It was smooth, but curved slightly, and had rounded pocks and bumps. Her hip was numb from the unyielding surface; she must not have moved much, if at all, while she slept.

She sat up, wincing in pain as the movement pulled on the cauterized wound. Her head spun with a brief bout of dizziness. She closed her eyes, willing it to pass.

"How are you feeling?" Asho's voice was quiet, but it echoed slightly.

After the dizziness receded, Aderes opened her eyes to see Asho sitting against a rocky wall across from her. They were in a small cave, roomy enough to accommodate both of them and their packs, which she spotted piled by the entrance, but too low-ceilinged for her to stand up without risk of head injury. Soft light at the entrance indicated either dusk or dawn—she wasn't sure which.

"Where—" Her dry throat locked on the words. She cleared her throat. "Where are we?"

"A cave."

Aderes flashed a scowl at him.

Asho offered her a water-skin. "Here. Peace offering."

She took it gratefully and drank until the last drop left the limp skin.

"I don't know where we are," Asho said. "Someplace safe, I hope. If the khafyri follow the horses' tracks, they won't find us here."

"What do you mean?"

"I had Devlin lead the horses away, to set a false trail." Sorrow filled his face at the mention of his dog, but Aderes couldn't care about that.

"The horses are gone?"

He nodded.

"Why would you do that? We need them. How am I supposed to find out what happened to Jarond without a horse? We need to go back."

"Aderes, that's suicide," Asho said. "The khafyri would capture or kill us. Besides, you are in no condition to ride, and they're miles from here by now, if they aren't looking for us. And I don't think they are. We've been here for a couple of days. You've been delirious with fever until now. You need to take it easy."

Aderes threw her blanket to the side and tried to stand. Pain lanced through her leg, and it buckled, sending her crashing to the floor. Her heart raced with even that small effort, and she realized just how weak the wound had made her.

Frustrated tears leaked down her face. "I can't just give up. Jarond's always been there for me. I need to do the same for him."

Asho scooted closer to her and reached out a hand to hesitantly rub her back. "I'm sorry. I wish I could help. But we're lucky to be alive."

"Lucky," she muttered scornfully.

"We are." His voice was firm. "And I promise you, once you're better, I will do whatever I can to help you find your brother . . ."

"If he's still alive." The words were a knife to Aderes's heart, a sharper cut than the gash on her leg, but she had to acknowledge them. She just prayed that they held no truth.

Chapter Thirty-Eight
Jarond

JAROND AWOKE TO the bouncing of a carriage. Every bump was a jolt of agony in his leg; it must've broken when his mount collapsed beneath him. Everything after that moment was a haze. Did Aderes escape? He struggled to remember.

As he regained lucidity, he realized that he wasn't alone. Damali lay on the bench seat across from him. She was unconscious, her hands bound in rune-carved shackles. Dried blood spiderwebbed across her face.

"Damali?" he whispered.

Jarond grimaced as he used his good leg and bound hands to push himself up until he was sitting. The carriage hit another bump and pain lanced through him.

The pain gradually subsided to a bearable level, and he looked out the windows. To one side rose pine-crowned mountains. Out the other window was an endless expanse of blue, which brightly reflected light from the sun, low in the sky. *The ocean,* he realized. *It's so vast.* Jarond tried the door handle, wondering if it would be possible to roll out and escape while the coach was moving. Locked. He looked around for anything to use as a weapon to defend himself, but the cabin was barren. His sword was gone, as was Damali's olkar dagger. He slumped in his seat, resigned to biding his time until an opportunity to fight or escape presented itself.

The sun sank lower toward the horizon as the carriage continued south, until finally they passed through an opening in a thick stone wall. Jarond stared out the window, trying to figure out where he was as the coach bounced down the streets of a small city. Someone must have cleared the way before them, since the crowds didn't slow their rapid progress. Before long the carriage stopped, and Jarond saw stone walls reaching skyward, far taller than those of Carwyn but still overshadowed by massive towers and a heavily fortified gatehouse, which contained a series of iron portcullises.

The door opened, and a hulking guardsman dragged Jarond out of the carriage. The muscles in his shoulders screamed in agony from their cramped position bound behind his back. He bit back a yelp at the hot piercing agony of his broken leg as he landed onto the cobblestones and was set upright. His injured leg buckled and another guardsman, nearly identical in size to the brute who had pulled him from the cramped box, caught his arm in a ham-sized fist and kept him from collapsing.

After untold hours of confinement in the stuffy carriage, the crisp salty breeze that hit Jarond's face was a welcome relief. He looked around, hoping to spot an avenue of escape, even with his broken leg, but his two captors dragged him across a small drawbridge to an iron-bound postern door. One of the guards pounded on it with a meaty fist, and it swung open to reveal a dark stone passage lit by a single torch burning against a soot-blackened wall. A man stood in the opening. By his clothes, he was clearly not a guard. Instead of the boiled leather and chain mail, he wore a wool tunic, basic but well-made, with a badge of a swooping eagle embroidered on the left breast.

"What d'ye want?" he demanded.

"Pris'ner," the guard on Jarond's right grunted.

"So what're ye botherin' me fer? Take the bugger down t' the dungeon."

"Orders," came the terse reply. "Tavek wants 'im in the eagle tow'r."

The man squinted at Jarond, taking in his dirty clothes and bedraggled state. "This little wretch? Well, come on then, bring him in."

He led the way down the short passageway, footsteps echoing in the narrow stone confines. The two guards followed, half-dragging and half-carrying Jarond as he did his best to keep weight off his injured leg. Still, he was mostly delirious with pain, unable to keep track of the turns of the passage and the doors they went through until they finally reached a large circular chamber hung with richly embroidered tapestries. The last rays of sunlight streamed into the room from a pair of large windows.

Jarond gaped, as fear jolted through him, at Tav Arawn seated behind a large, elaborately carved mahogany desk. He was writing, seemingly oblivious to having visitors. The steward and the guards waited to be noticed. With a final flourish, Arawn set his quill down and looked up. The steward made a low bow, which the guards clumsily imitated, forcing Jarond to his knees as they did so. Jarond gasped as his knees hit the soft rug underfoot and his broken leg twisted.

"Enough of that," Tav Arawn snapped in his smooth, crisp voice. "Leave us."

The guards released Jarond, bowed again, and left the room; even their large, lumbering bodies couldn't disguise how they scurried away like mice from a cat.

Jarond struggled to his feet, hampered by both his bound wrists and broken leg, but resolutely forced himself to stand despite the oppressive pain.

Arawn watched expressionlessly. "I admire your courage."

Jarond stared at him, surprised.

Arawn laughed softly. "Does that really come as a shock to you? I suppose you haven't had the years of experience I've had. The world is still black and white to you. Good and evil, that sort of thing. In your eyes, I wronged your sister and you defended her; to you, I am the evil one. And I suppose I haven't done much to disabuse you of that notion. After all, I generally don't take it lightly when someone attempts to kill me. Luckily for me, I am a bit more durable than you had surmised. I have to applaud you for your effort, however. It has been decades since a mortal has been quick enough to land a blow on me, let alone deal such a decisive blow as you did. Unfortunately for you, and to my great benefit, you were not in possession of this at the time."

He gestured to his desk. Damali's opalescent white blade glimmered softly in the light. Arawn picked it up; the light of the blade seemed to pulse as he delicately turned it in his fingers. "A great weapon, one whose powers I fear you haven't the least inkling of. I haven't heard of one in Sermund for many years. Its presence here is disturbing. Still, it has provided me with a great opportunity."

He placed the blade back on his desk, stood, and walked to directly in front of Jarond. A feral, predatory gleam filled his emerald eyes, and Jarond took a limping step back.

"Do not be afraid," Arawn said, his words curiously twisted.

Jarond sucked in a ragged breath at the sharp ivory gleam of Arawn's fangs. Ignoring his broken leg, he turned and took a half step before slim, strong hands grasped him on his arm and firmly behind his neck. Jarond felt a sharp pain as Arawn's mouth clenched his throat. With every wild beat of his heart, he could feel his life's blood leaving him, drained by the strong pull of Arawn's cold mouth. He thrashed and twisted, but Arawn's iron grip kept his mouth pressed to Jarond's neck. His vision blurred, darkening at the edges, and his head spun.

So, this is how it ends, he thought, his dizzy mind alarmingly unconcerned by the idea.

Arawn suddenly pulled away from his neck and released him. Jarond staggered and fell to the floor, a low groan of pain escaping him. From the corner of his eye, he saw a red stain seeping into the rug beneath him. He tried to stand up, but he couldn't even manage to roll into a seated position. He fought to keep focused as the khafyri's venom clouded his mind. Arawn returned to his desk, dabbing gently at his mouth with a silk kerchief.

Arawn, his face cleaned of any bloody evidence, picked up the dagger and faced Jarond. He approached Jarond, the feral gleam returning to his eyes as he stared at the blood trickling down Jarond's neck. The hungry look of a predator faded as he raised his eyes to capture Jarond's.

"I know you don't understand this now," he said, surprisingly gentle, as Jarond pushed himself across the floor, away from Arawn. "But one day, you'll understand the great gift that I am giving you, and you'll thank me for it."

Arawn lifted the dagger and drew it across his forearm. His pale skin parted smoothly, and blood welled up and spilled across the white blade. He held the dagger under the dripping ruby fountain, turning it until the blade pulsed red. The wound on his arm sealed shut, and Arawn approached Jarond.

"Brace yourself," he said. "This is going to hurt." Striking like a viper, he drove the dagger into Jarond's heart.

Jarond screamed as fiery pain exploded in his chest, lancing into the core of his being, ripping and tearing the fiber of his soul. A roaring tide of red and black clawed through his mind in an unending torment and agony. The black seeped into the red, fading the pain and Jarond's mind to nothingness.

Chapter Thirty-Nine
Asho

ASHO LEFT ADERES sleeping in the cave. He worried about her; she was still so weak from her injury. What if he had done more damage to her by cauterizing it? If only he had the power of healing like Makani.

Fresh sorrow washed over him. Asho had thought he was alone in the world for so long, and had been excited to learn that he had an uncle, only for Makani to be lost to him after such a short time together. He didn't know what to hope for: that Makani was alive and a captive, or dead and beyond the reach of any khafyri. From what he had learned from Makani, he knew that he would choose death over capture, but Asho couldn't wrap his head around that idea. Death was so crushingly final.

Asho sat on a boulder next to the stream that ran past their cave refuge. They were running low on supplies. There were probably fish living in the stream, but he had no idea how to catch one. He'd never had to forage for food before—at least not in the wilderness. Scrounging through leftovers and rubbish heaps was another matter. Maybe Aderes would have an idea for how they could get more food. But she was sleeping now, peaceful for once, and Asho didn't want to wake her and bring her back to the nightmare of real life.

Movement in the corner of his eye caught his attention. A lanky hare hopped down to the water's edge a short distance away. Asho froze. Food, if he could catch it. He remembered how Tycen had sent bolts of fire at his enemies. That would kill a rabbit.

Slowly, trying not to startle the hare, Asho lifted his hand and concentrated on the burning core within himself, focusing all his attention on his palm. A fireball materialized. The flames twisted, trying to escape his control, but Asho willed them to form a tight sphere. When he felt the fireball was ready, he looked at the rabbit. *Only one chance.*

He threw out his hand, using both the physical gesture and his mental effort to send the fireball streaking toward the hare. The animal bolted, but the fiery projectile smashed into it and exploded. A shower of sparks fell into the nearby brush, including a dried-out log, which quickly caught fire.

"*Paska,*" Asho cursed as the flames grew. What if he burned down the forest? Reacting to his fear, the blaze roared higher. Alarm spiked—he needed to get the fire under control before it grew any bigger.

Remembering Tycen's words about his emotions affecting his abilities, Asho closed his eyes and took a deep breath. *Calm,* he told himself. *Relax. Everything will be all right. You can do this.*

He opened his eyes; the flames had diminished, but the log was still dancing with flickering red and orange. Asho held out his hand, palm down, and willed the fire to subside. "Stop it," he said, speaking to the fire as if it were a living thing. "That's enough. Time for you to go away."

Sweat broke out across his body as he concentrated, and bit by bit, the fire died down to wisps of smoke. When the last spark extinguished itself, Asho let out a sigh of relief, a wobbly grin stretching across his face. He'd done it. He walked to where the carcass of the hare lay. The fur had been singed off, and it smelled as if the meat had started to cook. But it was food. They wouldn't go hungry. Not tonight at least.

Chapter Forty
Jarond

JAROND WOKE WITH a shudder. A mixture of clarity and confusion filled him. He knew where he was; the great wooden beams supporting the ceiling above him were unfamiliar, and yet he knew they were the supports for a tower floor in the great castle of the khafyri. But he also knew he should be dead. The blade shoved through his heart should have ensured it. And yet he wasn't. What was more, the pain in his broken leg was gone. Or, rather, it had migrated. A dry, burning sensation smoldered in his throat, the heat of crossing a thousand deserts with not a drop of water.

"Good, you're awake," Arawn said in a silky voice from across the room.

Jarond sat up with a start, noticing his hands were no longer bound.

"I've brought you a present." Arawn gestured toward the woman next to him, a middle-aged servant with a hollow, vacant look in her eyes.

"What did you do to me?" Jarond demanded.

"I've shared with you the life that flows through my veins," Arawn replied. "I've sired you."

"What do you mean?"

"All will become clear in time, I promise," Arawn said. "But for now, there are more urgent matters to attend to. The process is not yet complete. You must feed. If you come here, I'll show you how."

"No."

Arawn sighed, his face a mix of annoyance and amusement. "I suppose you must make this difficult. *Come here.*"

Jarond, his mind reeling, stood up and crossed the room to Arawn. He'd had every intention of staying where he was. Why then was he obeying? He ordered his legs to halt, but they refused to listen until he was in front of Arawn.

"Good," Arawn said. "Now, which would you prefer: neck or wrist?"

"I . . . what?" Jarond stammered, still stunned by his unintended obedience.

"There are, of course, other easily accessible blood-ways within a human body," Arawn continued. "But those are . . . shall we say, more private. If you wish to explore them, you'll have to do it without me. I would recommend waiting until you've mastered control with the basics, unless you don't mind leaving behind a few corpses. But from what I've observed of you, I doubt that will be to your taste. However, I have been wrong before. Sometimes the most reserved in their first lives discover that many former inhibitions disappear, and they end up being the ones who revel the most in their newfound powers. Only time, and you, can tell for sure. Now: neck or wrist?"

As Arawn spoke, dread built up in Jarond's gut, then coursed through him. He wanted to flee, to fight, but his feet stayed planted in front of Arawn. What was happening to him? A wave of nausea passed through him. "What did you do to me?" he whispered in horror.

"You *know*," Arawn said with quiet conviction. "You just don't want to believe it's possible. Now, I'm running out of patience. *Choose*. I order it."

Jarond stared at the woman next to Arawn, truly seeing her for the first time. Round scars covered her neck and wrists, set in evenly spaced pairs. She had a dreamy smile on her face, a vacant look in her eyes that told Jarond that she wasn't all the way there. His mouth opened, and he knew that a single word was about to issue forth. The only choice left to him was that word.

"Wrist," he whispered.

Arawn smiled. Jarond broke his gaze from the woman and saw Arawn's canines sharpen and lengthen as the smile turned into a silent snarl. Arawn lifted the woman's arm to his mouth and bit down, his fangs driving two narrow puncture wounds into the vein pulsing at her wrist. He held the woman's arm out to Jarond in a silent invitation. Blood welled up from the twin wounds, washing over her arm and merging on the underside to begin a steady drip-drip-drip to the floor.

Jarond stared at the welling blood, a confusing lust and desire filling his own veins. The pulse of the woman's heartbeat was mesmerizing, driving the blood from her pale wrist in steady spurts. He took half a step forward, need and desire consuming him. His hand was lifting toward the woman when his senses snapped back to him. What was he doing?

"No!" he vowed, hoarsely, weakly, and staggered a step backward. "No, I won't."

A sound of displeasure came from Arawn's throat. "One of the reasons I chose you was because of your strong spirit, but this is pointless. It will go so much easier if you don't fight it."

"You can't make me," Jarond said.

Arawn laughed. "Can't I? Have you learned nothing yet? Very well, my young neophyte, I command you: *Drink*."

The woman's wrist was at Jarond's mouth before he thought to protest. Warm, coppery liquid filled his mouth, and he swallowed. The sweet saltiness of it soothed his burning throat, quenching the thirst within him. He sucked at the wounds, greedy for more, the excess spilling out from the corners of his mouth and down his chin. The woman closed her eyes and moaned, an expression of rapture on her face.

He continued to drink, satisfaction filling him.

"Enough, or you'll kill her," Arawn said.

Jarond ignored him, too caught up in the experience to heed.

"I said *stop*."

He pulled away and felt a queer pain in his mouth, a pulling, tearing sensation that at once hurt and was rapturous. He ran his tongue over his teeth, searching for the source of the pain, and discovered long, sharp fangs in place of his dull canines.

The discovery brought him back to the horror of his reality. "No!" he cried out, dropping the woman's arm and staggering back several paces. "What have I done?"

"You've done quite well," came Arawn's calm reply. "Now, *pay attention*."

Jarond watched as Arawn lifted his hand to his mouth and pierced the tip of a finger with one fang. As thick red blood slowly welled up, he dabbed it on the two punctures on the woman's wrist. The weak trickle of blood from her ceased, and the two holes shrank to nothing, leaving behind another faint set of scars. "Unless you want your prey to bleed out or die from infection, it is best to tend to their wounds once you are finished feeding. Your venom will slow the blood flow once you are done, but only your blood will heal the wound, just as my blood healed your broken leg and all your other injuries. The blood donors at this castle are paid for their services, and I expect you to treat them well. *Do you understand?*"

Jarond jerked his head in an affirmative.

"Leave us now," Arawn told the woman, and she walked unsteadily out the door.

After she left, Arawn studied Jarond, an odd sort of pride and satisfaction on his face. "Congratulations. You are officially a neophyte, a former human who's been made khafyri. Now, I understand that you may want to cling onto what you remember of your humanity, but that is behind you now. There's no use in trying to go back. As your sire, it is my honor to teach you the aspects of your new life. There are a great many perks, to be certain, but there are also responsibilities and standards of behavior that I expect you to uphold. Your actions will reflect on me, and I hold my neophytes to a high standard."

Heavy knocking on the door interrupted him.

"Enter," Arawn called, and a burly guard clinking in mail opened the door and bowed. "Tav Arawn, forgive me, but a contingent of khafyri just arrived from the capital. Tav Naresh is with them."

Arawn cursed under his breath. "Of all the wretched timing . . ." He glanced back at Jarond. "I'm afraid your education shall have to be deferred to another teacher for the moment. Reka!"

Jarond heard swift, light footsteps cross the floor above and descend the tower stairs.

A young woman entered the room; Jarond guessed she was his age, maybe a year or two his elder. She wore a silk gown of beautiful emerald, which matched the stunning eyes set in her lovely, pale face.

"Yes, Father?" she said.

With an uncomfortable jolt of surprise, Jarond realized her eyes were the same green as Arawn's. Her father's. He swallowed convulsively. Could his life get any more surreal? Surely, he would wake up at any moment and discover this had all been a hellish nightmare.

"Reka, I must take care of business with Naresh. Will you please show Jarond around? And have the steward prepare rooms for him and provide him with fresh clothing." He glanced down at Jarond, as if noticing his state for the first time. "Actually, perhaps you should start with that last part." He smiled.

"Of course, Father," Reka replied.

"Jarond, do *not* give my daughter any trouble while I'm gone," Arawn ordered. "*Do you understand?*"

"Yes," Jarond muttered.

Arawn gave him one last searching look before turning and sweeping out the door, the guard following.

For a moment, they stared at one another.

"So, you are the human who tried to kill my father," Reka said.

Jarond felt his cheeks warm with unexpected embarrassment. "He started it."

Reka let out a peal of laughter. "I don't doubt that he did. Father is used to getting his way. It appears to me that he also is the one who finished it. That, too, is usually the case with him. He almost always gets his way when someone tries to cross him."

"Almost?" Jarond asked, hoping to gain some insight from her on how to break free from Arawn's grip.

Reka studied him. "Perhaps I'll tell you another time. For now, you need to get cleaned up. Follow me." She swept out the door, and Jarond followed, the order from Arawn making his feet move without a second thought.

Chapter Forty-One
Aderes

"YOU'RE NOT STRONG enough yet," Asho said. "We need to wait until your leg is healed."

Aderes scowled at him, frustration boiling through her. She knew he was right, but she could no longer stand lying hidden in the cave when she didn't know Jarond's fate. The unknowing was the worst part, worse even than the helplessness she felt with her injury.

"Then you go back," Aderes said. "Find the site of the battle and see if you can figure out what happened and where they went. I'll stay here and let my leg heal."

"Even if I could find that place again—and after our long escape in the dark, I know I couldn't—I can't leave you here alone. How would you get food? Our supplies have almost run out."

"I can fish in the creek."

"You fished all morning, and you didn't catch anything."

"But—" She sucked in her breath at the clatter of horseshoes on rocks. Had they been found?

"Stay behind me," Asho whispered. He crouched at the cave entrance and peered into the bright sunlight.

Aderes drew her belt knife with trembling fingers. The faint scars on her neck seemed to pulse. What she wouldn't give for a proper weapon. She had never missed Jarond more terribly.

A fireball took shape in Asho's hand. He might be able to stop any attackers. As long as they didn't have fire shields. Even Tycen hadn't been able to break through those.

The hoofbeats drew closer, echoing through the narrow canyon. She counted two sets. Had the khafyri split into different groups to track them down? Her pulse pounded in her ears. Could the khafyri hear it?

The sound of hooves stopped just before the horses reached the entrance to the cave. She clutched her knife tighter in her sweaty hand.

A massive dog, black with russet markings, came into view. Aderes tensed and then blinked in surprise.

"Devlin!" Asho cried.

Devlin bounded to him, wagging his tail and enthusiastically washing Asho's hands.

"You came back!"

Aderes struggled to her feet and limped to the mouth of the cave. Standing patiently outside were their two horses, sweaty and with scratched saddles from their trek through the forest, but healthy and sound. She smiled. They had mounts again. It didn't matter that she couldn't walk. She could ride. She could find Jarond.

Chapter Forty-Two
Arawn

ARAWN STRODE THROUGH the carved wooden doorway of the Eagle Tower, across the open space between the great hall and kitchens. Naresh and his contingent were dismounting by the twin-towered gatehouse. Black fury twisted Naresh's face into a scowl. The sight almost made Arawn smile, but he held it back. No need to fan Naresh's wrath until after Arawn had solidified the entitlement to his captive.

"You have no right to keep all the spoils of the hunt to yourself, Arawn," Naresh began without greeting. "My neophytes helped in your hunt. Kalei and Gerik even gave their lives to capture that changeling. You can't expect their help and then cut me out."

"I didn't," Arawn said, keeping his voice quiet and unruffled despite Naresh's rage. "They took the strieborna swords from the two changelings who were killed. An even split, I'd say."

"Navati said you took an olkar blade as well."

"Yes."

"I want it. Keep your damn captive. Give me the blade, and I'll go."

"It's too late. I already used it."

"*What?*" Naresh snarled, muscles coiling.

He stared calmly at Naresh, raising an eyebrow. They had discovered long ago who would win in a straight fight.

With visible effort, Naresh relaxed a bit, retracting his fangs. "Who did you use it on? I'll have to inform his father of his promotion when I return to the capital."

"The boy we captured. Jarond."

Naresh stared at him in disbelief. "*Seriously?* When you have a dozen noble knights that you could use to strengthen our political ties? You wasted it on a *captive?*"

Arawn shrugged. "I think he'll be useful."

Naresh laughed derisively. "So, you didn't learn from what happened last time you decided to bestow immortality on an unwilling human. Do you really think it will be any different this time?"

Anger flashed through Arawn, but he forced himself to stay polite. "We'll see how it goes."

Naresh emitted another scornful laugh. "Just remember, if it goes the same disastrous way as last time, my dungeons still have space. Always willing to take another prisoner from you."

"Is there anything else I can help you with?" Arawn asked with forced courtesy.

"No, I need to be returning to Serif. More important things to do there than in this backwater castle. Have fun with your neophyte. If he stabs you in the back, I'll take care of the mess. Again."

Naresh remounted his horse and trotted to the entrance. The double portcullises were already raised, and he and his party galloped across the lowered drawbridge.

Arawn watched Naresh leave. *Out of my way and no longer a problem. For now, at least.*

Chapter Forty-Three
Jarond

AFTER BATHING AND dressing in the clean clothes that were brought to him, Jarond followed Reka on a tour of Menai. His new home. He winced. *How can I get away from here? How do I escape, when Arawn can order me around so easily?* He even found himself automatically obeying Reka, since Arawn had ordered him to not cause her any problems.

The castle was massive, built to withstand siege or forays from sea raiders wishing to attack the coast or plunder the length of the Telnor River. Its colossal walls formed an uneven oval shape, divided by a central gate to form upper and lower wards, and were punctuated by seven towers spaced around the perimeter. The greatest tower, which overlooked the upper ward and had three spires at top instead of one, was the Eagle Tower, the residence of Arawn and his daughter. The Eagle Tower was set on the western end of the castle, closest to the ocean. The panoramic view of the great blue expanse would have taken Jarond's breath away, were he not so focused on studying the castle layout, hoping that somehow he would see something that would help him out of his predicament.

South of the Eagle Tower was the Spear Tower. Reka led him up a steep, sharply twisting stairway to the top floor. The octagonal chamber they entered filled the center of the tower. A narrow walkway, connecting the wall tops on either side of the tower, curved between the chamber and the outer wall, with a thin inner wall maintaining the room's privacy.

"The Spear Tower, like most of the upper ward, is human-free except for servants going about their duties," Reka said. "When khafyri visit, they stay on the first or second floor. You can have this room. My father's neophytes live here. For the most part, you'll have the tower to yourself. We don't have any khafyri visitors right now."

"Arawn has other neophytes?" Jarond asked. "What if they come back?"

"They all have dominions of their own now," Reka said. "When they visit, they stay in the guest chambers. It's been decades since someone lived in this room."

Jarond looked around the chamber. A hearth, empty and clean, filled one of the eight walls. The sparse furnishings were made from elegantly carved mahogany: a four-poster bed with maroon hangings, a tall wardrobe, and a desk with a matching chair.

"I'll have the tailor make you some garments suitable to your station," Reka said.

"And what is my station?" Jarond asked in a sour voice. "Prisoner? Lackey?"

Reka laughed—not mockingly, but with surprised amusement. "As an honored neophyte."

"*Honored?*" Jarond spat out.

Reka stopped laughing and looked at him with compassion in her emerald eyes. "Yes, honored," she said quietly. "I'm sorry that you don't feel that way now. My father can be quite offhand in his dealings with humans, and I know the change is a lot to take in at once—especially the bond of obedience—but in time, you'll see that he has given you a great gift."

"He can keep his gift. I don't want it."

"It's too late. The change is irreversible."

To his shame, Jarond felt tears well up. He turned away from her, but there was nowhere to go. He was trapped. Forever.

"The nobles in our service yearn for this opportunity," Reka said.

"Good for them. Arawn should have turned one of them instead," Jarond snapped.

Her hand touched his shoulder, and he flinched.

"I know that you were afraid of Father when he was pursuing you," she said. "But you're his neophyte now. You don't have to fear him anymore. Believe it or not, his other neophytes consider him to be a great sire."

"Are you required to say that of him?" Jarond asked. "Does he order you to think that way?"

"Arawn is my father, not my sire. I was born khafyri, not human. There is no sire bond between us the way there is with you and him. I don't always agree with him, but I do think he is a good sire. And a good father."

"How can you say that when he can force me to do whatever he wants?"

"Father rarely uses the sire bond to force obedience. It's different with you—after all, you tried to kill him and, I suspect, still want to kill him."

"Will kill him," Jarond muttered.

She sighed. "I'm sorry that Father turned you without your consent. I truly am. He shouldn't have done that."

Startled, Jarond looked at her. Honesty filled her face. "Really?"

"Yes. But it's done now, and there's nothing you can do about it. But think about this—Father could order you to be loyal to him. He could use the sire bond to change the essence of who you are. But he hasn't. And he won't.

Because there's something about you that he admires, which is why he chose to turn you, even though it will mean political backlash for him. I know Father uses his sire bond as little as possible—I've seen how he interacts with his other neophytes. Maybe if you stop thinking about how to murder him, he won't use it as much with you."

Jarond contemplated her words—could she be telling him the truth? He struggled to wrap his mind around the dizzying changes and information. His mind conjured images of Aderes, limp in Arawn's grip as he drank her blood. Tycen, so jovial and full of life, tumbling down from the sky to die at the hands of the khafyri below. Damali, so strong and kind-hearted, unconscious and bound in the carriage. He shook his head.

"No, I don't see it that way," he finally responded.

Reka sighed. "Well, give it some time. But until then, I'll show you around the rest of Menai."

Instead of returning down the stairs, they exited from the narrow passageway onto the top of the southern wall. Directly below them was the broad roof of the great hall. Across the way, Reka pointed out the Well Tower, which she said contained a cistern and granary, and the kitchens, nestled against the wall between the Well Tower and the Great Gatehouse.

They continued on the wall top until they reached the Red Tower, which stood across from the Great Gatehouse. The wall that divided Menai into two wards butted up against the Red Tower. Reka opened a door set into the wall of the tower, revealing a narrow passageway around the outer edge of the tower, similar to the walkway in the Spear Tower. When they exited the other side, the lower ward was visible below them.

"This is where the human servants and soldiers live and work," Reka said. "It's easier for everyone to have separate areas for them and us."

Three more towers were in the lower ward: the Granary Tower, with a secondary well, the Lord's Tower, for visiting human nobility, and the Chamberlain Tower, where the upper-class servants lived. The Lesser Gate tower opened to the east, and between the walls were barracks, stables, and the blacksmith's forge. A few soldiers sparred in the practice yard, and, with a jolt of surprise, Jarond recognized the monochromatic brown look of Sir Kayden among them.

They circled the lower ward atop the walls, and Jarond discovered things he hadn't noticed at first. A cistern for collecting rainwater dropped through the walls adjacent to the Chamberlain Tower. Between the Lesser Gate and the Lord's Tower was a spindly watch tower, a twisting staircase winding up to a tiny platform that was higher than even the Eagle Tower's three large spires.

On the other side of the castle, the Great Gatehouse formed the end of the lower ward. They crossed the span connecting the twin towers of the gateway. Jarond stopped to peer through the murder holes that punctured the floor. Any invaders attempting to break through the Great Gate would face a deadly rain from of rocks and scalding water from above as they battered their way through the two portcullises below.

Reka led him down the staircase in the far side of the gatehouse. They emerged at ground level in the upper ward, next to the kitchens. Jarond jerked to a stop when he saw Arawn striding toward the Eagle Tower.

"Father!" Reka called.

Arawn turned and altered his course to come to his daughter. "Is everything all right? Is Jarond behaving himself?"

Jarond tried to shrink into the stone wall behind him.

"Yes, Father," Reka said, then turned to smile at Jarond. "Come here and join us."

Jarond hesitated. He didn't feel forced to obey her, and he didn't want to get closer to Arawn. But Arawn could demand his obedience, and Reka had been kind to him. Despite everything. Reluctantly, he went to stand near Reka.

Arawn studied him for a minute, taking in his new, fine clothes. "Lord Taregan is visiting Menai. I have commanded the cooks to prepare a feast tonight. As my neophyte, you'll be seated at the high table."

Dread filled Jarond. He couldn't bear the thought of facing humans, of being seen as the monster he feared. There must be some way to return to his simple life as a guard. As a human. But somehow, if others saw him, perceived him as a khafyri, it would make it more real. More permanent.

"I don't want to go," he said.

Annoyance crossed Arawn's face. "Neither do I, but there are expectations you must fulfill, now that you are one of us. You need to learn your new place. Now, do I need to make this an official order?"

Jarond gritted his teeth. He couldn't decide which was worse: willingly going to the feast or being forced to do so.

Arawn sighed. "I don't have time for this. *Come to the feast tonight.*" Order delivered, he turned and walked away.

Jarond watched him go, anger, regret, and rebellion warring within him.

"He doesn't like it any more than you do," Reka said.

"But he has a choice. I don't."

"If you—"

"Leave me alone," Jarond said. "You don't know what it's like."

"I know more than you think," Reka snapped.

Jarond was surprised to hear anger in her voice. She stalked away toward the Eagle Tower.

Jarond almost called out to her, to find out what she meant. But he stopped himself. He had to find a way to get himself out of this trap, not get pulled further into the world of the khafyri.

Jarond returned to his room in the Spear Tower and threw himself on his bed. He stared at the ceiling, fruitlessly trying to figure out how to escape from Arawn's control. He had no idea what the future held for him. Except for attending the feast that night. He was bound to attend that.

Chapter Forty-Four
Aderes

ADERES'S LEG THROBBED with every step her horse took, but she refused to say anything about the pain. It would just give Asho one more argument for returning to the cave and staying hidden longer, instead of searching for her brother. It had already been hard enough to convince Asho to retrace their path to the scene of the battle.

They wouldn't have been able to make the journey at all if it weren't for Devlin. The loyal dog, returned after hopefully leaving a meandering, untraceable trail for any pursuers to follow, was using his keen nose to lead them back the way they'd fled on that awful night. Aderes knew she couldn't have found the site without him to guide them; never mind that her injured leg wouldn't have supported her for even a fraction of the distance.

Now the terrain was familiar once again: the dreadful box canyon, where they had been cornered by the khafyri. Her heart raced as they rode nearer. What would they find?

Aderes gagged on an awful stench and pulled her shirt up to cover her mouth. The unpleasant smell of sweat and dirt was a welcome shield against the foul odor that permeated the air. *What if Jarond is among the dead?* Her stomach heaved from the smell and the thought.

"Stay here," Asho said, voice muffled by his own shirt. "I'll go look."

"But—"

"Addie, if Jarond is dead, you don't want to see him like that. I don't want that to be the last memory you have of your brother. I'll go check. I'll tell you what I find."

Grateful to not have to face what lay ahead—even though it was her idea to come—Aderes nodded.

"Ride back down the canyon, so you don't have to keep smelling this," Asho said. "I'll be back soon."

"Thanks."

Several long, heart-wrenching moments passed before Asho returned, tears streaming down his face. Behind him, a plume of smoke reached for the sky.

Aderes saw the look on his face, and her heart broke. "No. No, Jarond wasn't there."

Asho shook his head. "No, he wasn't there. Neither was Damali. But Tycen and Makani are both dead." His voice broke.

"Oh gods," Aderes said. She had been so focused on finding her brother that she hadn't been thinking about what the deaths of the changelings would mean to Asho. "I'm so sorry, Asho. I'm sorry you had to see them."

"I burned the bodies," he said. "Had to be done."

"Is there anything I can do for you?"

"No. Let's just go."

They rode away, smoke rising in a twisting black plume behind them.

Chapter Forty-Five
Jarond

FROM THE SECOND tiered galley at the side of the great hall, Jarond watched the guests enter, laughing and talking, filling the long room with noise. He stood in the shadows, out of sight even if one of the noble lords or ladies glanced toward his overlook. Arawn had commanded his attendance; here he was, closer than he wished to be. Arawn had never officially ordered him to enter the hall.

At the high table, Arawn sat in the high seat, Lord Taregan in the place of honor at his right hand. From talking to the servant who brought him new sets of clothes, Jarond knew the feast was all part of Arawn's plan to get Lord Taregan to peacefully agree to an alliance with Arawn without realizing how much the proposed relationship favored the khafyri. Something about mines or minerals; Jarond didn't really care.

Lord Taregan and his lady were dressed in fine clothes, finer than anything Lord Kuval had worn back home at Castle Carwyn. Jarond quickly learned, while observing the humans in the great hall, how small and poor Carwyn was compared to the other noble fiefs in the land.

At that moment, Arawn looked up toward the galleries. A subtle smirk crossed his face when his eyes met Jarond's. There was no hiding in the shadows from that emerald gaze. Jarond met his stare defiantly, causing the smirk to widen. Arawn lifted his right hand and crooked a finger. Before Jarond could even think, his feet were moving along the gallery toward the stair down to the great hall.

He entered with the stragglers, a few lesser lords and the officers of the castle, all of whom took their seats below the salt. Jarond alone walked up the aisle between the long trestle tables to the high table, studiously ignoring the people raucously eating and drinking around him. A few stopped their activities to stare at him, wanting to see Arawn's latest neophyte for themselves. He halted a few paces before Arawn, within speaking distance but as far as he felt he was able to stretch his limits.

"Jarond," Arawn said amiably, as if he were an honored guest and not under compelled orders to be present. "How wonderful of you to join us. May

I present Lord Taregan and Lady Tarhe of Pentir? My lord, my lady, this is Jarond, my new neophyte."

Jarond stared sullenly at the lord and lady. It would take a direct order from Arawn for him to make an obeisance to them. To his surprise, both rose, and the lord made a shallow bow and the lady curtsied, her ample bosom straining against the low-cut bodice of her dress.

"Tav Jarond, it is an honor to meet you," the lord said graciously.

The lady peered at him beneath long lashes. "Such an honor to meet one such as you."

Jarond stared at them speechless.

Arawn laughed. "It seems my young neophyte is tongue-tied amongst such auspicious company. I shall have to teach him manners later on. May I interest you in a glass of wine? I have just received the finest Haseri red." He snapped his fingers, and a servant leapt forward to pour.

As soon as his noble guests were distracted, Arawn returned his gaze to Jarond. "Please, have a seat next to Reka." His daughter was seated at his left hand, an empty chair between her and the next diner.

Jarond hesitated; it hadn't been a direct order, so he didn't feel the overwhelming need to obey. Yet.

Reka smiled at him. "Come on, Jarond; I'm dreadfully bored up here. Father will be talking with Lord Taregan all evening; it would be unchivalrous to leave me to dine alone." Her brilliant white smile, set in a delicate round face, her green eyes inviting and warm, where her father's were unyielding hard emeralds, had him reacting in nearly the same fashion as an order from his sire. His legs carried him up the dais, and he sat in the carved wooden chair at her side.

She smiled again at him as the servants served the first course, a creamy mushroom soup. He flushed and looked down at his bowl, trying to focus on tearing up pieces of a soft roll, and not the way her smooth silk gown hugged the curve of her hips and bared the tops of her small breasts.

"I know that it is a lot for you to take in, but I'm glad you're here," Reka said. "Father hasn't turned anyone since I was a child, and there is not anyone near my age in all of Menai. It gets lonely sometimes; my kin treat me like I'm still a child, and the humans get skittish any time I try to talk to them. And the ones who aren't skittish are even worse; they always want something from my father, and are hoping they can get it through me."

"Not like I had much choice," Jarond muttered, pushing his soup around with a spoon. The scent of mushrooms and onions caused his stomach to twist and knot uncomfortably, but not in a way that made him want to take a bite.

Reka sighed. "It will get easier, you know."

"I don't want it to be easy," he spat. "I want it to go away."

"Here," Reka picked up the wine pitcher between her and Arawn and filled Jarond's goblet with the thick red liquid. "Drink. You'll feel better." She thrust the goblet toward him.

That close, the scent was nearly overpowering. Undiluted, unprotected, the liquid filled his nostrils with a coppery scent and filled his mind with desire. Saliva flooded his mouth, and he felt his other teeth lengthen reflexively.

"No," he said angrily, careful to keep his lips nearly closed. He thrust her hand—and the goblet—away.

She placed the brimming cup on the table in front of him. "It's humanely sourced. No deaths, no mess, willing donors. What more could you ask for?"

He gritted his teeth and shook his head, staring at the grain of the wooden table.

"It won't work, you know."

Puzzled, he looked at her before he could stop himself.

Sympathy filled her eyes. "You can't starve yourself to death. Fasting won't kill you. But it will weaken you. Physically and mentally. Eventually, you won't be able to resist. And when that time comes, you'll be so weak that you won't have the strength to stop yourself. You'll keep going until nothing is left. Nothing except a corpse and your guilt. So tell me, Jarond, what is so awful about having a drink?"

His jaw clenched. "You're wrong. I won't be like that. I won't do it."

"Do you think you're the first neophyte to believe that?"

"The others wanted it," Jarond replied. "I have never wanted to be a monster."

She laughed. "Do you really believe that you're the only unwilling convert in all of history? Please. I know you're smarter than that. Others have tried to resist their nature before you. All have failed. And in the end, they become killers because they weren't willing to take the step and embrace their new natures. If you continue down this path, you *will* become the monster you fear."

"I just . . . I can't."

"One way or the other, you will."

Jarond resolutely spooned up some soup. Although he knew Arawn employed the finest chefs, it tasted foul as he chewed. With great effort he swallowed, fighting to keep the small bite down as his stomach rebelled against it. Reka had no problem eating her own soup as she watched him grimace. He spooned up another mouthful, but was unable to force himself to lift the spoon to his lips.

"Why can't I eat?" he finally asked, dropping his spoon into his bowl with a wet thunk.

"Eating is a pleasure, not a necessity now," Reka replied. "Your body knows what you need, and until it gets it, it won't be willing to process unnecessary mass."

Jarond eyed the goblet before him as warily as he would face a viper. "How do I know you're telling me the truth? What if there's another way?"

She sighed, and then gently squeezed his hand. His fingers burned at her cool touch. "Those are two different questions. But I'm telling you the truth: I know of no other way. And I've seen many try, and fail."

"Nobody wants to be a monster, Jarond," she said after a moment of silence, her voice softer, more passionate. "What you are now is something I've been my entire life. You feel like you have no choice now; I've never had a choice. But I've learned to live without being a monster. Yes, I must do things that humans may find repulsive, but I've never fed on anyone who wasn't willing. And I've never lost control and killed anyone. The way you're going, I'm afraid you won't be able to say that for much longer. And from what I've learned about you, I fear the guilt would consume you. After all, forever is a long time to be carrying guilt around."

Chapter Forty-Six
Asho

ASHO AND ADERES, lost in their grief, rode west in silence, back toward the road. Before he'd seen Makani's body, Asho still hadn't decided whether death or capture was worse. He still didn't know. But now that he knew for certain Makani was dead, sorrow washed over him. Was he destined to lose everyone important to him? He looked at Aderes. Not her. He couldn't lose her too. He didn't know if his heart could bear another loss.

Two days of hard travel brought them back to the crossroad.

"We need to find Jarond," Aderes said, looking toward the south.

"Even if we knew where to start, there's nothing the two of us can do for him," Asho retorted. "I can barely control fire, and you have no weapons at all. We'd only end up captured or dead ourselves. And then we really wouldn't be able to help him."

"I can't just abandon him!" Aderes's voice was full of anguish.

"You aren't. Not really. We'll go to the changelings, get reinforcements. They have the power to challenge the khafyri."

"But why would they care about rescuing Jarond?"

Asho winced. He wished she hadn't thought of that. "I'm not going to lie to you, Addie. They probably won't care about your brother. But they will care about Damali—she was captured at the same time. Odds are, they are being kept in the same place. If we present it to the changelings as a rescue mission for one of their own, I think we could convince them to help. And then we can find Jarond at the same time."

Aderes hesitated, chewing on her lower lip as she stared to the south. Her shoulders slumped, and she turned to look at him, her eyes bright with unshed tears.

"I swear, Addie, I won't give up on Jarond. But now is not the time to go recklessly riding after him. We need to be smart about this."

Aderes nodded, a tear trickling down her cheek. She scrubbed it away with the palm of her hand.

"I think we should go to the coast," Asho said. "Your leg is taking a long time to heal. It will be easier to book passage on a ship instead of continuing to ride north."

"You're probably right," Aderes said. "But if we get to Varnstad and the changelings won't help us, I'll go after Jarond myself."

Chapter Forty-Seven
Jarond

JAROND PROWLED ALONG the wall tops of Menai. When he reached the western curtain wall, between the Eagle Tower and his own Spear Tower, he stopped and leaned against a parapet. The ocean stretched west farther than he could see, a great expanse of rolling blue, dotted by the occasional white sail of a trading galley or navy ship-of-the-line. Waves curled white fingers along the shoreline, crashing into the rocky base of the cliffs below the western wall. A clean salt breeze blew across his face, bringing with it a hint of rotting seaweed and other marine debris trapped along the jagged coastline. He closed his eyes and listened to the booming waves, using them to drown out the incessant, tempting heartbeats of the humans living and working in Menai.

The heavy steps of boots interrupted his brief peace. Jarond turned to glare at the guard marching across the ramparts toward him.

"Didn't mean to interrupt you, tavek," the guard said with a bow. "Just doin' my rounds."

Jarond barely heard the words, his attention captivated by the pulsing vein at the man's throat. He took a step toward the guard.

"Tavek?" the man asked, a hint of fear in his voice.

Jarond heard his heartbeat speed up. It was a tempting sound. Behind his closed lips, he felt his fangs extend.

The feeling of the sharp points snapped him back to reality. *What am I doing? I swore I wouldn't.* He stumbled backward in horror and turned his back to hide his abhorrent fangs from the guard's view.

"As you were, guardsman," he said, working to enunciate clearly around the encumbrances in his mouth.

The guard walked past him, keeping as far from Jarond as the narrow wall top allowed, and continued to march toward the Eagle Tower, his footsteps leaving more quickly than when he had approached.

Jarond turned and walked the other way, not paying attention to where his feet lead him. A faint tug in his mind pulled him to the northeast. He followed it, until he found himself at the top of the Lord's Tower, staring into the coastal mountain range.

Reka walked up to him. "Looking for anything in particular?"

He shook his head to clear it. "No. I don't know why I feel drawn that way more than any other."

"To escape from Father?"

He laughed bitterly. "Any direction is as good as the next for that. No, I don't know what it is."

She studied him for a moment. "Don't you have a sister?"

He hesitated, unwilling to give any information about himself.

"Is she your twin?"

"How did you know that?" he asked, shocked.

"I think I know what's happening to you. There's a blood bond between you."

"A what?"

"As humans, you shared the same blood. You were more than just siblings, you were twins. You shared a womb and came into this world together. That creates a powerful connection. I think what you are feeling is a connection to your sister. You are drawn to her."

Jarond turned to look over the ramparts. *Addie.* Miles away, but out there. Alive. And safe. Hopefully.

"You could bring her here."

"*What?*" Jarond was aghast. Bring Aderes here, to the home of monsters?

"She'd be safe here. I know you've only had a couple of days to adjust, but surely you've seen by now that you are more than human—and that Father isn't cruel to you the way you'd feared. Besides, it isn't as if Father needs your sister as leverage over you. You know that. And trust me, Father is very protective of his neophytes—and those they care about."

"But I'm not even allowed to leave here," Jarond said. The prospect of seeing Addie again was too tempting. But not to bring her here. Never that.

"Father would let you go if you asked."

Jarond flinched. Ask Arawn for a favor? He'd spent the last days avoiding his sire whenever possible.

"Isn't your sister worth swallowing your pride?"

JAROND KNOCKED HESITANTLY on the door to the Eagle Tower. What was he thinking? He was crazy to come here. Arawn would probably laugh at his request.

"Enter," Arawn called.

Jarond walked into the large chamber on the bottom floor. An ornate desk dominated the center space, and bookshelves filled the walls. He hadn't been back in this room since he was turned. He gazed at the spot where it had happened. The floor was bare and clean.

"Jarond," Arawn said in a surprised tone. "I didn't expect to see you here. What do you want?" The question had an air of curiosity, not the gruff snarl Jarond was expecting.

Now or never. "I want to go find my sister."

"Really." Arawn leaned back in his chair, linking his fingers together. "And how do you propose doing that?"

"Reka said I have a bond with her. That I can feel where she is."

"A blood bond? How interesting. She is your twin?"

He nodded.

"Very well. You may go."

Jarond stared at him. "What? Just . . . just like that?"

"Not quite."

Jarond braced himself for Arawn's order.

"First, take this." Arawn pulled a sheathed dagger out of his desk drawer and held it out.

Jarond walked forward and took the curved dagger. He unsheathed it, and saw the blade was sheer black. He frowned. It looked like Damali's olkar blade, only hers had been opalescent white.

"As this is the blade that was used to turn you, it is rightfully yours. Don't bother trying to kill me with it though; I sired you. The blade won't harm me." He paused. "Secondly, I could order you to return. But I don't want our relationship to be one of master and slave. So, here is my condition: Promise me that after you find your sister, you will return here with all due haste. If you wish, you may bring your sister with you. She will come to no harm here, either by my hand or anyone else's. But you must come back, with or without her."

"I promise," Jarond swore.

"Very well, you may go."

"Thank you." He forced the words out, hating to feel indebted to Arawn. As he opened the door to leave Eagle Tower, Arawn's last words followed him out.

"Do not disappoint me, Jarond. It will not end well for you."

Chapter Forty-Eight
Arawn

ARAWN SMILED AS he watched Jarond leave the Eagle Tower. He knew Naresh would chastise him, mock him for a fool, if he found out that he let his neophyte on such a long leash so soon. But Jarond needed to be tested and, from what Reka had told him, this show of confidence might be the final push needed to sway Jarond's loyalty. He would much rather have willing obedience than forced servitude from his subordinates. The difference in philosophy had been an area of contention between Naresh and him for decades, and Arawn was determined to be vindicated. And from what he'd observed, Jarond was honest almost to a fault. If he gave his word, he'd keep it. The trick would be in coming up with new incentives for Jarond to willingly obey—a challenge Arawn anticipated with pleasure.

Arawn finished going through the daily reports from his stewards and the correspondence from the fiefs under his domain and decided it was time to check on his captive again. Perhaps today the changeling would finally tell him what the unknown skriva mark on her arm represented. Or, perhaps, he would find out for himself—though ingesting a changeling's blood without knowing what powers accompanied it could be a dangerous task.

Arawn smirked as he recalled Naresh making that exact mistake. Naresh had been overeager when he'd gotten his first opportunity to drink changeling blood and experience their incredible gifts, and had bitten the man without realizing the jagged symbol on his arm stood for electrical power. The sudden surge caused Naresh to incinerate an entire squad of guardsmen, and for the following two weeks, Naresh sprouted lightning every time he'd lost his temper. Idiot had drained the changeling, quashing a one-time opportunity to practice control and master the power for himself. No, Arawn wouldn't make the same mistake as his longtime rival.

Arawn had ordered Damali to be placed in a relatively comfortable cell—a soft bed with warm blankets, a small, barred window that overlooked the ocean, and food delivered three times a day. Of course, the strieborna shackles still bound her arms, preventing her from being able to use her gifts, but the chain was long enough that it didn't hamper most activities.

Arawn stepped into the room containing Damali's cell. Damali was staring out the window, a light breeze ruffling her hair and bringing in a fresh, salty scent. Arawn closed the outer door, and Damali turned to him, scowling fiercely through the bars between them, though he could see the hidden fear lurking in her blue eyes.

"Tav Arawn," she spat, and he gave a small smile at her ability to make both his title and his name sound like a curse.

"Master Damali," he replied politely. "Have you reconsidered my offer of alliance? Help me, and the freedom of the castle will be yours."

"And just willingly give you my blood while I'm at it?"

"Either way, I will be taking your blood. It's entirely your choice as to whether this is a pleasant experience for you. Or not. It makes little difference to me."

"Never."

"So be it." He went to the small cupboard on the wall across from her cell and pulled out a wide-mouthed bottle and a thin-bladed knife. "I'll make a deal with you, though. Nothing too onerous. Tell me what the final skriva means, and I will abstain from taking blood from you. For one month."

She laughed derisively. "Still afraid of my powers harming you or those around you? Too bad. You'll just have to find out on your own what it means."

Arawn studied her, calculating. Was there something dangerous in her power, or was she bluffing? Sooner or later, he'd have to find out. He entered her cell, grabbed her shackles, and dragged her to the wall. She pulled back, but without her powers she was no match for his superior strength.

He lifted the chain to a hook set high on the wall, securing her in place. She kicked out, but he blocked the blow with one arm and stepped close to her, pinning her. He reached up and made a swift incision, holding the bottle under the wound to collect her blood. When the bottle was brimming, he corked it and healed her wounded wrist with a small prick to his finger.

He held her arm for a moment longer, staring at the marks. A circle bisected by a lightning bolt; That one symbolized the ability to shield against other powers. A series of jagged circles inside one another; the ability to detect the presence of nearby supernatural power. And the last, the one that was steel gray instead of black: two curves coming together into a point.

Arawn scowled as he stared at the final mark. The meaning was unknown, but the shape was familiar. But why? Where had he seen something that looked like that? It was like no rune he'd ever seen, he was certain.

Different from the others, not just because I don't know it's meaning. Gray instead of black, since it's an unmastered power. Then it hit him. What if it were black? Then it would look like . . .

A memory a hundred years old bubbled to the surface of his mind. Standing on the bloody, slippery deck of a warship as it beat laboriously away from the rocky coast. They'd been unprepared, caught off guard by the forces their enemies had mustered. They'd been expecting the attacks from land and air, but they weren't ready to face the threat below. The jarring *thump* of powerful creatures hitting the ships' hulls, splintering the planks. The sharp teeth waiting for hapless sailors to fall into the blood-red seas, ready to drag them down to cold, watery graves. The only sign above the surface of the massive beasts were ominous fins. Black fins, some straight, some curved, just like Damali's skriva. The distinct fin of . . .

"Tekula," he whispered, and felt Damali's muscles clench. He smiled in triumph, looking into her eyes. "You can shapeshift into a tekula."

"No," she said, but he could hear the lie.

Arawn broadened his smile. He'd figured it out. He unhooked the chain from the wall and left Damali, taking the bottle of blood with him. He still wasn't ready to test it—he knew that shapeshifting, especially into an aquatic creature, could go terribly wrong. But now, at least, he knew what to research to prepare for using the changeling's powers. It wouldn't be long now before he was ready to put his prisoner to her full use.

Chapter Forty-Nine
Jarond

THE RIDE NORTH along the Coastal Road was the fastest Jarond had traveled in his life, even faster than when he and Aderes fled from Carwyn. One look at who—or rather *what*—he was had hostlers scrambling to give him a fresh mount at every small coastal fief along his journey. The hours spent trotting and galloping in the saddle no longer bothered him—his tough khafyri skin and fast regenerative powers took care of any potential saddle sores that he would've acquired had he been human. The realization that he was free of normal human encumbrances was a bittersweet revelation, but he focused on the positive: the faster he traveled, the quicker he would see Addie again.

As Jarond traveled, he grew more accustomed to the enhanced sharpness of his senses, getting used to the fact that he usually heard—or smelled—other travelers before he saw them. The worst, though, was when he had to come into close proximity with humans, whether fellow travelers or inhabitants of the small fiefs. Heartbeats pulsed through the air, filling his mind with unwelcome desire, and the rich scent of blood promised to quench the dry burn in his throat.

I'm not a monster, he chanted to himself, as if constant repetition would make it true. *I will not be a monster.*

On the second day of travel, the breeze rolling down the coast from the north brought with it the scent of sweat and iron, and the sound of steel clashing against steel. Jarond paused, listening, then he cantered toward the sound of battle. A rocky outcropping rose in front of him, preventing him from seeing what he was charging toward, but as the road curved around the rocks, Jarond reined in his horse so that he could take in the scene of battle.

An overturned wagon lay on the western edge of the road, crates of merchandize spilled haphazardly around it. Two men crouched behind the protection of the wagon, trapped between it and the sea cliffs below as they steadily reloaded crossbows and fired at the bandits attacking them. A third merchant, with drawn and bloody sword, was engaged in a fierce—though clumsy, to Jarond's trained eye—battle with a ragtag bandit armed with a rusty scythe. Though the bandit's weapon was designed for cutting grass, not limbs, the superior reach of the pole gave him a slight edge against the merchant, who was being forced step by step back toward the cliff edge. Four more bandits, armed with longbows, were concealed in the pine trees to the right of the road, trading shots with the merchants. Two bodies—one bandit, one merchant—lay amongst the scattered crates.

Jarond charged toward the bandit archers, wishing that he had a sword. He didn't dare use the olkar blade on them—what if he somehow managed to turn one into a khafyri? It was a risk he couldn't take. *At least I don't have to worry about getting killed.*

He leapt from his horse as he drew closer and landed gracefully on his feet at a sprint. The bandits barely had the chance to register the new threat before he grabbed the first man's head and twisted sharply, snapping his neck with a sickening *crunch*. The bandit collapsed, dead before he even had the chance to scream.

Jarond broke a second bandit's neck and felt a punch in the ribs. An arrow protruded from the right side of his chest. With a growled scream of pain, he ripped the arrow from his flesh and raced toward the man who'd shot him. The bandit fumbled to nock another arrow, terror filling his eyes. Jarond yanked the bow from his grip and swung it at his head, the bow snapping in half as the bandit crumpled. The final archer turned to flee, but Jarond had his hands around his neck before he could take a step.

Jarond looked down at his chest; he needed to bind the wound before he lost too much blood. To his surprise, the puncture had already closed and the ache from it was a rapidly fading. Only his torn shirt, bearing a minor bloodstain around the hole in it, was evident of the injury that should've been life-threatening. *Another advantage of being what I am.* The thought filled him with mingled appreciation and bitterness.

As Jarond emerged from the woods, intending to deal with the final attacker, he saw the merchants had already killed him. The three surviving travelers stared in mingled awe and terror as Jarond approached, then they dropped to their knees, bowing their heads.

"Thank you, tavek," one said. "You saved our lives."

Jarond barely heard the words. Now that the heat of battle was over, he was captivated by the shallow gash on the swordsman's arm, which was quickly staining the man's torn shirtsleeve crimson. He took a step closer, feeling his fangs lengthen in response to his desire. Surely just a little wouldn't hurt.

No! Jarond wrenched his gaze from the wound, forcing himself to ignore the temptation. Though he wanted to continue to help the merchants, he knew his continued presence here would end in disaster. The fresh blood was too tempting.

"You're welcome," he said roughly, the words hampered by his fangs.

The humans still had their heads bowed respectfully, so they didn't see the monster standing before them. Jarond turned and strode away, clenching and unclenching his fists in frustration. His horse was grazing a short distance down the road, and as he mounted it, he felt the warring conflict raging within him. Could he face his sister like this? With the monster so close to the surface?

The blood bond was stronger now. He could feel her presence nearby, less than a day away. This close, the desire to see his sister again was almost painful. He couldn't go back without seeing her. Not after everything. *I won't hurt Addie. I won't. I just need to see her. Make sure she's safe. No matter what.*

Chapter Fifty
Aderes

ADERES WOKE WITH a start to the menacing sound of Devlin's growl. She sat up and looked across the glowing embers that were all that remained of their campfire. Asho was kneeling beside the snarling black dog, his eyes scanning the night in a vain effort to discern what Devlin saw in the dark. One of Asho's hands rested on Devlin's back, the other was held out in front of him, a fireball weakly flickering in his palm.

A small flame arose from the remains of their campfire as Aderes shifted to a crouch and drew her belt knife. The extra light gave just enough illumination for her to see a pair of eyes reflecting red in the shadows. Devlin's snarl increased in intensity as the eyes moved closer toward their camp. The eyes paused.

"It's okay. I'm not going to hurt you," a familiar voice said from the dark.

Devlin stopped growling and cocked his head in confusion as he stared at the dark figure stepping into the circle of radiance cast by the flickering flames.

"Jarond!" Aderes cried out, her knife falling to the ground as she rushed forward. "You're all right."

"Stop," Jarond commanded.

She skidded to a halt.

"Don't come closer. I . . . I'm not all right."

"What do you mean? How did you escape?"

"I didn't," Jarond said, a tremble in his voice. "Addie, look at me. Look what they did to me. I'm not myself anymore. Arawn . . . Arawn turned me, Addie. He made me one of them."

Aderes stared at her twin, horror rising. His sun-browned skin, his dark blond hair, they were the same as always, but his eyes, his deep blue eyes . . . they reflected the light of the fire, magnifying it, giving them a reddish glow beneath the familiar sapphire.

"No," she whispered, shaking her head. "No, he couldn't have. You're still you, you can't be a . . . a . . ." She felt tears roll down her cheeks.

"Khafyri," Asho spat. The tiny campfire burst into an inferno, reaching above his head. Devlin rumbled his own growled threat.

Jarond backed away from the towering flames, his hands held up. "I'm not here to hurt you. I just needed to see you. I needed to make sure you were safe. Arawn's given up the hunt for you, but I don't know about the others."

The flames died down to a low crackle, most of their fuel spent.

"How did you get away from him? And how did you find us?" Asho demanded.

Jarond laughed bitterly. "Arawn doesn't care what I do. He knows he can summon me anytime he wants. He's my sire, so I have to obey. As for how I found you . . ." He looked down, shame filling his face. "Blood. Addie and I have the same blood. I can find her anywhere."

Fear filled Aderes. She knew Jarond would never hurt her, but he wasn't Jarond anymore. He was . . . she couldn't even say the word in her own head. He was her brother. He couldn't be one of them.

"Jare, is there any way to get away from him? To break his hold on you? There has to be a way," Aderes pleaded.

Jarond ran a hand through his hair, his head bowed. Still himself. Then he looked up at her, and the ruby reflection of the fire shone in his eyes. "No, Addie. Believe me, I tried. But when he ordered me to—" He swallowed convulsively. "I have to obey him."

"Does Arawn still want me?"

"No, he doesn't care about you anymore. He actually said you could come to Menai. He promised you'd be safe."

"And you believed him?" Asho asked incredulously.

"I'm not sure. But either way, I don't want Addie in Menai. I don't want her to see—" He looked away into the dark, jaw clenched.

"But the khafyri aren't hunting us anymore?"

"No," Jarond said. "But it's still dangerous for you. The other khafyri want to catch any changeling they can find. And I didn't quite understand it before, but looking at you now, it's obvious you're a changeling. I can sense it."

"Then I need to go," Asho said. "If the khafyri see me with Aderes, she might get hurt. I can't take that risk." He rolled up his blanket and picked up his saddle.

"What are you talking about?" Aderes demanded. She felt as if the world was crumbling beneath her feet. "You can't go."

"I have to." Asho paused and gazed across the flickering embers to her. "The khafyri can sense what I am; I'll only endanger you by staying. I'll head for the border. Maybe I'll make it, maybe not, but at least you'll be safe."

Asho swung into the saddle. "Addie, I hope . . ." He shook his head. "Goodbye. Come, Devlin."

"Asho, wait!" Aderes called, but too late. He was gone, and a moment later, Devlin also disappeared into the night.

"I have to leave too," Jarond said.

"Jarond, no! You can't leave me alone."

"I have to. I don't want to hurt you. It's not safe around me anymore." He pulled a sheathed blade off his belt and handed it to her, along with a small, heavy sack that clinked as it moved. "Here. I don't know if it will still kill a khafyri, but it's the only thing I could think of to protect you. Use the money to buy passage north. Get as far from Sermund as you can."

Aderes drew the weapon. It looked like the olkar dagger that Damali had carried, except instead of a crystalline white blade, it was a smooth, shining black.

"What is it?" Aderes asked.

"It's Damali's olkar blade. It's how . . . how they turned me. The process changed the blade." Jarond hesitated. "Before I go, can I see your leg?"

"My leg? What? How do you know about my injury?"

Jarond flinched. "I can smell the dried blood. But I think I can help you."

Aderes sat on a log and pulled aside the bandage to reveal the poorly healed, cauterized gash. Jarond knelt next to her, examining the mutilated flesh, then with one swift movement, he brought his wrist to his mouth and bit down. Blood spurted from the wound, and Jarond held his arm over her leg, allowing the crimson liquid to fall on her mangled leg. Aderes froze, too shocked to react, and then stared in wonder as her burned and inflamed skin healed. Soon only smooth, unbroken skin remained, and the bite on Jarond's wrist had healed as well.

Jarond rocked back and stood up.

Adeles shot to her feet to stand next to him. She threw her arms around him and held him tight. "Please, Jarond, don't leave me."

Jarond stiffened. "Addie," he gasped. "Get away from me."

Hearing the desperation in his voice, she released him and stepped back. His breathing came in short, labored pants as he stared at her, a wild look in his eyes.

"I'm sorry," he whispered, and Aderes glimpsed a sharp flash of white. Without another word he spun and fled into the night.

Chapter Fifty-One
Asho

GUILT WARRED WITH Asho's belief that he'd made the right decision as he rode north, following a narrow track, his path lit by moonlight filtering through the trees. Was he truly protecting Addie by leaving her? What if she came across some other danger? Some threat that was *normal*—bandits or wolves or worse? But what could be worse than the khafyri? And they were after him, not her. So surely she was safer with his absence. He kept trying to convince himself of that as he kept riding, only stopping for a quick rest when the sun kissed the eastern peaks.

He traveled north for two days, following single-track paths made by hunters, miners, and other mountain men. He came across a few people during his trek, though he avoided any contact other than a nod of greeting. No need to get other innocent humans caught up in this blood feud between khafyri and changelings. His people. He still had a difficult time coming to terms with the fact that he wasn't human, though proof was in the flickering flames that he conjured each night to light a campfire to cook his meager meals.

Where was the border? Asho wished he had a map, then discarded the idea. Unlikely any of these narrow tracks would be marked on a map. Perhaps he had even crossed it already, passed some obscure landmark that divided one country from the next, divided danger from safety.

His horse suddenly nickered, with ears pricked forward. An answering whinny came from ahead, where Asho could see sunlight streaming through the dense pine trees. Cautiously, he rode to the break in the trees and looked out at a small grassy meadow.

A squad of soldiers stood near a stream in the middle, watering their horses. Asho's heart jackrabbited in his chest. *No need to panic. They're just human. They won't know what you are.*

He nudged his horse down the trail, doing his best to appear at ease. Then he saw her. The only woman among the squad of ten soldiers. Khafyri.

At the same moment, she looked up and locked her blue gaze with his, shock filling her eyes.

"Changeling!" she yelled. "Catch him!"

Asho dug his heels in, sending his mount galloping forward. The horse leapt the narrow stream just out of bow shot from the soldiers, who were scrambling into their saddles. He had precious seconds of leeway. If he didn't get out of sight, they would run him down. He might be able to use his pyromancer abilities, but he knew that an arrow would reach its mark before he would be able to take down all the guardsmen. After all, even Tycen hadn't been immune to arrows. And he was far from certain that he'd be able to kill the khafyri.

Asho rounded a bend in the trail and saw a steep slope to his right that was passable by horseback. If he could get over the ridge and out of sight before the squad rounded the bend, they might continue to follow the trail, away from him.

Devlin's heavy panting at his side matched his horse's labored breathing. The horse stumbled over a fallen branch, and Asho clung to the saddle to stay mounted. He didn't know how much farther the horse and Devlin could run.

He couldn't hear any sounds of pursuit behind him, but that didn't mean anything; despite his best efforts to flee silently, the racket of his steed and Devlin crashing through the underbrush masked almost all other sounds, except for the pounding of his own heartbeat.

The slope became steeper. His horse struggled to maintain the brutal pace, but Asho relentlessly pushed him forward. At the crest of the hill, the ground fell away in a steeper slant, and the horse slid through the loose loam as he struggled to keep its balance as they raced down the slope.

They broke out of the shaded cover of the trees, and Asho hauled back on the reins, forcing the horse to skid to a stop. Before them, the land ended in a rocky outcropping that formed the rim of a river canyon. He looked over the edge, searching for a path down, but the rocky cliff offered no escape from his pursuers. Far below, the green and white water of the river raged as it carved its way through the sheer canyon.

Hoofbeats sounded to his left; four guards cantered down the slope toward him. He bolted right along the rim of the gorge, hoping that the sheer cliff would break enough for him to scramble down to the river below.

Asho looked toward the forest on his right; maybe he could escape uphill. But the slope was steeper than where he had made his descent, and boulders were replacing the trees covering the slopes. The ridge was curving toward the river, and, with a flash of alarm, Asho realized it merged into a towering cliff face in front of him, cutting off any chance of continuing forward along the edge he was following. He glanced back: the approaching riders had spread out, blocking his retreat. The khafyri had joined the human guards, close enough that Asho saw her fanged smile. There was no escape, except for the sheer cliff edge and the churning river far below.

In desperation, Asho tried to summon a fireball. A faint flicker danced on his palm, then just as quickly disappeared. A short distance ahead of him, Devlin stopped, hemmed in by rocks on two sides and the long drop on the other.

Only one chance to escape. Asho threw himself off his horse, sprinted forward, and bent low to grab Devlin around his midriff. The massive dog was heavy, but Asho gripped him tightly in a rib-squeezing hug as his momentum took both of them into the open air above the river far below.

They plunged downward, the frothing white waters rising up rapidly to meet them. Asho didn't know if they would survive the fall, let alone the cold, turbulent waters of the river, but he knew that a quick death was preferable to life as a blood slave for the khafyri. He closed his eyes, bracing for impact.

Asho felt a brief, disorienting moment where he wasn't sure which way was up, then realized he was falling sideways instead of down. A split second later, he landed in wet grass, mud compressing under him and breaking his fall as he rolled several feet across slick foliage. He opened his eyes to blue sky, quickly obscured by a red tongue as Devlin washed his face.

Asho pushed Devlin away and sat up. Two women and three men stood before him. All wore matching brown uniforms with runes stitched along the edges. Their tunics were sleeveless, revealing skriva marks on their left arms. *Changelings.*

Behind them was a vertical circular opening in the air, just above the ground. The edges rippled and crackled; blue sky was visible through it, a contrast to the forested slopes that should have been seen from that angle. One of the men, who was facing the circle with his arms spread wide, brought his palms together, and the circle shrank and disappeared.

"What was *that?*" Asho asked, struggling to his feet. His body was bruised and battered, his muscles exhausted from the chase, but he didn't feel any broken bones.

"Portal," the man replied, turning to Asho. "I opened it underneath you after we saw you jump. Had to turn it though; otherwise, with the speed you'd picked up, you would've died when you hit the ground. This way, you got flung out sideways and were able to roll to a stop."

Asho looked around uncertainly. He stood on a grassy cliff top; across the wide river the mounted guardsmen and khafyri galloped away.

"They saw what happened, but they can't get you now," one of the men said. "You're safe here."

Asho looked at him. "Thank you. I thought I was a goner."

"Glad we were here to help," the man replied. "But who are you? You're a pyro, no? We thought we saw some flames."

Asho nodded.

"Where did you come from?"

"I'm Asho, son of Esme Linwood."

The five changelings shared looks of surprise.

"I grew up in Aldorn. I didn't know what I was until a few weeks ago, when Damali, Makani, and Tycen found me."

"You're the one!" the man exclaimed. "But what happened to them?"

Asho looked down, unable to meet their eyes. "Tycen and Makani are dead. Damali got captured. They helped me escape from the khafyri."

The five changelings clapped a fist to their hearts, bowing their heads as they murmured the three names. "Until we meet in the next life," they finished.

"We are the Vaktare unit," the man said, after a moment of silence. "We patrol this section of the border. We are sorry to hear of the loss of our brothers and sister, but we are thankful that you have made it safely to us, young Asho. We will take you to our outpost nearby. From there, we'll send for another unit to escort you to Lyndell, so you can begin your formal training. Come with us."

Without waiting for a response, the changeling turned away, the rest of Vaktare following. Asho and Devlin brought up the rear.

I made it. I can finally learn how to use these powers. Asho thought of Aderes. *I hope she's all right. Since she's human, she should be okay. As long as she stays away from her brother. Poor Jarond.* He shuddered as an awful realization swept through him. *What if I have to fight him someday? I don't think I can. I owe him my life. And Aderes would never forgive me if I killed her brother, no matter what he's become.*

Asho strode resolutely forward, trying to shake off the unwanted thoughts. *It won't come to that. I'll make sure it doesn't. Somehow, someway, in my training I will learn some way to stop Jarond without hurting him.* He smiled ruefully as he thought of how little he knew. *All I need to do first is master my pyromancer abilities and figure out what exactly this bond with Devlin entails. Then I'll be ready to make the impossible possible.*

Warm fur brushed his hand as Devlin nudged him. "You and me, Devlin, we'll get it done. The khafyri won't know what hit them." He laughed quietly "Lyndell, here we come."

Devlin barked in agreement.

Chapter Fifty-Two
Jarond

JAROND WALKED INTO his chambers and was surprised to see Reka lounging in the chair in front of the unlit fireplace.

"How did it go?" she asked softly.

"How did what go?" he returned bitterly.

"Seeing your sister. I thought you'd bring her back here, so you could protect her."

"I *did* protect her," he said savagely. "The thing I need to protect her from the most right now is *me*. I almost bit her! How could I live with myself if I—?"

"I'm sorry." Her green eyes were as soft as a blade of spring grass. "I can't say that I've ever felt the struggle that you are going through right now. It's been a part of me for too long; I've known no other life. But I do understand your pain. To have lived so long as a human, knowing human rights and wrongs, and then to suddenly be thrust into a different life, an unending life, that is not of your choosing. I am sorry that you are suffering. But I would be lying if I said that I was sorry that my father chose you."

"What do you mean?" he asked, bewildered.

"Khafyri are rarely born, and even more rarely made," she said. "There is nobody in this world that I have ever been close to. Humans have such short lifespans; gone to the grave as soon as a friendship is made. I've had a lonely life, and eternity is a long time to be alone." She walked to him, grabbed his face, and pulled him to her for a warm, gentle kiss.

With a groan of surrender mixed with passion, Jarond succumbed to the kiss, tasting the soft sweetness of Reka's mouth beneath his. When at last he emerged for air, Reka pulled his mouth to her throat.

"Do it," she whispered. "It will sustain you so that you don't have to feed on a human."

"I can't," he said, voice husky with desire and longing.

"Ever the human," she gently teased, then covered his mouth with her own once again.

His hands ran over her body, feeling the soft curves beneath her gown. He reached the row of buttons marching down the back and fumbled to get the tiny closures open. Instead of rebuking him, Reka tugged his shirt from where it was tucked into his pants.

The feel of her hands touching his bare skin under his shirt brought him back to his senses.

"Reka, wait," he said, heat rising in his face. "I can't. I've never . . . done anything like this before."

"There's a first time for everything," she whispered in his ear.

With a growl of desperation and frustration, he buried his face in her neck. "I can't," he gasped. "Not now."

He was surprised to feel her body shake with a slight chuckle.

"I can wait," Reka whispered. "We have all the time in the world."

He took a deep breath, inhaling the light floral scent of her skin. Underneath, he smelled an alluring scent, a sweet smell that had his parched throat burning. He felt a prickle in his mouth as his fangs began to elongate.

"I don't want to hurt you," he said, attempting to push Reka away, but she held on firmly and pulled his head to her throat once more.

"Do it!" she said, part demand, part plea.

Jarond surrendered, opening his mouth, fangs fully extended, and bit down. The warm, coppery sweetness of her blood filled his mouth as he finally experienced exquisite release, the pleasure giving him a high like none he had ever imagined. Reka stroked his hair, holding him against her. She was right; eternity would be a long time to spend alone.

Chapter Fifty-Three
Aderes

PORT DEREN WAS a sprawling, thriving city. Aderes was leery as she rode through the land-side gate, past a pair of guards in blue-and-white livery. What if Jarond was wrong, and the khafyri were looking for her? She had to risk it—she needed to book passage on a ship, and Port Deren was her only option, unless she wanted to ride south to Menai. She shuddered. She couldn't bear to think what was happening to her brother there.

The human guards at Port Deren looked bored as they slowly scanned the crowd for thieves and troublemakers. Aderes kept her eyes focused forward as she guided her gelding into the city. She made her way to the docks, giving the city's castle a wide berth, certain that khafyri lived there.

She reached the bustling dockyards and led her horse down the length of the wharf. In one area, naval ships were berthed, soldiers in leather armor standing guard by their gangplanks. Aderes walked past, head down to avoid attracting attention. She needed a merchant ship, not a fighting vessel.

Past the fleet, Aderes spotted dock workers bustling to load and unload various cargoes from massive wooden galleons. She nervously watched the commotion, the brawny, sweaty men shouting and cursing as they strained under heavy loads. Who could she approach to find out about booking passage north? She continued slowly down the docks, staying out of the way of the workers, looking for her opportunity.

The name of a ship caught her eye. *Earnest Evlar.* Surely that ship would be headed north, back to its namesake country. She hesitated by the bow, looking to see if she could spot an officer of the ship amongst the common dock hands, then took a deep breath and walked toward the busting gangway.

A burly man, sweaty and shirtless, with callused bare feet and muscle-bound arms, approached her. Clearly not the officer she hoped for. "Wha's a pretty li'l thing like you doin' here? You lookin' for some comp'ny?"

"Who is the captain of the *Earnest Evlar?*" Aderes asked.

"Capt'n? You don't need no capt'n. Ol' Markus here knows how to treat a woman right. Why don' you come wi' me, and we can get a drink?"

"No, thank you." Aderes turned away.

The man grabbed her arm with a meaty hand, his thick sausage fingers wrapping around her in an unbreakable grip.

"Don' be so uppity with me," Markus growled.

Aderes smelled tobacco and rum as he pulled her face close to his.

"I'll be a lot more fun to ride than tha' horse o' yers."

"Let me go." She pulled at her arm and tried to step back.

Markus tightened his grip. "Easy, there. We'll just step on o'er here fer—"

Aderes drew the olkar dagger from her belt with her free hand and pressed it against Markus's broad gut. "I said let me go."

Markus stared at the dagger, startled. "No need for tha' now. I'm just tryin' to show ya a good—"

"Markus!" a crisp voice yelled. "What are you doing with that girl?"

Markus released Aderes's arm and stepped back as an older man, lean and hard with salt-weathered skin, marched toward him. The newcomer wore an air of confidence as easily as his tailored, pea-green wool coat.

He stopped a pace away from them and lifted one dark eyebrow at the sailor. "Well? What are you still doing here? Get back to work."

Markus slouched off.

"Are you all right? Did he—where did you get *that?*" The man stared at the dagger that Aderes still clutched. The man suddenly bowed. "M'lady, please, forgive me. I should have been here sooner, to keep that lout from bothering you. What can I do to make it up to you?"

Aderes hid her surprise and sheathed the dagger; Jarond would have been pleased to see that it was a fluid motion, with no need for a downward glance despite her trembling fingers. She took a breath. Clearly the black olkar blade meant something to this man, gave her some sort of high status in his eyes. No doubt because of its ties to khafyri. She drew herself up in what she hoped was a haughty manner. "You can point me in the direction of the captain of the *Earnest Evlar.*"

"Easily done, m'lady." The man bowed again. "I am Captain Mathas, commander of that fine ship."

"Are you setting sail for Evlar soon?"

"Aye, m'lady. We leave on the dawn tide, bound for Port Vaynol."

"Do you have room for a passenger?"

Surprise flitted across the captain's face. "For you, m'lady?"

She nodded.

"Of course. We would be honored by the presence of a royal emissary on board our humble ship."

Royal emissary? What had she gotten herself into? She opened her mouth to deny the title, then hesitated. If the captain thought she was important, she would be safer aboard the ship. And once they reached Evlar, she could leave the ship—and false title—behind.

"How much for passage?" she asked, touching the coin purse on her belt.

"Nothing, m'lady. Not for a royal emissary, of course. Just be back here an hour before dawn. I'll have my first mate waiting for you, Lady . . ."

Aderes realized he wanted her name. "Aderes," she said, then immediately wished she had given him a false name instead. What if word of her reached the khafyri who ruled Port Deren? Too late now.

"My crew and I will be honored to provide you with passage to Port Vaynol, Lady Aderes." The captain bowed again, and then went back to supervise his crew and the dockhands in the loading and provisioning of the *Earnest Evlar*.

Aderes spent the rest of the afternoon preparing for her sea voyage. She found a horse trader and bade goodbye to her Kochi desert horse. She felt a pang of sadness as she walked away, saddlebags slung over one shoulder. She owed her life to that horse. She wished she could bring him along, but the *Earnest Evlar* wasn't equipped to transport livestock. Besides, the open ocean was no place for a desert-bred equine.

With the money she had planned to spend on ship fare, Aderes purchased new clothing and a small, fine trunk to carry it in. She couldn't show up with nothing but the clothes on her back if she wanted to reinforce Captain Mathas's assumption that she was a person of importance.

Finally, she found a modest but well-kept inn near the dockyards. After a long soak to draw out the tension in her muscles, Aderes gratefully sank into the soft mattress. Tomorrow would bring a new, blue horizon. If only Jarond were here with her. Aderes imagined that he would find life at sea to be a great adventure. *What is happening to you now, Jare?* she wondered as she fell into a restless sleep, tears rolling down her cheek onto the pillow.

THE SNAPPING OF sails in the salt air accompanied the rhythmic swishing of waves as the *Earnest Evlar* passed the breakwater of Port Deren, sleek bow pointed out to sea. The indigos and violets of dawn were painted with swaths of orange and red as the sun crept above the mountainous eastern horizon. Aderes stood at the rail, out of the way of the hard-pressed sailors, watching the walls and towers of Port Deren shrink behind the ship. She had made it.

She turned her back on the port, inhaling a deep lungful of crisp, clean salt air as she took in the wide expanse of blue and gray water in front of the ship. No turning back now. Her future felt as empty as the endless, flat seascape before her. Everything she had ever known, everyone she ever loved, was behind her.

Jare, what do I do without you? The ache she felt over the loss of her twin was compounded by the knowledge of what he had become, slave to the thing he hated most in the world. Aderes was adrift without his presence, his steadfast loyalty, his unwavering confidence. Arawn had taken him and broken him, twisted him into a creature that she barely recognized as her brother.

I swear, I will do whatever it takes to get you back. If you can be turned into a khafyri, there must be a way to turn you back. I will find it, even if I have to sail to the ends of the earth to do so. You've always been there to protect me; now it's my turn to do the same for you.

The *Earnest Evlar* cut through the water, bow swinging around until it pointed north. North, toward Evlar, and her future. The coast of Sermund receded as the ship moved out to sea. Away from the khafyri, away from danger. Her brother's sacrifice had enabled her to survive. She wouldn't let him down.

L. M. Filarsky graduated from Point Loma Nazarene University with a degree in Writing and a minor in Biology. She is the author of a children's book series, *The Star Horses*. Lauren lives in Northern California, where she divides her time between writing and riding.

For more information about Lauren's upcoming projects, visit thestarhorses.com and laurenfilarsky.com.